C000170523

Some Were In Time

Shift Happens Series Book Two

By

Robyn Peterman

Edition Notice

This book is a work of fiction. Names, characters, places, and incidents either are the product of the author's imagination or are used fictitiously. Any resemblance to actual persons, living or dead, businesses, companies, events, or locales is coincidental.

This book contains content that may not be suitable for young readers 17 and under.

No part of this book may be reproduced, or stored in a retrieval system, or transmitted in any form or by any means, electronic, mechanical, photocopying, recording, or otherwise, without express written permission of the author/publisher.

Cover art by Rebecca Poole of *dreams2media*
Edited by Mary Yakovets

Copyright © 2015 Robyn Peterman
All rights reserved.

What others are saying about this book

"Uproariously witty, deliciously provocative, and just plain fun! No one delivers side-splitting humor and mouth-watering sensuality like Robyn Peterman. This is entertainment at its absolute finest!"

~ **DARYNDA JONES**
NY Times Bestselling Author of the *CHARLEY DAVIDSON* Series

Acknowledgements

Writing is singular sport, but putting a book out is not. It takes a village and I am blessed to have an awesome village with great landscaping and tons of sunshine!

Rebecca, your covers rock and so do you. Thank you.

Mary, your editing has saved me from myself many times. This is a very good thing.

Melissa, Jennifer and Donna your input has been more valuable than you could ever imagine. I love you!

My Pimpettes, you ladies are the bomb and I am humbled that you pimp for me!

And last but not least, my family. Thank you for understanding that I have to let the voices out of my head and put them on paper! I love you all so much and none of this would be worth it without you.

Dedication

For Donna, you make this ride so much more fun.
Thank you.

Prologue

"Just walk quietly and no one will get hurt."

A menacing dude with a long black trench coat, questionable breath and sunglasses growled out the order.

"Oh my god, could you be dressed more cliché?" I laughed and rolled my eyes. "You do realize I've torn the head off a Dragon?"

I hissed as I got shoved along a side corridor in the airport. This was not how my Jamaican vacation was supposed to end—not at all.

"You do realize if you don't shut up and move, you will cause many innocent human deaths," he ground out as he grabbed my arm in a grip I was fairly sure had snapped a bone. Thankfully we were out of the main part of the airport and there were no innocent humans around.

There were two goons on me but there were six on my mate, Hank.

"Smith, you son of a bitch, I don't care how many men you have on me. You touch her again and all of you will die violently in less than one minute," Hank threatened through clenched teeth.

Hank's fangs descended as he got angrier at our tormentors, which made him look hotter than hell, and his deadly Alpha magic swirled around him causing the goons to quickly back away.

"You know this douche?" I turned and slammed my knee viciously into Smith's man jewels, sending him to the floor in a blubbering heap.

"Nice shot," Hank said, congratulating me. I ducked a left hook from my other guard dog right before I connected the palm of my hand to his nose, jamming it up into his forehead.

"Thank you," I said with a smirk and a curtsey. "Seriously, who are these losers?"

I knew they were Werewolves, but I'd never had the displeasure of meeting them until now.

"They're colleagues of ours," Hank said with disgust as he stepped on Smith's head and aligned himself with me.

It was now two against six as Smith and his buddy were writhing on the floor in agony.

"These are WTF agents?" I asked, shocked at how easy it had been to take them down.

Both Hank and I were undercover agents for our national governing Council, unfortunately named WTF—Werewolf Treaty Federation. I had a difficult time buying that these idiots were too.

Hank nodded curtly and the six still standing began silently glancing at each other, trying to figure out what to do next. Clearly the now soprano Smith had been in charge.

"I'd suggest you tell us what you want," Hank said in a voice the made the hair on my neck stand on end. "You have five seconds or I'll let the love of my life have at your nuts. When she's done I'll rip your heads clean off of your bodies."

God, my man was sexy.

"Angela wants to talk to you," one stuttered as they all kept their distance from me and my castrating knee.

"Well, asking would have been a hell of a lot easier," I muttered with an eye roll.

"She's here?" Hank asked.

"Down the hall, first door on the right," another answered.

"We can make our own way there—*alone*," Hank stated firmly. "You will remove Frick and Frack and if I see you again, it will be the last time anyone sees you. Ever."

"And he means that, buttheads," I informed them as I stuck out my tongue.

"Not really helping here, Essie," Hank said.

"Whoops, sorry."

"We clear?" Hank inquired of the remaining agents.

They nodded and quickly hauled Smith and the other one back down the hallway.

"Angela's got some splainin' to do," I said as I grabbed Hank's hand and marched down the hall.

***

The interior of the room in the bowels of the airport left much to be desired—as did the company.

"Essie, you and Hank have five days left before you will report to Chicago," Angela told us grimly as she yanked at the hair on the right side of her head. "What happened to your escorts?"

My boss wasn't extremely pulled together on a good day, but today she was a freakin' mess. She sported huge circles under her eyes and her short, cropped hair was standing straight up on her head. Her suit was a wrinkled disaster and if I was correct, the rusty blob on the lapel proved she'd just eaten a chilidog without a napkin.

"Well, let's see," I replied with sarcastic glee. "One will have to have his nose surgically removed from his hairline. And the other, I believe his name is Smith, will never be able to father children due to the painful fact that his man bits are now embedded in his esophagus. Hank scared the rest of your pathetic henchmen off. And just so you know, Angela, I'm still on my vacation before I go back to work and potentially get torn to bits by some Dragons. Don't you think this is overkill?"

"I hate puns," she grumbled.

"Not intended," I shot back as I stared at her hard. "What gives? Why in the hell are you skulking around the Atlanta airport sending inept gofers to rough us up? You ever heard of email or a phone?"

I was surprised at how quiet Hank was considering the last time we'd met with Angela he told her how it was going to be—not the other way around. His narrowed gaze hadn't left my boss since we'd entered the room.

Granny and my BFF Dwayne were getting the car so they were missing out on the fun, but Angela never missed a beat. She clearly only wanted to talk with Hank and me.

"Phones can be bugged and email can be hacked," she stated wearily.

"True, but you haven't said anything worth knowing," Hank shot back softly through gritted teeth.

Angela blanched a bit and started in on the hair on the left side of her head. If she kept it up she'd be bald by the time we were done talking.

"Who's going to bug your phone?" I demanded.

My stomach clenched as Angela stared at the ceiling for a long moment. As far as I knew this was definitely not normal protocol.

"You'll be working with another undercover agent," Angela said. Ignoring my question, she let go of her hair to pull a flask from her purse and take a healthy swig.

"Who's the agent and who's bugging your phone?" I asked as I thought about asking for a sip. This day was quickly turning to crap.

I'd been so happy for the last week. Jamaica was paradise and coming back to the real world was something I didn't think I had to do for a few more days. The last several weeks had been a whirlwind of nightmare inducing incidents that were sure to land me in therapy for a couple of years. I just wanted to pretend I didn't have to kill anything for five more days. Was that too much to ask?

"Council doesn't know I'm here," she said as she gave up on the flask and pulled a full bottle of whiskey out of her purse. "Something is going down and I needed to connect in person."

"Would you like to be a bit more cryptic?" I snapped.

She heaved a large sigh and took a huge belt off the bottle. "I'm sorry about the greeting. My mistake. I'm just a little jumpy right now."

"As awesome as that is to know, you still haven't answered any of my questions," I said. "Spill or we're out. You don't own our butts again until five days from now."

"Hence the henchmen," she said.

"You've got three seconds to start talking," Hank informed her tightly.

"Fine," she grumbled. "There's intense infighting amongst the Council as to whether or not we're going to do a big reveal to the humans."

"Very bad idea," I said as I shook my head and shuddered. We had enough problems living in regular society without being hunted by humans who

10

would most likely think we were dangerous freaks of nature.

"I happen to agree with you, but I'm not on the Council. I simply work for the imbeciles," she said. "At this point I have suspicions that the Dragons are involved."

"How?" Hank asked.

"Well, if I knew I wouldn't have abducted your asses in the airport," she yelled and then gulped down the rest of the whiskey. "I'm sorry. Forgot my manners. You want a swig?"

She held out the empty bottle.

"I'm good," I said. "So what exactly are we supposed to do about that?"

"Along with finding out if the Dragons are trying to crossbreed species, I need you to ascertain if they're in cahoots with any of our Council members."

"Mission impossible," I muttered under my breath.

"And that's why I'm assigning another agent to work with the two of you," Angela went on. "You'll rendezvous in Chicago with the agent in five days. The Council is on a retreat in Wisconsin and will be back in session by the time you have to report."

"Why the hell would anybody go to Wisconsin for a retreat?" I asked, confused. "I mean, I'd pick some place cool like Hawaii or Europe or Spain. No, wait, Spain is in Europe. My bad."

Angela gaped at me like I had two heads. I decided to ignore that. However, I thought my point was valid.

"Who's the agent?" Hank asked, getting the conversation back on track. "What's his name?"

"It's a her and her name is Dima," Angela said.

"Absolutely not," Hank hissed and bared his fangs.

"You have to realize that I have no choice here," she said nervously trying to plead her case. "I'm

*

11

taking too many chances as is. I would never do it this way if life as we know it wasn't at stake."

"It's a very bad choice," Hank snapped.

"Lost here," I cut in with a raised hand. "Who the hell is *Dima*?"

"The question should be—what the hell is Dima?" Hank suggested with a calm that belied his anger.

"Okay, I'll bite. What the hell is Dima?"

Angela tried to take another pull off of her now empty bottle and shrugged her shoulders. "A Dragon. Dima is a Dragon."

"There's a clusterhump in the making," I said with a laugh born of utter shock. "The whiskey has clearly eaten your brain. Call me crazy, but I don't think the Dragon will want to work with me considering I ripped the head off of one of her kinsmen last week."

"She's a double agent," Angela explained. "She's on our payroll."

"Which means she's on theirs too," Hank said. "Shitty idea."

"You got a better one?" Angela asked, completely frazzled. "Because if you do, I'm all ears."

Hank's jaw worked rapidly and I could tell he was about to lose it on Angela. I really wasn't in the mood for a bloodbath. As angry as I was at my boss at the moment, I liked her. We still had five days of very well earned vacation left and I didn't want to deal with the guilt Hank would have for ending Angela's life. It would wreak havoc on my sex life. That was unacceptable.

"We'll work with her," I said as Hank's head whipped to me in surprise. "But she will drink the serum that prohibits the Dragon shift. She'll have to stay hopped up on it the entire time we work with her or it's a no go."

"Brains and beauty," Hank murmured as he grabbed me and planted a hot one on my lips.

"She won't be able to defend herself," Angela said hesitantly.

"Yep. But more importantly she won't be able to kill us. Those are our terms. Take 'em or leave 'em," I told her.

"I'll take them," Angela said after a long pause.

"Alrighty then. I'd say it's been nice seeing you, but it hasn't. We're leaving now and if any of your flunkies try to stop us it will be the last thing they ever do. I have five more days of deathless freedom and I am taking them," I said in a voice I usually reserved for the outdoors.

Hank stood and I followed him out of the room, leaving a defeated looking Angela behind. Not my problem.

"Here's the deal," Hank said decisively as we walked back down the hallway. "We are going to pretend this didn't happen. We won't talk about it or think about it until we have to leave Georgia and report to Chicago."

"I can work with that," I agreed. "You wanna know what would help a lot?"

"What?"

"Sex. Lots of sex."

"I can work with that," he replied with a panty-melting grin that made me want to jump him in the airport.

"Good. Let's go enjoy the rest of our vacation," I said as I slapped his very fine rear end.

"As you wish, my mate. As you wish."

Chapter 1

"Dang, it's beautiful here," I shouted to no one as I sped solo down the country road that wound along the sparkling blue ocean. Two days after the heinous meeting with Angela I was doing fairly well not thinking about what lay ahead. I was home and still had three more days of blissful vacation. Hung Island, Georgia was as close to paradise as you could get. I'd tried to run away a year ago, but fate and some psycho Were Dragons brought me back and I couldn't have been happier.

I pressed down on the accelerator and held my breath. On one side the ocean whipped by me in a blur—on the other side tall grasses and rolling hills. The siren of the police cruiser that rode up my ass from out of nowhere made my stomach clench. I blew out a long sigh and pulled over.

"Ma'am?"

"Yes?" I asked as I rolled down my window and peeked out from behind my sunglasses.

In the early morning glare of the sun the sheriff looked huge—hotter than hell and ginormous.

"You were driving forty-five miles over the speed limit."

I couldn't see his eyes as they were behind aviators, but the rest of his face matched his smokin' hot bod. "Are you sure, Sheriff?" I gave him my best sexy smile and a giggle.

His full lips thinned as he rocked back on his heels. "Speed detectors don't lie. License and registration, ma'am."

"You got it, Hot Stuff," I said as I handed over the requested paperwork.

Ignoring my wildly inappropriate endearment, he looked at the papers carefully while I did the same to him. God, they sure built them nice around here.

"I'm going to have to ask you to step out of your car."

"Really?" I asked as I bit down on my lip to keep from squealing with excitement.

"Yes. Step out of the car and place your hands on the hood."

"Can I put on some lip gloss first?" I asked politely.

"No ma'am, you cannot. Out of the car now. It would be a shame to have to cuff you and bring you downtown."

Today was the best day ever.

I stepped out of the car and brushed his massive chest *accidentally* with one of my breasts as I made my way to the hood of my car. His quick intake of breath was music to my ears and I knew the pants of his uniform had just gotten tighter.

"Like this?" I placed my hands on the hood and spread my legs so my miniskirt hiked up to the level of indecent.

"Jesus Christ, Essie. You left the house wearing *that*?" Hank, our local sheriff and my sexy mate, griped as he yanked my skirt back over my bottom. "Where in the hell are you going dressed like that?"

15

His normally green eyes had turned icy blue with desire.

"To try on wedding dresses," I told him as I jumped him and wrapped my legs around his waist. "Don't you like it?"

"In the privacy of our bedroom it would be great, but in public where any man can see the color of your panties—no."

"Thong," I corrected him.

"Worse," he replied.

"Aren't you gonna feel me up and check for weapons?" I asked as I placed little kisses along his lips. "I am a deadly secret agent."

"What I want to do, *deadly secret agent*, is put you over my knee and spank you for going out in public dressed like this."

"Works for me," I said as I tangled my fingers in his thick dark hair and laid a big one on him.

"God, you taste good," he muttered as our tongues tangled. He grabbed my ass and ground me into his happy camper. "Can't get enough of you."

"Then don't," I whispered against his lips.

"You wanna take the chance of someone from town driving by and seeing me take you on top of your car?" he inquired as his hand crept under my shirt and caressed my breast.

"Um, no… we could get in the back seat," I suggested as I arched into his talented hand.

"I don't fit in your car, Essie," Hank said.

He was right. He was huge and my car was tiny.

"Didn't you drive the cruiser?" I asked as I glanced around. My eyes landed on his motorcycle and I sighed dramatically. "You are woefully under prepared today, my fiancé."

"You are correct, my fiancée," he answered with a huge grin on his face. "And P.S.— you're driving the wrong way if you're going to the bridal shop."

"I know that," I said. "I knew you were working this stretch this morning. I was hoping to get arrested and felt up by a sexy sheriff."

"As appealing as that sounds—and trust me it's appealing," he said as he pressed his painfully hard lower half against me. "I actually am working at the moment and you have an appointment. Please tell me you have a change of clothes in the car."

"Nope. Can't tell you that," I said as I slid to the ground, wiggling all the way. "As long as I'm not bent over a car my ass will feel no wind."

Hank ran his hand through his hair in frustration and backed me up against the passenger door. "Who will be at your fitting?"

"Granny, Dwayne and the bridal shop gals," I said, knowing he would be fine with that crew. Granny was my Granny and Dwayne was my three hundred year old gay Vampyre best friend.

"Species?"

"Of the shop gals?" I asked.

"Yep."

"It's Lori and Layla. They're Were Weasels," I told him as I bent over far more than necessary to get back in my car.

"You're killing me, Essie," he growled. His wolf was close to the surface and I was so turned on I needed to get the hell out of Dodge before I took *him* on the hood of my car.

"I know, Hank," I shot back. "It's my job."

"Be careful, my little Werewolf," he said as he gave me one last scorching kiss.

"Careful is my middle name," I said as I gunned the engine of my small piece of crap and peeled out.

Through my rearview mirror I spotted the love of my life and I giggled. His hands were in his hair and he was looking up to the Heavens like he was praying.

***

"Oh my God, I look fabu," Dwayne squealed as he pranced around the bridal shop wearing a full-on princess wedding gown with a sequined bodice.

The Were Weasels, Lori and Layla, who owed Bring on the Bride were speechless. Actually I was speechless too. Almost. We'd been here for three hours and I was ready to punch somebody in the head.

"Um, is he planning on buying that?" Lori whispered to me as we watched him defy gravity, do a leap across the room and land in the splits.

"Hell if I know," I muttered. "Dwayne?"

"Yes, doll?" he asked as he gracefully rolled out of the splits and hopped to his feet.

"You gonna buy that dress?"

"Do you think I should? White's not really my color, but I love what this neckline does for my pecs." He examined himself critically in the trio of full-length mirrors.

"First of all," I snapped. "We're here for me. You are not getting married—I am. You have tried on fourteen dresses. I have tried on two. There is something wrong with this picture."

"Oh honey, let him be," my granny said without looking up as she played Scrabble on her phone. "How often is Dwayne going to be allowed to go in a store and try on wedding dresses without getting arrested? Son of a bitch," she shouted and slapped her phone. "This Scrabble bastard cheats. What in the hell is a *zyzzyva*? Total bullshit word. I tell you what... I'm gonna find him and skin him alive."

"I thought you played with the computer," I said, slightly confused.

"I do."

"Alrighty then." I pressed the bridge of my nose and wondered how refocus the attention back onto myself... where it was supposed to be to start with. "Dwayne, remove the dress. I'm not wearing white, so neither are you."

Granny's eyes narrowed dangerously and I scooted away. "What color you wearin', sugar plum?" she asked in a deadly quiet voice.

I debated telling her. We were in public and I hoped that would mean I wouldn't get my butt handed to me when I sprung the color on her.

"Granny," Dwayne interrupted my inner debate. "Just in case you didn't know, Essie is *not* a virgin. I would think the church would go up in flames if she wore white."

"Actually, I would think it would be more apt to explode with you wearing a dress," I told Dwayne—my Vampyre BFF.

"But you promised," he whined as he stomped the blush pink four-inch stilettos he had tried on.

"Fine," I relented. "But you're not wearing white and it has to have sleeves. I don't want to catch a glimpse of your armpit hair on my wedding day."

"Good point, well made," he said. "However, I could get my pits waxed... "

"No," I yelled in unison with Lori and Layla.

"It was just a suggestion," Dwayne said with a pout.

"Um, we have four brides waiting," Layla said nervously. "Would you like to try anything else on today or should we make another appointment?"

"I think I'm good," Dwayne said as he slipped out of his gown.

"She was talking to me," I informed him with an eye roll and a laugh.

"Whoops, my bad," he said as he walked buck ass naked except for the stilettos back to the fitting room to get his clothes.

"Holy shit," Lori gasped as she turned several shades of red and began frantically gathering all the dresses Dwayne had tried on. "We'll have to have all of these dry cleaned now."

"Sorry about that," I mumbled as I yanked Granny and a mostly clothed Dwayne out of the shop. "I'll call and make another appointment."

"Don't hurry," Layla said sweetly. "Oh my God, I meant we'll see you soon," she stuttered as she hustled away in embarrassment.

"Those Weasels are a bit odd," Dwayne said, buttoning his pants as we walked across the street to the diner for lunch.

"Oh, they're nice girls," Granny said as she dropkicked her phone into the fountain in the middle of the town square. "They're just not used to peckers touching the inside of their dresses before they've been sold."

"Oh dear lord," Dwayne gasped, completely mortified. "I'll wear panties next time."

"There will be no next time," I muttered as I retrieved my Granny's phone from the water.

"Well, aren't you a party pooper," Dwayne huffed.

"Yep," I told him. "And you…" I dangled Granny's now useless cell phone in her face. "I am not getting you a new phone. This is the third one this week you've destroyed."

"No problem," she said with an evil little grin on her face. "I'll play Scrabble on your laptop."

"That's just awesome," I said in defeat.

No getting felt up, no dress and soon no laptop. This day rocked.

Chapter 2

"I've got the pictures back from Jamaica." Dwayne squealed as he pulled a large envelope out of his man-purse and slapped it down on the table of our booth. "Granny, you are gonna flip!"

Hank, Granny, Dwayne and I had just spent an awesome week in Jamaica. I'd gotten engaged, sunburned and had more fantabulous sex with Hank than I'd ever had in my life. Jamaica was now my favorite place in the world. Of course Hank and I were already mated, which in the Werewolf world was as good as married, but since we inhabited the human world too we decided to tie the knot.

"Please tell me you didn't snap one of Granny in her thong bikini," I pleaded. I took a huge sip of my Coke and said a quick prayer to all the angels and saints.

"Oh for heaven's sake, no. But I did get some gritty yet artistic nudes of her," Dwayne said with glee.

"Left side or right?" Granny inquired as she carefully folded her straw wrapper into a small football.

"Right," he answered as he examined a few shots.

"Good, because my right boob is slightly bigger than the left one. Wanna show my best assets."

"Okay, let's start today over." I positioned my fingers in a goal post so that Granny could flick her paper football. "We have three days left in Hung before we have to report to Chicago. I need to pick out a wedding dress."

"And invitations," Dwayne interrupted.

"Yes, invitations. And we have to brief Junior so he can take over the Pack," I continued.

"And pick out your flowers and a cake," Dwayne added.

"Yep—cake and flowers. And we have to make sure Granny can still shoot a gun straight," I said, trying to steer the conversation back on track of what was actually important.

"I resent that, sugar lips," Granny said as she downloaded Scrabble onto Dwayne's phone.

"And we have to get a caterer and a band and a photographer and a..." Dwayne reeled off his list like an auctioneer on crack.

"I'm gonna elope," I hissed as a large and ugly headache exploded between my eyebrows.

There was silence.

Blessed silence.

And then there were tears.

"Do you hate me?" Dwayne blubbered.

"Um... no?" I answered wondering if this was a trick question.

"Well, I am feeling hate. I have only been in one wedding in my three hundred years. The bride was an absolute cow and the groom had three teeth."

I winced at the image he'd just planted in my brain and hoped this was going to be one of his shorter diatribes.

"There were a total of three blind people and four others that no one knew at the wedding and I had to wear a robe."

"Why in tarnation were you wearing a bathrobe?" Granny asked.

I kicked her under the table. We did not need to encourage these nightmare-inducing stories.

"It wasn't a bathrobe," Dwayne huffed indignantly. "I have far better taste than that. It was a clerical robe."

"I'm about to ask a question that I'm sure I don't want the answer to, but… why were you wearing a clerical robe?" Because as much as I didn't want to hear the rest of the story, my morbid curiosity always got the better of me.

"It was when I was a Catholic priest," he said as if that were even a little bit logical.

"I got nothing," I mumbled as I held up my hand and tried to get Donna Jean's attention so we could order, eat and leave.

"I wasn't an *actual* priest," Dwayne explained. "It was because I was bald. The monastery was full of hair-impaired fellas and I fit right in. It was winter and they were an unending blood supply. It was totally awesome. Plus those holy men had a wonderful glee club and they let me sing tenor."

"You ate monks?" I asked as the headache moved to my temples.

"Noooooooooo, I just sipped. They were a bit bland, but what would you expect?"

I decided to ignore him and move on. Sometimes that was the easiest thing to do with Dwayne. The waitress, Donna Jean, was clearly on her break as she was sitting at the counter and had taken off her shoes. She was a Were Fox and had bunions. That was a mystery to me since all the Weres I knew were exempt from most human ailments. Granny said she was just lazy and I tended to agree.

"Guys, we're out of here," I said as I stood to leave. "Donna Jean has her shoes off. That means she's about to go out back and have a smoke which she'll make Chauncey hold so she can pretend that she quit. Getting fed is out of the question."

"Seeing as Dwayne doesn't eat food and I had five breakfast burritos this morning, I'm good with that," Granny said.

I gaped at her and wondered where she put it. She was tiny—looked like a young slim Sophia Loren. She was eighty but didn't look a day over forty. Werewolves aged very slowly.

"Doesn't anyone want to hear about my time as a man of God?" Dwayne asked, a bit miffed.

"You weren't a real priest, were you?" I asked as I slurped down the rest of my soda.

"Oh heavens, no."

I paused and placed my glass back on the table. "Oh my God, all their lives that woman and her three-toothed husband thought they were legally married."

"Sweet Baby Jesus in a thong," Dwayne gasped as he paled even more than his usual shade. "I never thought about that. There could be thousands of toothless bastards running around the world thinking they're legitimate. Sweet mother of Lady Gaga," Dwayne wailed, attracting the attention of everyone in the small diner. "What have I done?"

In his distress he began to levitate. I quickly yanked him back into the booth before anyone saw him. I did not want to explain Vampyres to unsuspecting humans. It was enough to digest that the Council wanted the Werewolves out of the closet. Vampyres would cause mass hysteria.

"What's done is done," Granny stated with a chuckle. "Who knows if they even procreated? Were they Weres?"

"They were Were Cows," Dwayne whispered in a strangled voice.

A burst of laughter escaped my lips and I had to sit back down so I didn't fall. "Oh. My. Hell," I said as I wiped the tears from my eyes. "There are no such things as Were Cows."

I looked to Granny for conformation, but she had paled a whiter shade than Dwayne. In fact, I was certain she was about to puke. What in the mother humper was going on here?

"There is no such thing as a Were Cow, right?" I repeated in a whisper so the humans in the diner wouldn't hear. They lived blissfully unaware of the paranormal world around them and I wanted to keep it that way.

"Yes, there is," Granny muttered tightly and shook her head.

"So wait," I said to Dwayne. "When you said she was an absolute cow, you meant Were Cow—not that she was fat?"

"For Cher's sake," Dwayne said as if I was two years old. "All Were Cows are fat and yes, when I said Cow I meant Cow—fat, magical and deadlier than a Dragon."

Again in his agitation he started to float to the ceiling.

Again I yanked him back down.

My smile was now gone. How in the hell was there a species I didn't know about? Cows? There were freakin' Were Cows—and they were dangerous? This was too much.

"Where's the camera?" I asked.

"What camera? My hair is a mess," Granny said alarmed as she ducked under the table in terror.

25

"Never mind." It was too much to hope I was being punked. "Out. Now," I snapped at my dysfunctional little posse. "We're going over to the sheriff's office to talk to Junior."

"That's good," Granny said as she cased the diner for cameras. "We'll have privacy there."

"Can Junior hack?" Dwayne asked as he slung his man purse over his shoulder.

"Why?" I asked as I dragged them out of yet another establishment.

"Because I have a potential bovine bloodbath on my hands," he replied hysterically.

"I'm not sure how much worse this day could get." I heaved a huge sigh and grabbed Dwayne's phone from Granny. The least I could do was save the harmless electronic's life.

"Trust me, if Junior can't hack his way into a few probably obsolete sites, this day could go to hell in a handbasket pretty damn fast," Dwayne said as he rushed ahead.

That's when I noticed he was still wearing the blush pink stilettos from the bridal shop. There was one good thing at least—I could turn Dwayne in for shoplifting. If he had to spend a couple of hours in the pokey maybe I'd have a little peace.

***

"He stole them," I announced to Junior as we entered the sheriff's office with the first real smile on my face since Hank had pulled me over for speeding a couple of hours ago.

"It was an accident," Dwayne whined as he gave me the stink eye.

Granny chuckled with delight.

"Well, boy, you stretched the livin' hell out of those shoes," Junior said with a huge grin on his handsome face as he examined the stilettos Dwayne had grudgingly handed over.

Junior was Hank's older brother by two years. By all rights he should have been the Alpha of the Georgia Wolf Pack, but when their father had retired Junior was too busy chasing skirts and partying so Hank had stepped up.

Hank, besides being hotter than asphalt in August and *my fiancé*, was an outstanding alpha—deadly and fair. Surprisingly there wasn't an ounce of hostility or competition between the brothers. In a twist of fate, their mother had given birth to two Alpha boys.

"You know I'm richer than Midas. I would never steal shoes," Dwayne pled his case as we all grinned.

"That may be so, but the evidence speaks differently," Junior said in his official deputy sheriff voice. "You're gonna have to return the shoes, pay for them and offer up your services for twenty-four hours to the gals at the shop."

Dwayne's scream of pleasure made my stomach drop to my toes and Granny cackle with laughter. The girls were gonna crap.

"Um… Junior, not sure that's the best plan," I said as diplomatically as I could.

"Sure it is," Junior said with a satisfied smirk as he sat back and plopped his cowboy boot clad feet up on his messy desk. "Those bridal Weasels are trying to poison Sandy Moongie's mind against going out with me. Serves them right if Dwayne goes in and shakes it up a little."

Shaking it up was an understatement. Dwayne would have them hosting full on bridal drag shows if he had twenty-four hours. However, Junior's reasoning was interesting.

"Junior, I'm sure your man-whore reputation might be part of the issue," I said as I knocked his feet off of his desk.

"Those days are behind me," he explained.

"Since when?"

"Um... I'm guessin' it's been about a week, give or take a day," he said.

My eye roll was one of the largest I'd ever produced. I knew Junior had it bad for Sandy. The entire reason I had come back to Hung Island, Georgia was that I'd been sent down here undercover by the WTF to find out who was kidnapping Weres. It had turned out to be some egomaniacal Were Dragons who were trying to crossbreed species and take over the paranormal world. They were now dead thanks to a disastrous mind meld by Dwayne that killed two and my ripping off the head of the third.

Sandy had been one of the kidnapped Weres we had saved and she was far too smart to get involved with Junior...

"It's gonna take more than a week—*give or take a few days*, to get rid of your well-earned reputation," I told him.

"Two weeks?" he asked.

"Um... more like a year or so," Granny informed him.

"Dang it, I don't have a year," Junior grumbled as he stood up and accidently knocked everything off of his desk. He paced the office and we all backed up. Junior was huge and dangerously clumsy when he was agitated. "Some dumbass Were dude could snap her up in that time."

"Guess you should have thought about that when you were doing the horizontal hula with half of Georgia," Dwayne offered unhelpfully.

"Oh my hell," Junior said as he sat back down and dropped his head into his hands. "I'm gonna have to dedicate every waking minute I have to getting Sandy to believe I've finished my man hooker phase."

"He's really off the charts MENSA?" Dwayne whispered skeptically.

We all watched Junior scribble out a list of how he was going to get rid of his gigolo rep.

"Yep," I whispered back. "He's brilliant."

"Junior, you chatted with Hank yet?" Granny inquired as she sat down next to him and started her own list to help him out.

"Nope, you guys just got back two days ago. He told me we'd talk later today," Junior said as he peeked over at Granny's list and gasped. "Would I have to go to church and confess my sins? Sandy's dad is the preacher. I just feel that that might a little awkward and potentially deadly after we mate and all."

"Hell's bells, you're right, Junior. Preacher Moongie would skin you alive," she agreed as she crossed that one off the list. "You might not know how to keep your possum in your pants, but you're a nice boy. You don't deserve to die because you can't keep your flesh sword in your grundies."

"Thank you," he said.

"Welcome."

"Is it time for me to do my community service at the shop?" Dwayne asked as he bounced up and down like a kid on Christmas morning.

"Don't you want to know if Junior can hack?" I reminded him.

"Oh dear god, yes," Dwayne said as he slipped his heels back on. "Junior, I have a little bitty problem on my hands."

"Potentially a cluster womper of epic proportions," Granny added.

"Yes," Dwayne admitted. "It seems like I might have posed as a priest a couple hundred years ago and might have accidentally performed an illegal wedding. It was an oversight on my part. I was so

29

excited to get to wear something that resembled a dress without getting my ass kicked that I possibly got carried away."

"You lost me," Junior said.

"I performed an unlicensed and illegal wedding between two... umm..." Dwayne was at a loss.

"Two what?" Junior asked.

"Cows," Dwayne choked out.

"So what?" Junior said with a laugh and a shrug. "Two cows can't get married in Georgia. That would be a gay marriage. And let me go on record and say I'm all for gay marriage. However, for it to be legal it would have to be a cow and a bull, and as far as I know most people don't hold weddings for their farm animals. Bulls are bigger man whores than me. Old Farmer McDonald only has one bull and about thirty cows. That son of a bovine gets around."

"He's really MENSA?" Dwayne asked again.

"Yep," Junior said sadly. "But don't spread it around. It hurts my rep with the ladies."

"Oh my god," I huffed as I sat down, knowing this was going to take a while. "I thought you were giving up the ladies for Sandy."

"Sweet Jesus, you're right." Junior slapped his head and scribbled a few more to do's on his list. "I'm gonna take out an ad in the paper about my brains."

"That's an alarmingly fantastic idea," Dwayne said kindly. "But I'm not talking about farm animals. I unlawfully wedded two Were Cows."

The silence was deafening as we watched Junior take in what Dwayne had said.

Junior's laugh when he relaxed was large and loud. "You almost got me. You are one slick Vamp." Junior shook his head and slapped his knee, knocking the coffee maker into the water cooler.

"Not joking here," Dwayne said without a trace of humor on his beautiful undead face.

"He's really not," Granny added as she put an arm around Dwayne.

Junior was up and pacing again. I pulled my feet up so he didn't step on them and break my toes. Of course they would heal quickly, but it would hurt. He stopped and stared at the wall for a full minute. We stayed silent and watched. His burst of movement scared the hell out of all of us as he ran to his computer and punched keys a mile a minute.

Granny patted Dwayne's bald head as he heaved a huge and dramatic sigh, which was ridiculous because Vampyres didn't breathe. For having such huge fingers, Junior typed faster than anyone I'd ever seen.

"Holy sheeeeeot," he said as he wiped some sweat from his brow. "You might be in luck. They seem to be extinct."

"Are you sure?" Dwayne asked hopefully.

"Not entirely," he admitted as he scrolled the site he was on. "I'll have to hack into some more databases to be sure."

"Okay, let me get this straight," I said sarcastically. "A species of Were I did not know existed is now extinct? How in the hell does a Were species go extinct?"

"Apparently the female Cow often ate the male after he impregnated her," Junior read from the screen. "God dang, that's sick," he muttered. "They didn't even kill the poor bastards before they ate them—chowed down while they were still kickin'. After a while it seems they ran out of males and they became a lesbian society. That served to be a problem as far as numbers went."

I was really grateful I hadn't eaten any lunch because my stomach was churning.

"Thank Tina Louise, that is fabulous news," Dwayne said as he dropped down on a chair and let his head fall back on his shoulders. "Death by bovine tusk is so messy."

"They have tusks?" I asked yet another question I didn't really want the answer to.

"Had. Had tusks," Dwayne corrected me.

"That's not definitive though, is it, Junior?" Granny asked quietly.

"I'm gonna have to do a little more research, but it looks pretty good that they died off."

"How long is the extra research gonna take?" Granny asked.

"Don't know—a few weeks possibly," he said. "I'll have to call in some geek favors on this one."

"I'll pay you," Dwayne offered.

"Hell to the no." Junior chuckled. "You're my sister-in-law's best friend and her man of honor in the wedding. I consider this family duty."

There was silence.

Blessed silence.

And then there was blubbering.

Again.

"I do not know what I did to deserve this kind of love," Dwayne sobbed. "I love all of you so much it makes my fangs hurt. Junior, I would like to give you the gift of some of my blood."

"No," I yelled as I dove across the room and sat on Dwayne before he opened up a vein for Junior.

When we had gotten ready to take down the Dragons, Dwayne had made me drink some of his blood. It made me stronger and my sense of smell had kicked into overdrive. However, it also enabled me to rip the head off a Dragon with my bare hands without even realizing I had done it. In the end it was what saved Hank's and my life, but it was scary and wrong—and it still hadn't left my system. Dwayne thought it would only last a few days, but we were going on a few weeks at this point and I still felt the residual effects.

"No blood exchange," I said firmly. "A nice waffle iron will suffice."

"Or a new coffee pot," Granny suggested as she eyed the one Junior had just demolished.

"How about a Hummer?" Dwayne asked.

"Oh my god, Dwayne, that is so inappropriate," I yelled.

"What?" he asked, bewildered. "I was talking about a car."

"Oh. Sorry," I muttered.

"Anyhoo," Granny interjected, saving me from myself and my dirty mind. "I think it's time for the shoplifting Vampyre to do his community service. Let's go, bloodsucker," she said affectionately to Dwayne. "Those Were Weasels will have no idea what hit them."

"Looks like I missed a party," a very familiar and insanely sexy voice said from the doorway as he took in the mess with a shake of his head. "Junior, you're gonna need to reel it in."

"Little bro bro," Junior yelled as he trapped Hank in a bear hug. "I've missed you and your judgmental ass."

"Missed you too," Hank told him as he disengaged himself and copped a quick feel of my rear end. "You got time to talk?"

"Yep," Junior said as he discreetly tried to pick up the office.

"I have to go run the bridal shop because I stole some shoes," Dwayne announced with delight. He was positively orgasmic about his community service. "Come on. Granny. We have work to do."

Dwayne flounced out of the sheriff's office with a giggling Granny following behind him.

"Should I even ask?" Hank inquired with a wince.

"Nope." I grinned and settled myself on his lap.

"So what's the scoop?" Junior asked as he sat back down behind the desk.

"Well, first off I want to know if you'll be my best man in the wedding," Hank asked.

"I'd be honored, my brother," he answered with emotion.

I felt my throat get tight and I was so happy I was witnessing this moment—a moment I never thought would come. I had stupidly and mistakenly thought Hank had cheated on me and had left Hung Island without talking to him. I was impulsive like that. However, I'd grown up in the year I was away and had become an accomplished agent for the WTF. I was now a deadly fighting machine and I still got my guy. Irony of all ironies, Hank had also secretly joined WTF because he thought I wasn't coming back. Now we both were owned and employed by our governing Council. Hence the talk with Junior…

"I understand that Dwayne is wearing a dress," Junior said cautiously. "While I think that is brave and appalling, I just want to put it out there that… "

"You'll be in a tux, man," Hank said quickly.

"Thank Jesus." Junior heaved a huge sigh of relief and I bit back my laugh. The thought of Junior in a dress was so wrong it was awesome.

"So what else you got?" he asked Hank.

Hank gently moved me off his lap and went to his brother.

"It's come time for you to step up to your rightful place," he said quietly.

"Whoa, whoa, whoa," Junior yelled as he jumped to his feet, taking the bookshelf behind him down. "I have a list." He shoved the paper in Hank's face. "I have to bag Sandy Moongie… Wait." He groaned and slapped himself in the head. "I do not mean bag. I mean, I do mean bag, but not until we've gone on at least two dates." He glanced over at me for approval.

"Fifteen dates and I'm being conservative," I said.

"Are you serious?" he shouted. "This is going to be harder than I thought. Maybe I should confess to her father."

"Confess what?" Hank asked, bewildered.

"My sins."

"Holy shit." Hank whistled and laughed. "You're a dead man walking."

"I know," Junior said morosely. "Now do you understand why this is a *really* bad time for me to become the Alpha and sheriff?"

"I'm WTF now. I can't be the alpha anymore," Hank said.

"What the hell? When did you join the Werewolf Treaty Federation?" Junior demanded as he realized the ramifications of Hank's enlistment.

"About a year ago—right after Essie did."

"Did you know about this?" Junior asked in a high-pitched voice as he rambled around the office leaving disaster in his wake.

"Only for a week," I admitted.

"Wait, so you went to Chicago and joined WTF? What did you do—stalk Essie for a year?"

"Pretty much," I said as Hank shrugged and grinned at me.

"Wow, that's kinda hot," Junior said grudgingly.

"Right?" I agreed.

"We have a mission and we leave in three days," Hank told a now pale Junior.

"Son of a beeotch," Junior muttered as he dropped onto the couch and stared at the ceiling. "This just sucks."

"Junior, you're ready," Hank said firmly. "You've been ready for a while, but you never would have challenged me. This is the way it should be. You're

fair, smarter than hell and deadly. The Georgia Pack
will be lucky to have you."

"Do you think being Alpha will help me get
Sandy?" he asked, totally serious.

"Oh my god," I mumbled wondering if an Alpha
that thought with his wanker was going to be a huge
clusterhump.

"Um... possibly, but you're gonna have to put
Sandy on the back burner for a while," Hank told him.
"You have to have your shit together to lead the
Wolves and all the other Weres in Georgia. Your
pecker is going to have to stay in your pants."

"I can do that," Junior said somewhat doubtfully.
"It would prove to the world I'm not a man whore
and then Sandy would have to go out with me."

I exchanged a covert glance with Hank who was
biting his lip.

"Okay," Hank said encouragingly. "That's a good
start. You are going to use your big head, not your
little one."

"It's not little," Junior cut in.

"Whatever," Hank grunted in frustration. "You're
gonna keep it in your pants and dedicate yourself to
governing our people and keeping them safe. You
follow?"

Junior sat in silence and digested the information
for a long moment.

"Yep. I can do this. You're right. It's time, but the
pants thing is gonna be hard. No pun intended," he
said honestly.

I rolled my eyes and gave Junior a hug. "You are
strong, brilliant and compassionate. You will be an
outstanding leader."

"You forgot good-looking." Junior amended my
list with a wink.

"And humble," Hank added sarcastically as he
took his brothers hand in his own and shook it.

Both Hank and I went to our knees in respect for our new Alpha. Junior was overwhelmed for a second and then gently laid his hands on our heads. I felt his magic entwined with Hank's fill the room. I was awed as I closed my eyes and let their power wash through me. Junior was going to be fine.

I just hoped our mission in Chicago would work out as well.

Chapter 3

"It was glorious," Dwayne gushed as he danced around the shooting range. "Layla was balled up in the corner with the peignoir sets rocking like she was insane, but Lori pulled up her big girl panties and got with the program fast."

"Yep." Granny laughed. "Dwayne insisted we all wear wedding gowns and parade up and down Main Street for two hours."

"Um... oookay," I mumbled.

I noted Hank's completely confused expression and Junior's ear-to-ear grin. Thankfully they'd removed their gowns and were back in their regular clothes. Granny now wore a colorful peasant skirt, jeweled sandals and a boob tube. Dwayne wore skinny jeans, starched wife beater and low heeled pumps.

"It was their highest sales day of the year," Dwayne boasted. "Lori offered me a permanent job at the shop."

"And Layla puked in a potted plant," Granny added.

"What did you tell them?" I asked as I examined the array of weapons on the table. We'd met up at the gun range after hours to get some practice in and to make sure Granny was up to snuff.

"I told them they could only have me for three more days because I have to go kill some stuff in Chicago. However, I offered to Skype with customers twice a week," Dwayne said, quite pleased with the compromise he'd worked out.

Granny slipped on her ear protectors and picked up a Beretta 92. I put mine on and picked out a Glock 22. Junior, Hank and Dwayne stood back and watched.

"You want me to kill him or maim him?" Granny asked as she squinted at the targets.

"You think you're good enough to choose?" I inquired with a grin.

"Little girl, I'm as good as they get."

"Maim," I challenged.

She took aim and nailed every non-kill spot on the body, missing all major arteries and organs.

"Holy sheeeot." Junior whistled and applauded. "Nice work, Granny."

"Can I kill him now?" she asked as she chuckled.

I shouldn't have doubted my granny's skills. She was one freakin' surprise after another. The most major being I'd just found out she'd been WTF before I was born. She'd been partnered with my overworked and grumpy boss Angela. Angela had worked her way up the WTF food chain and Granny had gotten out. Of course she had voluntarily gone back in for this next assignment and I was worried. If anything happened to her my world would not be okay.

"Kill him," I said.

With one clean shot right through the heart of the paper target, he was dead.

"Think you can beat that?" she asked with a smirk.

"Not think—*know*," I informed her cockily.

"Be my guest, sugar puss."

My pleasure," I said as I raised my gun, kicked off my flip-flops and aimed.

And I killed him.

Shot him thorough the heart ten times and only made one hole.

One small hole.

"He's dead," I announced to my shocked audience.

"Guns down," Hank said with a huge grin on his face as he approached the targets.

"What in the hell was that?" Junior shouted. "I heard the damn gun go off ten times but I only see one hole."

"I'm that good," I said silkily.

"Damn right you are," Dwayne said as he put his arms around me and squeezed. "Boys, move. Let her show you the other thing."

"What other thing?" Granny asked as Hank and Junior hightailed it out of the way.

"Oh, hell to the no," Junior moaned as he and Hank jack-knifed forward in anticipation.

"Geld him," Dwayne instructed.

And I did. I shot his balls clean off his body and then some. Hank, Junior and Dwayne were all leaning forward and wincing in solidarity with the paper man who had just gotten his jewels blown to Kingdom Come.

"That is some fine shootin', honey bun," Granny yelled with pride. "Hank, I'd suggest you stay on my granddaughter's good side."

"Noted," Hank said as he shook his head and laughed.

"Do we really need to be here?" Dwayne whined. "All of you can shoot the teats off of a cow with your eyes shut. I need to start packing for Chicago."

"What do you have to pack?" I asked. We'd been in Georgia for two weeks and Dwayne had brought one suitcase—one large suitcase, but only one.

"I shopped," he told me.

"Nuff said," I replied.

"Speaking of Cows..." Junior said.

"Did you find anything else out?" Dwayne paled and dropped dramatically down on a chair.

"No, not yet, but I have some friends looking into it."

"Want to get me up to speed here?" Hank asked as he and I put the weapons away.

"Dwayne?" I gave him a look and he groaned.

"Fine," he huffed. "A few hundred years ago I kinda sorta married some cows."

"Holy hell," Hank muttered with disgust. "Vampyres marry farm animals?"

"Were Cows," Dwayne hissed. "And I didn't marry them. I pretended to marry them."

"I am so lost," Hank said as he ran his hands through his hair.

Hank had known Dwayne for a year. It was one of the ways he'd secretly kept tabs on me after I had run away because I stupidly thought he had cheated on me. I was training in Chicago and trying to have a new life, which wasn't working out all that well. I was freakin' miserable without Hank. He befriended my BFF under a fake name and since Dwayne had no filter whatsoever, Hank had been able to find out all he wanted to know. Most people would think that was psychotic and stalkerish. After I got over being pissed, I thought it was hot. Hank had always known we were true mates even if I was too dumb and immature to realize it.

Werewolves could mate with whomever they wanted. Some lasted and some didn't. We had long lives and over-active sex drives. If you didn't find

41

your true mate you often had several relationships in a lifetime. True mates belonged together. If they had crossed paths, even as children, they would never be happy with someone else. Hank was my true mate and luckily we had a second chance.

"Let me simplify this," Granny said as she put her hand over Dwayne's mouth so he wouldn't spout more redonkulous bullcrap. "Dwayne posed as a priest and performed an illegal wedding for two Were Cows. It's really not all his fault. He was enamored with the outfit, so he made a poor choice."

Dwayne nodded in agreement with Granny's summation.

"Still lost," Hank said.

"Bottom line," Granny continued as she seemed to realize her version had a few holes in it. "There might be thousands of illegitimate Were Cows roaming the earth that will want a piece of Dwayne. From what I remember reading back in school, they're *extremely* religious and would take issue with being Cow bastards."

Hank shut his eyes and took a breath in through his nose and blew it out through his mouth. This was never a good sign. It was all kinds of sexy, but it usually meant he wasn't happy.

"Good news is I hacked into a few databases and it looks like they're extinct," Junior said, watching his brother carefully.

"Your info is wrong," Hank said quietly. "They're not extinct."

"What?" Dwayne screeched.

"They. Are. Not. Extinct," Hank repeated tightly. "There aren't many, but they definitely still exist."

"What the hell?" I groused. "Does everyone know about Were Cows except for me?"

"Yep." Granny answered as she adjusted her boob tube and narrowed her eyes at me. "You skipped a lot of Were history in high school and college."

That shut me up because she was correct. Balls, now I wondered what else I missed.

"Rumor has it they're working with the Dragons," Hank said.

"Well, Dwayne, you're screwed. That could be inconvenient since we're going after the Dragons," Granny muttered the obvious.

"I'm going to hurl," Dwayne whimpered.

"Vamps can't puke," I reminded him.

"Watch me," he hissed.

"We have no clue if they're related to the Cows that Dwayne duped," Junior said reasonably. "What was the surname of the couple?"

"Dung," Dwayne answered.

I waited for the punchline. It didn't come.

Chicago was going to be very interesting.

***

"I got a Hummer," Dwayne shouted as he flopped down on my granny's plastic slipcovered couch. Granny's house was literally a museum to junk. She had more knickknacks than Dwayne had shoes— Dwayne had several hundred pairs of shoes. Thankfully we wore the same size seven.

I froze in terror. I was unsure if he meant a car or a blowjob. It took all I had not to ask. I wasn't going there again.

"There is no way all my luggage will fit in your tiny metal death trap. Not to mention my legs were cramped for days after we drove down," he informed me as he smoothed out his shirt.

Shirt was pushing it. It was a wife-beater with Hello Kitty in pink sequins plastered on the front. I was certain his booty shorts were going to make his legs stick to the plastic covered couch.

I heaved a huge sigh of relief and laughed. "A Hummer guzzles gas and is ugly," I said as I popped a cookie in my mouth.

"Yes, but it doesn't smell like old French fries like your car does."

"Point," I agreed. "How many suitcases do you have?"

"Eight."

"Eight?" I gasped and squinted my eyes at him. How did a person go from one suitcase to eight in two weeks?

"I have to bring wedding gowns for my bi-weekly Skype sessions with the customers from Bring on the Bride. I want to wear gowns from the shop, considering that's what we're trying to sell," he explained logically.

As if anything Dwayne said or did was logical...

"Alrighty then," I replied as I wondered if he packed any gowns in my size.

"I did," he squealed as he clapped his hands with glee.

"Are you reading my mind?" I demanded.

"Nope, your face. I can only read minds of people I share blood with... *oh shit*," he muttered. "Maybe I did read your mind."

Dwayne began to immediately rearrange the miniature plaster rabbit family that was the centerpiece on the coffee table and I paced the room in agitation. Just as he started to refold the afghans into a fort pile I lost it.

"Dwayne, I thought you said your blood would leave my system in a few days," I snapped. "It's been weeks and I'm still feeling itchy."

"Itchy or bitchy?" he inquired with raised eyebrows that would have touched his hairline if he had any hair.

"Touché," I said, biting back my grin. There was no way I was going to let on that he made a good one.

"Essie, the operative word in your sentence was *thought*. I had no clue it would last," he said in a world-weary tone. Dwayne was as flighty as they came, but sometimes I could hear in his voice that he had lived lifetimes—and they hadn't been happy.

I closed my eyes and calmed myself. As much as I didn't want any of Dwayne's frighteningly unstable powers, it was what had saved Hank's life and my own. The strength of the Vampyre blood I'd ingested had allowed me to rip the head off of a Dragon with my bare hands. Killing the bad guy didn't bother me a bit—it was him or us. The simple fact that I didn't realize I had done it until after the fact was what I had a difficult time wrapping my head around. I knew I was being a baby about it, but it scared the hell out of me—and I was not a weenie.

I glanced over at my friend. He was slumped over like a bald, deflated, sequined blow-up doll.

"I agreed to take your blood. It's as much my fault as anyone else's," I said as I sat down beside him and laid my head on his shoulder.

"I'm sorry," he said quietly, "but I don't regret doing it. I wouldn't want to go on if you weren't in my world."

The seriousness of his tone and words humbled me. I wrapped my arms around him and held on tight. I loved him and losing him would destroy me too.

"I'm not going anywhere," I promised. "However, if I am stuck with your blood you're gonna have to teach me how to control the heinous super powers I've gained."

"Deal." He grinned and tweaked my nose. "Wanna try on dresses?"

"Do I have a choice?" I moaned and laughed.

"No, beautiful missy, you don't."

"I knew you were gonna say that," I muttered sarcastically.

"Did you read my mind?" he asked with wide eyes.

"Oh crap," I yelled as my eyes grew even wider than his. "I certainly hope not."

"So do I." Dwayne's voice sounded uncharacteristically hollow. "So do I."

Chapter 4

The sheriff's office looked like a cyclone had hit it. Clearly Junior had been spending a lot of time here coming to grips with his new Alpha status. He was a disheveled mess. His hair was sticking straight up and his shirt was buttoned wrong. It made me want to hug him. Hank put his hand on his brother's shoulder to stop his nervous pacing.

"Relax, big bro. It's all good," Hank told him.

Junior nodded, sat down and started bouncing his knees like a baby was on them. My beautiful man grinned and shook his head at his brother.

"We have one more day here before we leave for Chicago," Hank said as he tossed Junior a stress ball. "Everything is in order. The elders of the Pack have accepted Junior as the new Alpha and the official ceremony will be held tonight."

"What should I wear?" Dwayne asked.

"Actually, Dwayne, you're not exactly invited. It's just for Wolves," I explained gently.

"Well, that's beyond rude," he huffed. "Who is the one who mind melded those two insane Dragons and saved everyone's butts?"

"Um… that would be you," Junior said as he turned an alarming green hue and tried not to gag.

I'd missed Dwayne's mind meld death show as I was out saving the kidnapping victims and yanking off the head of the third Dragon, but it was apparently something that would be forever branded into the minds of those that had witnessed it. There were a few Weres still in therapy after that one— stinky Dragon guts had covered several city blocks.

"It's just gonna be a bunch of nekkid Werewolves dancing around and then going all furry," Granny said as she downplayed the magical ceremony and patted Dwayne's head like a dog.

"But that sounds like fun," he moped. "I want to get naked and furry too."

"Dude," I reminded him and I joined in on the petting. "You're a Vampyre. You don't shift."

"I know that," he said with an eye roll. "But I have a fabu faux fur coat that I could slip into after the naked dance."

That left everyone speechless.

"I'll see what I can do," Hank muttered as he handed me a folder.

"What's this?" I asked as I opened it. My heart leapt to my throat and my eyes filled quickly with tears. It was a folder with information on my parents.

"Thank you," I whispered. My hands shook and my stomach clenched. "How did you get this?"

"Junior hacked some sites. It's not complete. We still have some work to do," he said as he put his arm around me and led me to the couch.

I nodded my thanks to a now still Junior and leaned into Hank.

Until very recently I'd believed my parents had died in a tragic car accident when I was a baby. I had no memories of them except for the beautiful stories Granny had told me. Once Granny realized I'd joined the Were Wolf Treaty Federation, she let loose on a few details that she'd neglected to inform me of during my childhood...

My parents had died in a car crash, but it wasn't an accident. They had been the highest-level WTF undercover agents and they'd been taken out. The case was left unsolved which made no sense whatsoever. WTF got to the bottom of everything. It stunk of a cover up and if it was the last thing I did, I would find out what really happened to my parents.

"Baby, they would not want you to die tryin' to solve the mystery. They loved you something fierce. They would want you to have a happy life," Granny said quietly as she looked over my shoulder at copies of old newspaper articles and death certificates.

"I believe that," I said slowly as I touched the yellowed picture of my mother and father's faces, "but if the WTF covered up my parents' death, what else have they covered up?"

"Good point, well made," Dwayne said. "We need to take those bastards down."

"We don't know for sure that it was WTF," Junior cut in before Dwayne went into a blood-curdling, therapy-inducing story of how we should do it.

"I'd bet my left boob, *it's the bigger one*, that they know what happened," Granny said without an ounce of embarrassment.

"Wait," Dwayne said, confused. "I thought the right one was bigger."

Granny grabbed her bosom and felt herself up.

"Oh my god," Junior mumbled. "I don't know where to look right now. This is just wrong on so many levels." He shut his eyes and squeezed the stress ball with a vengeance.

Hank stared at the ceiling while my grandmother ascertained which breast was larger. How was this happening?

"Dang it, you're right. The right one is bigger. I'll bet my right boob that WTF knows what happened." She amended her earlier statement.

"Mammaries aside, I will find out what happened and I will make whomever was responsible pay," I promised.

"It's gonna be a cluster whomper of a bunghole to get the Council to tell you anything." Granny slid in next to me and gently caressed the picture of her daughter and son-in-law.

"No, it won't," I said.

"How you figuring that?" Junior asked as he opened his eyes, hoping it was safe due to the fact that the conversation had moved on from boobs.

"Simple," I said as I stood up and took the stress ball from Junior. "We go after the Dragons and figure out what the hell they're doing and who's behind it, and then we withhold that information from the Council until I get mine."

"Damn, my girl is hot and smart," Hank said with a sexy lopsided grin that made me want to tackle him to the ground and make him see Jesus.

"Do we get to kill some Dragons?" Dwayne asked hopefully.

"If they deserve it, then yes," I said as I took the folder back from Granny and hugged it close to my chest.

"How are you guys gonna make that work? Aren't you taking orders from the Council?" Junior asked as he put his hand back out for the stress ball.

I reluctantly handed it over. I was definitely going to have to get one of those things.

"Hell to the no." Granny cackled. "Our boy Hank here laid down the law with that dumbass Angela. We are going off the grid and we only report to her."

"Dayum boy." Junior whistled and slapped Hank on the back. "What level of WTF are you?"

That was a really good question. Why hadn't I thought to ask that? When my boss Angela had come down to Hung Island after the Dragon debacle, Hank explained to her how it was going to be—not the other way around as I had expected. She flinched and whined a little and then pulled some hair out of the left side of her head, but she agreed. It shocked the hell out of me. Angela was very high up in the organization...

"Yeah," I said as my eyes narrowed at the love of my life. "What level are you?"

He paused and considered his answer. Shrugging, he blew out a long breath. "My level doesn't exist."

"Meaning?" I demanded, not liking the way this was heading.

"Meaning he's as high as you get before you become Council," Dwayne guessed as he pulled out a hundred dollar bill and waved it around. "Anyone want to place a bet?"

"Is he right?" I asked as I yanked the money out of Dwayne's hand and shoved it back down his shirt.

How was he a higher level than I was if he'd been in less time than me? Oh my god, was I jealous of the man I loved? I took the damn stress ball back, closed my eyes and took a few cleansing breaths. I could feel all eyes on me, but I didn't care. My brain raced and then something clicked. Hard. I dropped the ball and slid to the floor.

No. I wasn't jealous. I was petrified.

I knew in my gut the Council had something to do with the death of my highest level parents and now my mate was the same level. I wasn't gifted with premonition, but this little twist made all the bells go off in my brain.

"How many other Weres are at the same level?" I asked Hank tersely.

He eyed me with concern and then shrugged. "I have no idea."

"Junior, I need you to hack in and find out who's at Hank's level. It has to be recorded somewhere," I said as I put my thoughts together as I spoke them. "Research all agents at that level over the past fifty years and tell me if they are alive or dead. If they're dead find the death certificates, and if they're alive I want addresses."

"Holy hell, Essie," Dwayne gushed with joy. "If I was straight I would totally fight Hank for your ass."

"Thank you," I said.

"Wait what?" Hank yelled. "You're mine."

"I know," I told him. "Dwayne was just giving me an unfiltered and inappropriate compliment."

"It's true," Dwayne concurred. "I'd bang the hell out of Granny too if I enjoyed hoohoos."

"TMI, Dwayne," I muttered.

Junior shut his eyes again and put his hands over his ears. "Sweet baby Jesus in a jock strap, I can't unhear any of this."

"Dwayne, I'd just like to say I find that flattering." Granny smiled as she adjusted her boob tube and blew him a kiss.

"I would pop you in a minute if I went that way," Dwayne assured her. "Being gay has never been so difficult. However, I love being gay and wouldn't trade it for all the cows in... "

"*Stop*," Junior shouted as he scooped up the stress ball from the floor. "I have entirely too much going on here to have this in my brain. I too find Granny attractive, uneven bosom and all."

"Thank you," Granny said politely.

"You're welcome. And I'm not sayin' shit about Essie's hotter than Hades looks because Hank would remove my scrotum."

"Damn right," Hank snapped.

"But we gotta get back on track here," Junior said in his outdoor voice. "How in the hell am I supposed to be Alpha *and* sheriff *and* hack in to Council databases to find super agents *and* find out if the Were Cows Dwayne didn't marry are still alive and want to kill his undead ass?"

"Can't you multitask?" Dwayne asked politely.

Junior's grunt of fury made Dwayne back up.

"You're going to have to have help," Hank agreed. "Who in town has outstanding computer skills?"

My grin was enormous and everyone stared at me like I'd lost it. "I know who has mad computer skills." I bit down on my lip to keep from laughing.

"Who?" Junior asked as he squinted at me in distrust and pretty much tore the stress ball in half.

Pausing for dramatic effect—a skill I'd learned well from Dwayne... "Sandy Moongie is absolutely brilliant on the computer."

All eyes flew to Junior and we waited.

"Multitasking will be no problem at all," he informed us with a grin that practically split his handsome face. "No problem at all.

***

"So, Mister Sexy Pants," I said as I curled up on the couch in our cute little cottage on the outskirts of town, "you're some kind of super uper duper agent?"

"Does that bother you?" Hank asked as he dropped down beside me and let his head fall back on the cushions.

His scent and proximity made my inner wolf want to talk fast and get down to business faster. We were finally alone after far too much time with Granny, Junior and Dwayne and I wanted him something bad.

"No. I thought it did, but mostly it makes me worry," I told him honestly as I traced his lips with my finger. "How'd it happen?"

"How did what happed?" he asked as he sucked my finger into his mouth and nipped it.

"Gaahhhh," I grunted as I yanked back my finger and got in his redonkulously gorgeous face. "How did you become a level whatever-the-hell-you-are agent?"

"Council put me in a cage with a Dragon and I came out alive."

"Oh my god," I shouted and punched him in the arm. That was asking for death. "Are you insane? Why would you agree to do that?"

He sat silently and crossed his arms over his chest—a sure sign this conversation wasn't going my way. I *hated* when stuff didn't go my way.

"Did my punch to your arm make you hard of hearing?" I demanded.

"You have a damn fine left hook," he said with a smirk, completely deflecting. His lips found the spot on my neck that made me see Jesus. My inner hooker Wolf literally purred like a damn cat. However, I was not falling for the *I'll give you a massive orgasm so we don't have to talk ploy.*

"Nope," I said as I backed away with difficulty and gave him the look. "Answer my question."

"Didn't have a choice," he said as he stood up and walked to the kitchen. "You want a Coke?"

"No! I want an answer and then I want to have sex until I forget my name. You do realize I can withhold panty privileges until you talk."

I followed him into the kitchen and blocked the fridge.

"You gonna leave me?" he asked.

I was so confused I laughed. "What kind of question is that?"

"A real one," he answered as he planted his very fine butt on the edge of the counter.

I blew out a long sigh and slid down the fridge to the floor. "Of course I'm not going to leave you. That's a dumb thing to say."

"There are two things that would destroy me, Essie." He stared at the ceiling. "You leaving me and you dying."

"Ditto," I said, "but you still didn't answer my question."

Hank lifted me off the floor and sat me on the counter like I weighed nothing. He then proceeded to fill a Styrofoam cup with the tiny rabbit turd shaped ice that I was addicted to and filled the cup with Coke. He added a straw and put it in my hands. His jaw worked furiously the entire time and I could tell he was thinking hard.

"I bought time," he said tightly as he paced the kitchen like a caged tiger.

"Bought time for what?" I yelled. Did he have a death wish? "Bought time till they put you in a cage with *two* Dragons? Bought time till they tell you to do some stupid ass bull honkey thing that will kill you dead? Bought time for..."

"I bought time for you," he said harshly and then ran his hands through his hair in frustration. "I bought time for you."

I was stunned to silence. What was he talking about? Even my special drink, with my special cup, ice, and straw didn't give me any comfort.

"I bought time for you, baby," Hank whispered. He stood in front of me and pressed his forehead to mine.

"I don't understand."

Hank brushed a feather soft kiss to my lips and cupped my face in his large hands. "Apparently some on the Council want you taken out. I made a deal that they didn't think I would come out of alive. I lived through it. The deal was witnessed by the entire Council so it had to be honored."

My body shook, not with fear—with fury. "Those old wankers want me dead? Why? What the hell did I do for our governing freakin' council to want me dead? I mean, I know I illegally used the company credit card to buy shoes and maybe I used it a couple of times at Victoria's Secret and possibly at Neimans six or eight times, but that shouldn't equate to my demise. Why do they want me eliminated?"

"They never said. If I had to guess I would have to say your theory about the Council being involved somehow with your parents' death is spot on. Someone wants you gone before you can dig."

"Which one?" I yelled as I hopped off the counter and practically downed my drink. "Balls."

I pressed my fingers to the bridge of my nose to try and ease the brain freeze my gulping just caused.

Hank put his hands on my head and massaged. His magic flowed through his fingertips and the explosion in my head eased.

"I don't know which one—or ones. But I swear on my life I'll find out and kill them," he said in a voice that made the hair on my neck stand up.

"You won't have to," I said as I wrapped my arms tightly around the man who was willing to die for me. "I'm gonna find them first. Wait, how many are there again?"

"You really skipped a lot of Were History classes in school."

"They were boring," I snapped. "Just tell me how many."

"Twelve."

"I could take on twelve," I said hesitantly.

"You will not take on twelve old and insanely powerful Werewolves," he stated with narrowed eyes.

"I didn't say I was going to do it all at once," I muttered with an eye roll.

"We, as in *WE*, will figure out who wants you dead and *WE* will deal with them together. You understand?"

Hank had gone all Alpha on me and it was hot. It took everything I had to stay on task and not rip his clothes off his body.

"I hear you."

"Why do I feel like that wasn't exactly an agreement?" He grabbed me and pulled me close. "You and I are now us. Hell, we've always been us, but now that we're mated we are officially an us. There will be no going rogue. We protect what is ours. You're mine and I'm yours. Period."

As I breathed him in I realized how utterly amazing and brilliant he was.

"Oh my hell." I gasped and pulled back. "That's why you cut that deal with Angela."

He nodded and tucked my wild hair behind my ears. "Yep."

When my boss had come to Georgia Hank had made terms that were unheard of with the WTF. Conditions had been negotiated that Hank, Dwayne, Granny and myself would go off the radar completely. We wouldn't be monitored or in any kind of database. We would answer to no one but Angela and when the mission was done, we had a free pass out of the WTF. Apparently the Dragons were that much of an issue.

"I thought I loved you all that I could, but I love you even more," I whispered against his lips.

"You wanna prove it?" he asked as he pressed himself against me with a grin.

"That could be arranged," I said as I slid off the counter and walked away with a hip swing that made him groan. "I was planning on taking a shower. Wanna join me?"

"You don't have to ask twice," he said as he picked me up and sprinted to the master bath.

"Your hearing seems to work just fine now." I giggled as he grabbed my ass and kicked off his shoes.

"Yep. Get naked. Now."

"Yes, sir." I saluted him before I tore my shirt over my head and kicked out of my fabulous mini skirt and wedge heeled sandals. My bra and panties disappeared in a frenzy of groping hands, nips and kisses. My inner wolf howled with delight.

"God, you're sexy," Hank muttered as he pulled me into the shower and plastered his rockin' hot body against mine. "I am so in love with you."

"Back at ya, big guy," I said as I ran my hands over his massive chest and six-pack abs. He was truly a work of art. Water sluiced down his body, enabling my hands to slip over him with ease.

My fangs descended and I felt my eyes turn icy blue with desire. The cinnamon scent of lust unique to Werewolves laced the steamy air and my breathing became labored as Hank's hands molded my breasts and hips, causing little zings of heat everywhere he touched.

"How in the hell does this keep getting better?"

"Don't know. Don't care," he mumbled as his mouth lowered to my breasts.

My nipples went into overdrive and I arched my back, begging for attention. Tangling my fingers in his hair, I held on as my knees grew weaker with every lick and nip. He dropped to his knees and his lips and teeth teased my most sensitive spot. An explosion of lust unfurled in my belly and I came with a scream.

"So responsive." He moaned as he made his way back up my shaking body.

The sharp gnawing pleasure of aftershocks tore through me as he lifted me and wrapped my legs around his waist.

"Wait," I stammered as my brain began to function again. "I want to return the favor." I tried to slip from his arms and find the prize, but he held me fast.

"If you touch my dick with your lips this will be over before it begins," Hank ground out as his fangs punctured the skin of my neck, sending me into explosive orgasm number two.

"Oh my god," I gasped. "I'm gonna pass out and drown in the shower."

"I gotcha, baby," he growled in my ear, driving my need to a fever pitch.

"I just came twice with less than a minute in between. I should be dead," I mumbled as I scraped his shoulder with my fangs.

"Let's go for one more together, lover," he whispered in my ear. A shudder rocked my body.

"I could make that work." A soft cry left my lips as I felt the head of his erection press at my opening. "You feel so good," I hissed as my nails raked down his back.

"It only gets better," he ground out as he entered me with one swift thrust.

We both cried out and sweet and slow time was over. His thrusts were wild and I met them with joyous abandon. We mated and made love like the animals we were. A tingling started between my legs and I ground myself against him.

"I'm close," I said frantically as I took his lips in a violent kiss.

"Bite me," he demanded against my lips. "Now."

As I sunk my fangs into the smooth skin of his shoulder he did the same to me. Blinding color ripped across my vision as I screamed in ecstasy. My body tightened like a vise around him and the sounds that came from deep in his chest prolonged my orgasm almost to the point of pain. His roar as he came got tangled with my scream. I dropped my head to his chest and gasped for air. Hank held me tight and whispered words of love in my ear. Everything was right with my world.

I didn't care who wanted me dead or that I hadn't found a wedding dress or that Were Cows were something that existed. I was in the arms of the man I loved more than my own life. Tomorrow would be a new day, but this very moment was perfection.

"I'm dead," I grunted. "I'm fairly sure you just screwed me to death."

His chuckle made me grin, but I was too wrecked to pick up my head to glare at him.

"You feel alive to me," he said as he sat me on the shower bench and proceeded to gently wash my entire body—including my hair.

"You are a keeper," I mumbled and he rinsed me and pressed a sweet kiss to my lips.

I watched him clean himself with the same efficiency he used in his daily life. If I'd had the energy I would have copped a feel, but all I could do was sit back and enjoy the show—and it was a very good show.

"We have twenty minutes to get ready before we leave for the ceremony." Hank exited the shower and handed me a fluffy bath sheet. "You gonna be able to walk out of there?" he inquired with a cocky grin.

I was still a useless but very satisfied noodle. I stuck my tongue out at him as I gingerly rose and followed him into our bedroom.

"How dressy are we going?" I asked as I pawed through my closet.

"Just wear something that will be easy to take off for the shift," he said as he pulled on some loose pants and a collared shirt.

He could make a garbage bag look hot.

"Okay." I grabbed a sundress that was easy to slip out of and stepped into my Prada sandals. I considered flip-flops, but that kind of hurt my soul. My legs looked far better in heels and even though I was a wanted woman, I planned on going out in style.

"Oh," Hank said absently as he twisted one of my wet curls in his fingers. "I was able to procure an invite for Dwayne."

"Oh my god." I laughed. "This could turn out to be a shit show."

Hank's grin made my heart flip. "You are correct, my mate."

I shook my head and grabbed my purse. "Did you tell him not to bring the faux fur?"

"Of course not." Hank laughed. "I can't wait to see the elder's faces when he pulls that baby out."

"You're really bad," I said with a light punch to his arm.

"Actually," he said with a smirk, "I'm really good."

I giggled and gave him a kiss. I certainly couldn't argue with that logic.

Chapter 5

"Um, Dwayne, what in the Hell are you wearing?" I asked as I took in his ensemble.

"Drawstring gauchos and a spandex tear-away halter top," he answered. "You like?"

"Is that a trick question?" I asked as I bit back my giggle.

"Doll face," Dwayne informed me with raised brows, "this is all the rage right now. I'll let you borrow the gauchos whenever, but I'll probably destroy the top when I tear it from my body later."

"Thanks, but I'll pass," I mumbled as I glanced around the clearing.

"Where are the boys?" Dwayne asked, referring to Hank and Junior.

"At the big house with their dad getting ready," I told him.

We were on Hank and Junior's parents' property. The Wilsons owned several hundred acres of the most beautiful and lush land on the island. Magic hung thick in the air and I wrapped my arms around my waist and breathed it in. My wolf itched to come out and play. I hadn't shifted enough lately. Hank, Granny and I had shifted in Jamaica and played on the beach twice while Dwayne kept watch, but it wasn't the same as shifting with my Pack.

"OMG," Dwayne whispered. "You should get married here. It's fabu."

"You know what? You're right. This place is perfect," I told a delighted Dwayne truthfully. "I'll have to ask... "

"Ester?" an imperious female voice demanded. "Is that you over there skulking with the Vampyre?"

"Damn it," I hissed and wondered if I could make a break for it. I'd hate to miss Junior's ceremony, but dealing with Junior and Hank's mom was tantamount to a living hell.

"Do you want me to mind meld her?" Dwayne asked with wide eyes.

She clearly scared him too. I shook my head and stepped bravely in front of my BFF.

"Hello, Mrs. Wilson," I choked out as I glanced around wildly for Hank, Granny or Junior.

All the Weres in the immediate vicinity stopped what they were doing and watched. Several pushed each other out of the way to get a better view.

Crapballs.

"From what I understand you'll be calling me mother soon—not that anyone bothered to inform me," she purred silkily as her eyes flashed with anger and her fists clenched at her sides.

There was excited whispering amongst the Pack as they waited for a showdown.

"*Does she have any daughters?*" Dwayne asked frantically in my head. My very pissed soon to be mother-in-law's fangs descended, much to the delight of the crowd.

"*Oh my freakin hell! Are you inside my head?*" I asked.

"*Yep, and you're in mine. Answer the question,*" he insisted.

"We are so going to talk about this new party trick later," I said.

"The question?"

God, he was a nag.

"No. No, she has no daughters."

"That is the answer I was hoping for. Ask her to help you find a dress," he told me as his voice bounced around loudly in my brain.

"Hell no," I shot back. *"I'd rather remove my boob with a dull butter knife."*

"That can be arranged," Dwayne snapped, *"but right now you will ask that heinous woman who looks like she wants you dead to help you find a dress."*

"Ester," Mrs. Wilson hissed as she advanced on me and the crowd drew closer. "I find your silence to be rude. I have no idea what my son sees in you and I think… "

"Will you help me find my wedding dress?" I shouted at the top of my lungs, causing everyone to clap their hands over their ears… including Mrs. Wilson.

Her silence was deafening and I wanted to curl up and die, but not before I decapitated Dwayne.

She slowly peeled her perfectly manicured hands from her ears and looked down at the ground as her body began to tremble. She was so going to try to kill me. What a clusterhump. Tonight was supposed to be an evening of celebration and magic and now it was turning into a death match. My heart thumped in my chest so loudly I was sure everyone could hear it. I could kill a Dragon, but Hank's mom scared the pants off me.

It was so going to suck if she tried to off me. Hank might be unhappy if I tore his mother's head off… I mean, I knew they didn't get along, but me killing her could put a real crimp in my sex life.

She looked up and her eyes were glassy. Pulling a perfectly starched white lacey handkerchief from her ample bosom, she dabbed at her eyes. What the Hell was happening? Did she feel bad that she wanted to kill me? I really didn't want to kill her, but if she left me no choice…

"What did you say?" she asked so softly I had to lean in to hear.

"I, um… I forgot," I choked out. This could not be happening.

"She asked you to help her select a wedding gown. Actually, what she meant to say was do you still have yours? She would be honored to wear it," Dwayne cut in as he casually smoothed out the wrinkles in his gauchos as if the future of my life wasn't pending.

"*You are so dead,*" I threatened.

"*Already dead. Doesn't scare me,*" he shot back.

"Do you really want to wear my dress?" Mrs. Wilson asked in a high-pitched voice. Her tears now flowed freely.

What was going on here? Did she want me to wear her dress? Confusion didn't begin to cover my rioting emotions. I was ready for a smack-down and now I was negotiating a dress? Shit, when did she get married? It had to be at least thirty or forty years ago. Her dress was probably poofy and horrid. I wanted something strapless and simple… A painful pinch from Dwayne halted my inner monologue.

"*Tell her you want to wear her damn dress,*" he shouted inside my head.

"*It's probably fugly,*" I shrieked in a panicked tone.

"*You have a choice here,*" Dwayne explained. "*Wear a heinous, more than likely white wedding gown and live reasonably non-deadly holiday seasons with your mother in law—or get your ass handed to you.*"

"*I think I could take her,*" I said with confidence.

"*Just don't see that going over real well.*"

"Point. Do I really have to wear her dress?"

"Yes. Yes, you do."

"You suck so bad," I snarled at him. *"You will pay for this."*

"Doll face?"

"Yes?"

"Everyone is staring at you," Dwayne said.

He was correct. They were all watching me to see what I was going to say. I knew half of them probably were hoping for a fight. We really were a violent species. However, there would be no bloodshed tonight. I hoped...

"Yes, Mrs. Wilson, I would be humbled and honored to wear your dress," I said as I tried not to gag on my words. I was certain it would have huge sleeves and a train from hell.

She whipped around on the blood-thirsty crowd, scaring the hell out of them. I was glad to see it wasn't just me...

"Did you hear that?" she shouted, getting the attention of the entire Pack. "My daughter wants to wear my wedding gown at her nuptials."

The crowd went wild and Mrs. Wilson took a bow. This was all kinds of weird, but I was quite sure I was going to live through the evening now. I knew in my heart the gown would be awful, but it did save me from having to try on any more.

Next thing I knew I was in a rib-crunching hug from Mrs. Wilson. Getting beaten to death was one thing, getting loved to death was another. However, they both hurt.

"Go for the home run while you're ahead," Dwayne insisted.

I couldn't see him as I was trapped in Mrs. Wilson's enormous cleavage, but I could hear him... and he had a point.

"Can we get married here?" I knew it came out muffled, but she heard it. I was certain that she liked the idea because I heard my sternum crack.

"Oh dear sweet baby Jesus, all the angels and saints, the Goddess, Mother Earth, all my ancestors and Dolce and Gabbana, my prayers have been answered! We'll be hosting the nuptials of my son and my darling daughter-in-law on our land. Praise Buddha," she shouted.

Again the crowd went nuts.

"Boy, she really hit a large cross-section of deities," Dwayne observed.

"Can you pry me out of her knockers?" I begged, still unable to see anything except the cavern between her bosoms.

"I'll give it a shot," he said. "Mrs. Wilson, you truly have the gams to pull off some gauchos," Dwayne gushed.

"Oh, do you think so?" she asked, flattered as she dropped me to the ground and moved in to examine Dwayne's fashion disaster that covered his lower half.

As I sat sprawled on the grass I tried to regulate my breathing. My future mother-in-law had one hell of a deadly hug. It reminded me yet again to stay on her good side. I'd hate to get introduced to her left hook.

"Are you okay?" Sandy Moongie asked quietly as she squatted down next to me and gently lifted my chin.

Sandy and I had gone to high school together and I adored her. Heavy and shy in her teen years, she had slimmed down and looked like a damned super model now—wild blonde curls framed her heart-shaped face and her cornflower blue eyes were huge. She had been one of the gals I'd saved from the Dragons and we were bonded for life.

"Will be in about thirty seconds," I replied with a weak grin. "She's a scary mother humper."

"You got that right. So… I'm not sure whether to say thank you or to tackle your ass for telling Hank and his brother that I'm a computer whiz."

My grin was now large. I luuurved that she wouldn't call Junior by name. I was certain she had it as bad as he did.

"What?" she asked as her eyes narrowed.

"Nothing," I said. I put my hands out to Sandy for some help up. My ribs were still burning from the loving I'd just received from Mrs. Wilson.

"Will you ever call her mom?" Sandy asked as she pulled me to my feet.

That gave me pause and indigestion. "Oh my hell, do you think I'll have to?"

"Don't know." She shrugged and laughed. "Knowing her, she'll make you call her Mrs. Wilson the rest of her unnaturally long life."

"I'd bet my life her dress is butthole fugly," I muttered as I checked my midsection for blood or a protruding rib.

Sandy bit at her full lips and stared at the ground.

"Tell me," I hissed as I yanked her away from the Pack so we wouldn't be heard.

"She wore one similar to what my mother wore," she said slowly while trying not to laugh.

"And?" I demanded.

"It's freakin awful—huge, with sleeves bigger than my head and acres of material… and a rhinestone tiara veil," she gasped out, barely containing herself.

"Is it white?"

"Of course it's white," she said, confused.

"Son of a bitch, Dwayne is dead," I muttered as I spun around and started to march back into the fray to behead my BFF.

"Oh shit," she muttered. "Come back here."

"Look, I have to maim Dwayne for getting me into this or at least spill something on his gauchos that will permanently stain them," I explained impatiently as I walked back to her. "Can this wait?"

"No, it can't," she said as she twisted her hands. "I know Junior will brief you guys on this, but it looks like one of his geeky friends accidently put Dwayne's name into the search engine with the Were Cows." Sandy paled considerably and her eyes were wide.

"What does that mean?" I asked, fairly sure I knew.

"It means the Cows could know Dwayne is alive and well," she said.

"That is sucktastic," I yelled catching the attention of the group admiring Dwayne's heinous ensemble. From the looks of it, he and Mrs. Wilson were now besties. I smiled and waved as I dragged Sandy farther into the woods.

"What else do you know?"

"That's really about it. Junior let the geek guy have it so bad I was hurtin' when he was done," she said with a shudder.

"Did you think it was hot?" I asked.

"What the hell kind of question is that?" she asked as heat crept up her cheeks.

"A legit one," I said. "Answer it."

Sandy rolled her eyes and I giggled.

"Fine," she huffed. "It was hot, but Junior is such a knob I'm not going there."

"You do realize you just called your Alpha a knob," I informed her.

"Shit," she mumbled. She walked farther into the woods, leaned on a tree and resumed chewing on her lips.

"Look, if it helps, he's given up his man-whore ways," I told her.

Her eyebrows shot up and she snorted with disgust. "When? Last week?"

"Well, um... yeah."

"Priceless," Sandy said with another eye roll. "Come on, we need to get back. The knob is going to be inducted soon."

She started back to the clearing and I gently took her arm.

"Sandy, he's really not a knob," I told her.

She blew out a long sigh and her shoulders slumped forward.

"Essie, he really is."

"Well, okay—he is, but he's trying very hard not to be," I said, working to plead his case. I knew I should be freaking about the Were Cows, but I could only handle one thing at a time. Helping Junior out was the easiest of the jobs I had at the moment... maybe.

"Essie, it will take a miracle or a castration for that boy to keep his pecker in his pants," Sandy stated in a resigned voice. "Do I think he's hot? Yes. Brilliant? Absolutely. Would I like to ride him till he's blind? You bet. The Werewolf for me? Not in a million years. So while I appreciate you trying to de-knob Junior, your case is falling on deaf ears."

"Okay," I said as I let go of her arm and continued back to the Pack.

"Okay?" she sputtered. "That's all you have to say?"

"Yep—once a knob always a knob," I agreed with a nod of my head. "You are absolutely correct. People cannot change. They can't grow up or realize the error of their weenies—whoops, I meant ways. You should stay far away from him because he wants you something awful. Do you want me to find someone else to do the computer work?"

She just stared at me in shocked silence. It took all I had not to pump my fists over my head and yell *Victory*.

"Well?" I asked. "Do you?"

"Um… no. I can, you know, do the stuff and um… no, you don't have to replace me," she stuttered, not making eye contact.

"Okay. You ready to go back?"

She nodded curtly and slapped me hard on the back of my head. "You suck, Ester Elizabeth McGee. You know that, don't you?"

"I have heard it before." I grinned and smacked her back. "But you love me anyway."

Sandy made a very unladylike grunt and stomped ahead of me. "I will make you pay," she said angrily, but I could hear the frustrated laugh trying to escape.

"I've heard that before too," I said with a huge grin.

One job down… so many more to go.

***

Dwayne was literally holding hands with Mrs. Wilson when we reached the Pack. She was all aflutter and had pinned her dress together between her legs. She was now sporting an alarming make shift version of gauchos. I was going to have to rethink Dwayne's decapitation. Only a true BFF would make nice with my enemy and keep her occupied so I wouldn't put my foot in my mouth and start World War III.

A hush fell over the crowd as our new Alpha, our old Alpha and their father, our retired Alpha, walked over the hill together and approached the Pack.

Dressed in loose fitting black clothing, their power danced around and bathed the clearing. Splashes of colorful light flitted around them and shot out over the delighted crowd. The hair on my neck stood up and I was again awed at the raw and beautiful enchantment of the Werewolves. Hank and Junior quietly stood with their father on a raised stage. Torches burned brightly, illuminating the heightened area as the sky darkened in dusk. Magic swirled through the air and lightning bugs lit the excited faces of the Pack. I glanced quickly over at Dwayne, whose mouth was open in astonishment.

"We are here tonight to pledge our loyalty and obedience to the new Alpha of the Georgia Pack," Mr. Wilson said with great joy. "I am humbled to have sired two Alphas."

"You didn't have to give birth to them," Mrs. Wilson grumbled good-naturedly.

The Pack laughed as did Mr. Wilson, Hank and Junior.

"You are correct, my beautiful mate," Mr. Wilson agreed. "I am eternally grateful to you. Our blessings are many," he said as he gave her a wink. "And now we share our blessings with our people."

The crowd howled and I howled right along with my Pack. Granny came up behind me and wrapped her arms around my waist. Her love sunk right into me and I made a very important decision.

"Will you give me away at my wedding?" I whispered as I placed my hands over hers.

Granny froze and then squeezed me tighter. "You gonna wear Sadie Wilson's buttass nasty gown?"

"Um... yep."

Holy hell, how fugly was the dress?

"You're gonna looked like a puff ball with sequins and rhinestones," she whispered gleefully.

Question answered.

"Understood. It was a life or death decision," I hissed under my breath. "Answer the other question."

She got right up next to my ear and gave me a kiss. "Nothing in this world would make me prouder.

You are the light of my life and delivering you to the man who loves and deserves you will be one of my finest moments. I love you, baby girl."

"I love you too, Granny," I choked out as my eyes filled and my world felt so right.

"I wish your daddy was alive to walk you, but I will do him and your mamma proud." Her eyes were misty now too. I took her hand and placed it on my cheek, then leaned into it for comfort as I had when I was a child. I had no clue what this woman had given up to raise me, but I was so endlessly grateful that she did. I may have lost my parents, but I had never lost unconditional love. She was everything to me.

"Enough of the sappy crap." She grinned and wiped my tears. "We better listen up or Jack Wilson will have our butts."

She was right. Hank and Junior's father was a good and kind man, but he was an Alpha.

"Nuff said," I whispered as I turned back to the action on the stage.

A beautiful ruby encrusted knife had been drawn by Mr. Wilson and he held it up for the Pack to see.

"Jacob David Wilson, do you solemnly swear to protect the Pack and lead with fairness and integrity?"

"I do, Father," Junior answered.

I almost giggled. Sometimes I forget Junior had another name... Granny pinched my backside and I immediately sobered up.

"Do you promise to put the Pack above all others until the day you are blessed with a mate who shall rule by your side?" Mr. Wilson asked.

Junior's eyes scanned the crowd and landed on Sandy. She tried to look away, but Junior's gaze was so intense no one could have looked away. Her body trembled and her eyes blazed with both anger and desire. Junior had his work cut out for him in that department.

"I do, Father," he said with a grin and a wink to Sandy.

"Henry James Wilson, do you willingly cede the title of Alpha of the Georgia Pack to your brother, knowing this shall never change? He will rule the Pack and you will now be one of his subjects."

"With honor, humility and love I do," Hank said as he embraced his brother.

"Then in the name of our ancestors and all that we hold as fair and good, I name you, Jacob, Alpha of the Georgia Pack. Jacob David Wilson, Henry James Wilson—hold out your hands."

With quick and decisive slashes from the glittering knife, Mr. Wilson sliced his sons' hands and brought them together over his head. As their blood mixed and the power of the Pack Alpha was transferred the crowd fell to their knees. The soft ground beneath me trembled with magic. I raised my eyes back to the stage and had to put my hand up to shield them from the blast of golden light that exploded and burned brightly between Hank and Junior's clasped hands.

Shouts of joy began to burst from the kneeling crowd. Clapping and whistling soon followed. A cool wind blew and the mist floated around us. Hank caught my eye and mouthed, *I love you.* I almost cried with pride. He was so strong and good and mine. I had no clue what I had done to deserve him, but I was keeping him until the day I left this earth. I also felt the distinct need to rush the stage and jump his sexy ass.

"Is it time to get naked and furry?" Dwayne yelled over the crowd, thankfully stopping me from making good on my inappropriate plan.

"Almost," I shouted back as I hugged him. "Thank you for befriending the viper."

"She's really not that bad and she looks wonderful in gauchos!"

"Did you bring your faux fur?" I asked, not touching the newly discovered merits of Mrs. Wilson.

"You bet I did, doll baby." Dwayne's eyes lit up almost as brightly as the magic still floating around us.

The shift was about to be Dwayned... no one would ever be the same.

Chapter 6

"I proudly introduce to you our new Alpha, Jacob David Wilson," Mr. Wilson bellowed as he hugged both of his sons.

"Isn't it amazing?" I asked Dwayne. I grasped his hand and let myself get lost in the pure joy and excitement of my Pack.

"In all my years I have never seen anything so beautiful," Dwayne said reverently. "Vampyres don't like each other much so we really don't get together often. Our gatherings tend to end in a decapitation."

"Then I'm so happy you're here," I said. I wrapped my arms around my best friend and held on tight.

"You have no clue what that means to me," he said as he hugged me back. "No clue."

"What are you going to do while we run?" I asked, feeling bad about leaving him here alone.

"Oh honey pie, I'm coming with you."

"How?" I asked, a bit confused.

"You'll see." His grin was positively evil and totally contagious.

"God help us all," I muttered.

"And all the angels and saints, the Goddess, Mother Earth, all our ancestors and Dolce and Gabbana," Dwayne recited with a smirk.

"You forgot Buddha," I reminded him.

"Damn it, you're correct—and Buddha," he amended. "Can we get naked yet?"

I rolled my eyes and laughed. "In a minute. Just listen."

All eyes were fixed on the stage as Junior stepped forward and his father and Hank stepped back. The crowd quieted and waited.

"I am humbled and honored to be your new Alpha. I come from a long line of Alphas that have taught me well. I will do everything in my power to respect the bravery and memory of those that have come before me or I will die trying," Junior shouted to the Pack.

Gone was the clumsy man that could destroy an office by simply pacing. On the stage stood a powerful force to be reckoned with. He seemed to be even bigger than his already enormous self and magic swirled around him like a moving kaleidoscope.

"I promise to protect you and to govern with a fair and honest hand. I also swear to destroy anything that risks the health and happiness of our people."

That got a bloodthirsty whoop from the crowd. What did I expect? We *were* Werewolves.

"Alright people," Junior bellowed with a wide grin followed by a howl. "It's time to get nekkid and run!"

There was the Junior I knew.

The whoops were now so loud I couldn't hear my own thoughts. Clothes were flying and skin turned to fur quickly. Dwayne had a somewhat shocked and amused crowd around him as he stripped to a Lady Gaga song. He had put his phone in a cordless dock and was going to town. I fell down laughing as he tore away his halter and tossed it up high. It was caught midair by a set of fangs that belonged to a delighted Mrs. Wilson. I had seen everything now. She shimmied over and continued her de-robing in time with the Gaga. I prayed to Dolce and Gabbana that this would not become a new ritual.

Hank came up behind me and stopped dead in his tracks.

"What the hell is happening?" he asked as he winced at the site of his partially clad mother twerking with the very gay Vampyre.

"I'm pretty sure Hell just froze over," I said as I observed the disaster unfolding.

It simply got more disturbing as Mr. Wilson joined his mate in the dance party.

"Let's get out of here before this degenerates into something I'll need therapy for," Hank insisted as he pulled me away from the show.

"Agreed," I said as I followed him into the woods. My wolf was close to the surface and wanted out badly.

"You ready baby?" Hank asked as he tore his clothes off.

"So ready," I said as I joined him.

I closed my eyes and drew on the power of my inner wolf. She was there and waiting for me happily. I let the magic engulf me and my body tingled from my head to my toes. A magic so wondrous and rare it always left me breathless. My skin changed to fur, my bones shifted painlessly and my body became what it was supposed to be. My wolf—my strong and beautiful wolf.

Hank's wolf was as gorgeous as his human form. His shiny chocolate coat glistened in the moonlight that filtered through the trees. He was huge. My wolf was small in comparison, but I was fast. His eyes were still the same intense green and they stared at me with amusement.

"You like what you see?" he asked as his voice invaded my brain.

In wolf form the Pack was still able to communicate. A mated pair could communicate perfectly even from great distances because of the mating bite and shared blood. With other Pack members we had to be in close range. The only other wolf that could communicate with ease and complete clarity to our people was our Alpha.

"You'll do," I replied cockily.

His laugh bounced around in my head and I nipped playfully at his hind legs until he pinned me and howled with victory.

"You suck," I accused. *"If I had a running start you'd never best me."*

"Be my guest, my beautiful wolf," he dared with narrowed eyes as he let me up.

I needed a little distraction if I was going to make good on my boast... I limped pathetically as I got to my feet and favored my left hind leg.

"Oh baby, are you okay?" Hank got low and examined my paw. It was all I needed. I took off like a bat out of hell. Shrieking with delight I left him in the dust.

"You'll pay for that," he threatened as he took off on the chase.

"I keep hearing that one tonight," I squealed as I raced through the woods I knew like the back of my hand.

Being smaller I had the advantage of being able to go under brush as opposed to over. It gave me an edge that I used wisely. As I ran the wind blew through my fur. I felt free, happy and alive. I would miss Hung Island when we left, but I knew we'd always come back.

"Gaining on you, pretty girl," Hank huffed inside my head.

"*Maybe,*" I shot back, "*but I'm still winning!*"

I whipped past Granny's wolf. She was trotting around with some of her buddies including Lori and Layla. I wondered for a moment if the shop gals had seen Dwayne's striptease and I honestly hoped they hadn't. Poor Layla was liable to loose it.

"*You better run, girlie,*" Granny shouted with a gleeful cackle. "*I can hear him coming.*"

I came to a clearing and skidded to a halt. I caught the scent of a non-shifter deer and I lost precious seconds. To hunt or not to hunt... that is the question. Unfortunately my brief pause put an end to both choices. Damn that Shakespeare.

Hank jumped me from behind and we rolled down the hill laughing like children. Paws and muzzles and tails were undistinguishable as we tumbled forward all tangled up in each other. We landed with a thud by a gurgling stream.

"*Uncle?*" Hank asked as my wolf lay pinned beneath him.

"*Fine. Uncle,*" I huffed. "*But it wasn't 'cause I actually lost. I scented a deer and my wolf wanted to hunt.*"

"*Excuses, excuses,*" Hanks said drolly as he let me up.

We went to the stream and drank like we hadn't had water in weeks.

"*God, that was fun,*" I said with water dripping from my muzzle. "*I really love being in my wolf form when it's for fun. Not for the job when I'm trying to sniff out a bad guy.*"

"*Couldn't agree more,*" he said as he nuzzled me.

"*You wanna hunt?*" I asked as I pressed my side to his.

"*In a minute. Let's just be lazy for a few,*" he said as he knocked my paws out from under me, causing me to land on his furry chest.

"*Works for me*," I said as I cuddled with my big wolf. "*Oh my god, I have to tell you about the conversation I had with your mother. It was positively...*"

I stopped on a dime, jumped to my feet and growled low in my throat. Something huge and furry flew over our heads. Hank leapt and tried to yank it out of the air, but it was too fast.

"*What in the hell was that*," he growled as we went butt to butt and circled, looking for danger.

"*I have no idea. Crap,*" I snapped. "*Is this something else I missed by skipping Were History?*"

"*Nope,*" he answered tersely. "*Wolves do not fly. However, if that was a wolf it was one of the mangiest wolves I've ever seen.*"

Wolves did not fly... but Vampyres did.

If we could get in each other's heads in human form maybe I could tear Dwayne a new butthole in wolf form. It was worth a try.

"*Dwayne, you idiot, is that you?*" I shouted as I scanned the air above me.

"*Yessssss,*" he squealed. "*And you tell Hank I resent that. I am not mangy. This faux fur cost six thousand dollars.*"

"*Tell him he overpaid,*" Hank said. "*Wait. Am I hearing Dwayne in my head?*"

"*Oh my god,*" I yelled. "*Are you?*"

Hank shook his big furry head and stilled. "*Say something, Dwayne,*" he said slowly.

"*I think you could pull off gauchos with your ass,*" Dwayne volunteered.

"*How is this happening? It's not natural. And I would rather chew glass and swallow it than wear gauchos,*" Hank muttered as he paced in tight circles. "*You can hear him too, Essie?*"

"*I can, but I've shared blood with him,*" I told Hank.

Dwayne hovered above us and flapped his arms like a bird.

"*Do you have to do that to fly? I didn't think... oh my freakin' hell, Dwayne! Button the bottom of your coat. Your man bits are blowing in the wind.*" I groaned as I buried my muzzle in my paws.

"*When did you become such a prude?*" Dwayne huffed as he adjusted his coat.

"*I'm not a prude,*" I snapped. "*It's just alarming to look up and see my BFF's weenie and friends bouncing in the breeze.*"

"*Fair point, well made,*" he said. "*I would find it disturbing to glance up at a faceful of your knockers too.*"

"*As appalling as this conversation has gotten, I still want to know how I'm communicating with Dwayne,*" Hank said.

"*I can only guess that because we've both shared Essie's blood we can hear each other,*" Dwayne surmised.

It was the only explanation that made any sense. Dwayne floated down and landed gracefully in front of us. Hank was correct. The coat was awful.

"*Did you really pay six thousand dollars for that?*" I asked.

"*Hell to the no!*" Dwayne laughed as he modeled his scary fur. "*Got it at the thrift shop for thirty-two dollars and seventy-five cents.*"

"*I still say you overpaid,*" Hank said as he sat down on his haunches and stared at Dwayne. "*As bizarre as this communication thing is, it may come in handy in Chicago.*"

"*Hey now,*" I grumbled as I butted Hank with my head. "*We still have about ten hours of vacation left. No talking about our impending deaths.*"

"*You're right baby. I have a better idea anyway.*"

"*What's that?*" Dwayne asked as he picked twigs and leaves out of his hairy mess of a wolf costume.

"*How about we go scare the hell out of the Pack with the flying mangy Werewolf?*" Hank's wolf grinned, which would look frightening if you didn't know him.

"*That is fabulous,*" I squealed.

"*While I wholeheartedly agree with the devious activity,*" Dwayne said with a hand on his hip and his brows raised high, "*if you call me mangy one more time, I will fly over your head and pee on you.*"

"*Okay, that's just gross,*" I said as I shuddered.

"*What if we just call you nappy?*"

"*I prefer kinky,*" he informed us with a grin.

"*Of course you do.*" I rolled my eyes and chuffed. "*Alright, kinky Vamp, you ready to go have some fun with the wolves?*"

"*Oh my god,*" Dwayne shrieked as he levitated and did flips in the air. "*I haven't had this much fun since I went fishing naked in the Bermuda Triangle with Hemingway, some Pygmy fellas and a Were Skunk named Herm.*"

Both Hank and I were smart enough not to touch that one. However, even if we wanted to we couldn't. Dwayne had taken off screaming like a banshee to terrorize the Pack. I realized I hadn't told my BFF about the Were Cows knowing about him, but I didn't want to ruin his fun.

Tomorrow was back to reality. Tonight was for fun.

"*You ready to watch Dwayne make a mockery of our scared rituals?*" Hank inquired as he nipped at my ear.

"*Yep. This will be a night that will go down in history.*"

"*God help us all.*"

Chapter 7

"Well, would you look at that?" Granny gasped and pulled out her new cell phone that I had gotten for her... the one I swore I wouldn't buy. "When Dwayne sleeps he looks dead."

She started snapping pictures.

"He's always dead," I said as I glanced over my shoulder at my best bud.

Good lord, Granny was right. He was laid out on the backseat of the Hummer like a cadaver without rigor mortis. Dwayne had worn himself out last night. Junior's induction would live in infamy due to the kinky Vamp scaring years off of most of the Pack's lives. A group of teenage boy wolves had taken a chunk out of Dwayne's hind-quarter before they realized he wasn't a hairy flying Demon from Hell. They were mortified and extremely apologetic, but Dwayne brushed it off and healed right back up in less than five minutes. He then entertained the Pack with songs and stories from his time as a pirate. A debilitating and educational time was had by all.

Mrs. Wilson even offered to put Dwayne's faux fur in storage for the next time he wanted to join in on a Pack shift. Needless to say my fellow Werewolves were appalled, but no one questioned Mrs. Wilson. No one.

"I know he's *dead*," Granny said, "but he looks *really* dead."

"Is he?" I asked, alarmed. He couldn't be. I was almost certain Vamps turned to dust when they died. However, since I'd forgone most of my paranormal education because I skipped all my classes, I wasn't entirely sure.

"How in tarnation can I tell? It's not like the boy has a pulse." Granny got up in his face and blew on him.

"What in the name of Christina Aguilera are you doing?" a drowsy Dwayne mumbled as he swatted at Granny's head.

"Making sure you weren't dead, bloodsucker," she answered as she popped him back.

"Considering that I am, I don't really see the point. And you seriously need a mint," he said as he pinched his nostrils closed. "Hank, are we there yet?"

Hank's lips compressed in annoyance and he said absolutely nothing as he maneuvered the Hummer in and out of traffic on our way to Chicago. Of course, before Dwayne had passed out he'd asked the same question of Hank at least thirty times.

"He's not going to answer me, is he?" Dwayne whispered loudly.

"Nope," I told him. "He's not."

"Fine by me, it's a fabulously smooth ride. Are you all enjoying my Hummer?" he asked with an innocent grin.

"Oh my god." I laughed and then groaned. "You totally bought this car so you could legally say hummer all the time without getting in trouble."

"Guilty," he sang and then high-fived Granny.

"Dwayne," Hank said with a chuckle. "We need to talk."

"About Hummers?" he asked.

"Uhhh no, about Were Cows."

"Dear god, did Junior find out more?"

"Yes and no," Hank said as he turned off on an exit and parked the humongous vehicle at a deserted rest stop. "Your name was accidently tied in on an Internet search and the Cows are now possibly aware of you."

Dwayne's silence was scary, but his levitation that plastered him to the ceiling of the car was downright frightening.

"Um, Dwayne?" I whispered. "Can I do anything for you?"

"No, doll, I just need to work out my anger issues for a minute," he replied as if he weren't hanging like a human bat.

"Okay."

"Maybe they're not related to the Cows you married," Granny said as she reached up and patted his kneecap.

"Did we get a surname?" Dwayne inquired calmly as he dangled.

"Yep," Hank said hesitantly.

"Dung?" Dwayne asked even more calmly.

Crap, if the answer was yes, would Dwayne blow off the roof of the car?

"Yes, it's Dung," Hank answered and then held his breath.

"Well, that's suckerific," Dwayne screeched as he dropped from the ceiling to the floor with a thud. "I'm going have to go find them before they find me."

"Why would you do that?" I demanded. "They want you dead."

"True," he said. "But in order for me to have any kind of upper hand, I can't wait for them to ambush me. If anything happened to one of you guys I would have to decapitate myself and that is very difficult."

"Whoa, so you're just gonna go off on your own and kill a bunch of Dungs?" I snapped. "I forbid you to do this alone."

"Essie, you are not the boss of me," Dwayne said with a sad smile.

"I am the boss of everybody," I informed him loudly. "Just ask Hank."

Hank shrugged and grinned. Granny just patted Dwayne's head like he was a dog.

"She's correct," Granny told Dwayne.

"That she's the boss of everyone?" Dwayne asked, confused.

"Hell to the no! I'm the boss of everyone," Granny said. "Always have been, always will be. However, Essie is correct about you not going off half-cocked and getting into it with the Cow Dungs."

"The Dung Cows," Dwayne corrected her.

"What?"

Now Granny was confused.

"Bottom line," I ground out, not wanting to get into a semantics debate that could take hours. "We're a family. We work together. First the Dragons, then the Dungs, and then the Council. You understand me?"

"I'm farklempt," Dwayne blubbered as he fluttered his hand in front of his watery eyes. "Not really used to having backup."

"Well, now you have it, and if you go off by yourself *I* will decapitate you," I said as I bent over the passenger seat and gave him a hug.

"That is the nicest thing anyone has ever said to me," he said as he sniffled.

"You're welcome." I laughed and rolled my eyes.

"Everyone out of the car," Hank directed. "Stretch your legs and prepared to get stabbed."

"Sweet hell, is this a Werewolf thing?" Dwayne asked as he got out.

•

87

"Nope," Hank said as he pulled a sharp pocketknife from the glove compartment. "It's a safety thing. We're all getting homing transmitters put in so Junior can track us if we get separated."

Hank quickly inserted the small knife into both Granny and Dwayne's hips and placed tiny metal chips inside them. They healed immediately. He then sliced his own hip and slid a transmitter under his skin.

"Why doesn't Essie have to get stabbed?" Dwayne complained as he stared at his healing hip.

"Because I already have one in my butt," I said as I narrowed my eyes at my mate.

Hank didn't give me a heads up when he stabbed me in the ass two weeks ago to plant a transmitter in me. We were going after the Dragons and time was of the essence…

"Would you have let me stab you in the butt if I told you I was going to?" he asked as he crossed his arms over his chest and gave me a lopsided grin.

"Yes," I said, not making eye contact. I could throw down with the best of them, but I really hated getting stabbed.

"Really?" he prodded.

"Yes, really," I snapped. "You might have had to chase me down for an hour."

"Or two," Granny chimed in.

"Fine. It was better to just blindly stab my ass. You happy?"

"Yep," he said as he grabbed me and swung me around.

"You're a dork."

"I'm your dork," he shot back and punctuated it with a kiss.

"Are we going to stand here and watch you two suck face or are we gonna go get some Dragons?" Granny asked with a grin.

"Actually, Dwayne made a fine point," Hank said as he gave me one last peck and then got all sexy serious.

"On my god, I did?" Dwayne asked.

"The element of surprise will go a long way in not getting gored by the Cows," he said. "We are heading into Indiana in the next hour."

"Yes? And?" I needed some facts—not hints.

"The Dung's main compound is right outside Indianapolis. I saw we pay the Cows a visit before they extend an invite."

"Won't this screw with Angela's schedule?" Granny asked gleefully.

Soon I'd have to get the full story from Granny about her time partnering with my boss.

"Do I look like I care?" Hank inquired with an evil smirk.

"Nope, you don't," I said. "Furthermore, I think making Angela and her Dragon buddy come to us somewhere outside of Chicago is safer."

"Brilliant! Damn, I should marry you," Hank yelled.

"You already are." I laughed and held up my left hand, showing off my beautiful ring.

"I sure am a smart guy."

I threw my arms around his neck and laid a big one on his full beautiful lips. "Yes, you certainly are."

***

"Is this a joke?" I asked as we stood at the rickety wooden gate of a compound with a stench that made my eyes water. The enormous hand painted sign read, *DUNG FARM. We Moo For You. All Trespassers Will Be Eaten. Open To The Public On Mondays For Milk. Bring Your Own Damn Jug.*

"I told you they weren't very bright," Dwayne whispered as he held his nose. "They eat their mates. Which begs the question, how are they still here?"

"Maybe they're hermaphrodites and can impregnate themselves," Granny suggested. "You know, they take themselves out to a nice dinner and then dance a little and then feel themselves up and get all randy and then WHAM. Next thing you know... preggers."

That pretty much rendered everyone silent while we contemplated her absurdly wrong and horrifying nugget.

"I'm gonna have to go with a no goddamned way on that theory," Hank choked out as he put his hand over his mouth to keep from hurling.

"I'm with Hank on that one," I said as I struggled not to gag.

"Just a thought," Granny huffed defensively. "I don't hear you brainiacs coming up with a logical possibility."

"It's a fine hypothesis," Dwayne told her with a weak thumbs up. "It's simply a bit vomit-inducing."

"It might be," Granny agreed with a shudder, "but it makes sense."

"God, I really hope you're wrong," I said, joining her with a shudder of my own.

We had parked the Hummer at a Krispy Kreme about five miles away and hoofed it to the Were Cow's lair. Granny had polished off a dozen doughnuts on our hike and still complained about being hungry.

Indiana was flat with very little brush—no place to hide. Thankfully we had waited till dark to approach.

"Do we have a plan?" I asked.

"It's a dairy farm," Hank stated the obvious.

"Yep."

"I'm thirsty. Let's go in and buy some milk," Hank said with a grin.

"Um, it's ten at night on a Tuesday," I said, just in case no one else had actually read the entire sign. I was all for walking in and shaking it up; I just wanted to make sure we all had the intel.

"Oh my Donna Summer, this is exciting," Dwayne squealed as he bobbed up and down. "Of course we could be walking into a bloody and violent death, but it's just so naughty. Reminds me of the time I streaked in Pamplona at the Running of the Bulls about eighty years ago. I lost my left leg and my right test… "

"Stop," I said as I slapped my hand over Dwayne's mouth. "I just can't. Not right now."

"Later?" he asked.

"Possibly," I muttered.

"Anyhoo, thankfully it all grew back," he explained.

"That's… great," Hank said with a wince. "Back to the matter at hand—we go in diamond formation. I'm in front, Dwayne in back in case they recognize him, and Essie and Granny flank my sides. If it goes bad quickly we shift and go back-to-back. Dwayne, be prepared to do a mind meld."

"Oh dude," I moaned and paled. "I was hoping to never see one of those."

"They are a bit messy and stinky," Dwayne admitted, "but they get the job done."

"It couldn't reek any more than this place already does," Granny grumbled as she pulled a colorful scarf out of her cleavage and tied it over her nose. "Anybody want a kerchief?"

She pulled several more out of her bra and handed them out. On any other day, I'd hesitate to wear something that had been nestled in my Granny's bosom for twenty-four hours, but the stench was horrific. We looked like a band of designer burglars.

91

"Everyone armed?" Hank questioned as he checked his guns and knives.

"Yep," I said as I felt for my Glock.

"Locked and loaded," Granny said.

"Dwayne does not need weapons," my BFF reminded us. "Dwayne *is* a weapon."

Hank shook his head and looked up to the Heavens for a moment. "Let's do it."

"Wait," I spluttered. "Is there anything I need to know about a Were Cow before we go in... considering I was, you know... absent the day it was studied in school."

The laughter from my posse made me want to punch them in their heads. However, I knew I deserved it.

"I get it," I admitted sheepishly. "I do get it, but giving me shit aside, is there anything I should be aware of?"

"When they shift they're roughly the size of a Hummer," Dwayne said with a smirk.

"You really enjoyed saying that," I said as my eyes narrowed at him.

"Yes. Yes, I did."

"Anything else?" I asked and then instantly regretted it.

"Stay the hell away from their asses," Granny instructed.

"I don't want to ask why—but *why*?" I could tell Granny was going to explain whether I wanted to know or not. I was simply expediting.

Hank just pinched the bridge of his nose and stared off into the darkening sky. I was unsure if he already knew all of this information or if he was simply too smart to have opened a can of worms—or ass.

"Because they blow wind that can singe the hair right off your head. The Were Cows' gastric explosions are directly responsible for the Greenhouse Effect," Granny said.

"Bull crap," I said as I rolled my eyes.

"That too," she added.

"Wait—what?" Following her train of thought was headache inducing.

"Were Cow patties are destroying our ozone too." She shook her head with disgust. "Their rectal issues are gonna be the end of the world. I really think they should have their rear ends permanently plugged up."

"They'd simply start producing killer stanky burps," Dwayne told Granny.

"Sweet Jesus in a mini skirt, you're right."

"Oookay guys, I think that's probably enough," I stammered.

Note to self: stop asking questions of Granny and Dwayne. Or at least make sure my stomach is empty if questions are necessary.

"Remember how they said Mrs. O'Leary's cow started the Chicago Fire?" Dwayne asked.

"That was totally disproven," I argued.

"More like covered up," Dwayne sniffed. "A Were Cow ate twenty-six pounds of baked beans and tooted next to the lantern that started it all. Damn thing blew up like a bomb."

"Enough," Hank said in frustration as he ran his hands through his hair and gave Dwayne and Granny a look that would have scared the hell out of most people. Granny and Dwayne were not most people. "Most importantly, if they shift don't let them gore you. The tips of their tusks are poisonous. Also, their hooves are razor sharp so… "

"I really think the ass part is more important," Granny interrupted Hank. "Of course, Dwayne would be fine because he's bald."

"And don't step in their poo poo—it will eat your foot right off your body," Dwayne added.

"I'm actually really sorry I asked." My gag reflex was so close to the surface I had to pace it off.

"Okay," Hank said as the color began to come back into his face. "We ready now?"

"I was born ready," Granny crowed.

"Of course you were," I mumbled as I swallowed carefully to make sure nothing was going to come back up.

"I would just like to say that I love all of you and if you die tonight, please accept my sincerest apologies." Dwayne hugged each of us and then dropped to the ground and did eleven one-handed pushups.

"Does that help?" I asked as I watched him.

"Not at all," he replied.

"Move it," Hank said in exasperation.

I grinned and slapped his butt. Even annoyed he was hotter than asphalt in August.

The dirt road was rutted and uneven. Rusted-out junk cars and garbage littered the fields on either side. Up ahead I spotted several rundown trailers. The entire place made me sad. What could have been beautiful property in its stark simplicity was an unkempt pathetic disaster.

"This confuses me some," Granny said quietly as she took in the abject poverty. "How does a powerful species come to this?"

"Don't know," Hank said tersely. "Maybe it's a cover to keep people away."

"Possibly," I whispered, "but I don't detect power here. I smell desperation."

"I feel sick," Dwayne said. "If I'm the cause of this… "

"How could you be the cause of this?" I asked.

"I don't know." He wrung his hands and then wrapped them around himself. "I don't know, but I have a bad feeling."

I did too, but not one of fear for my life—one of fear for the state that the Cows had gotten themselves into.

"Desperate people do desperate things," Hank reminded us. "Stay alert and let's find out what's really happening here. Do not kill unless provoked."

"You think they're in the trailers?" Dwayne inquired as he pointed down the road.

"Or possibly out grazing and farting in the fields?" Granny suggested.

"Um... nope," I said as I put up a hand to halt our movement. My other hand went to my pocket and attached itself to my gun. "Cows. Twenty feet away on our left."

"What the hell?" Dwayne gasped and levitated slightly.

"Down, boy," Hank ground out as he yanked Dwayne out of the air. "They don't seem aggressive—mostly confused."

"Um, I'm kind of confused." I tilted my head to see if that would clarify what I was staring at.

There were eight sexually ambiguous people watching us closely. Their hair was cropped short and they wore dirty baggy jeans and oversized work shirts. Were they men or women? I had no freakin' clue. I was scared to ask. Being Southern, I had manners, but this was a conundrum... and it was bugging the crap out of me.

"My theory is starting to make more sense now, isn't it?" Granny muttered under her breath.

"Actually, yes," Dwayne told her.

"What you be wantin'?" the one in the front grunted in a voice that could have been a feminine male or a masculine female.

95

Mystery still not solved. I moved slightly for a better view, trying to detect if there were any boobs evident.

"Came to buy some milk," Hank said agreeably with a neighborly wave.

"That girlie right there could use some," another grumbled as it pointed at me. "She's so skinny she could fall through her butt and hang herself."

"I'm sorry, what the hell did you just say?" I shouted. This was unbelievable. A group of Androgynous Pats were insulting me? This was not working for me...

"You can't take the truth then you can just walk your emaciated carcass right back to where you came from," the first one snorted with an indifferent shrug.

"Yep," my insulter backed the leader up. "And don't let the gate hit ya where the good Lord split ya."

"What is this? A bad redneck comedy show?" I mumbled. I was not too skinny—at all.

"Shhh," Granny whispered. "I wanna hear what else they have to say. This is some good stuff."

"You ain't human," the leader yelled. "What is ya?"

"We're wolves," Hank said with a calm that belied the tension I could feel coming off of him. "Heard your milk was good and thought we'd stop and try it."

"Wolves. Interesting," she said, puzzled. "Thought we was the only Were Species left in the world."

They all nodded sadly and hung their heads. What was happening here? I was tempted to go up and hug the grubby crew.

"Where did you hear that?" I asked as I took a small step forward.

"We read poop patties," the leader announced proudly. "We learned about forty years ago that we were the only ones left. I'm kinda flabbergasted at the moment."

They all nodded and stared at us as we all tried to keep the contents of our stomachs in place and stared right back at them.

"Huh," I said, searching for something appropriate to follow that one.

"I regret all those doughnuts now," Granny muttered.

"I'm Essie. This is Hank and my granny, Bobbie Sue," I said as I took another tentative step forward and held out my hand.

"Francis," the leader said as she took my hand and shook it.

Well, that certainly didn't help the sexual identity crisis. As they reeled off their names I got more confused than ever—Pat, Mickey, Terry, Lee, Harley, Morgan and Jamie.

Damn it, this was going to drive me bonkers.

"That one there in the back ain't no Werewolf," Pat said as she pointed at Dwayne.

"That's correct," Dwayne said carefully. "I'm a Vampyre named... Dracula."

"Well, I'll be damned," the one named Mickey yelled and smacked its forehead so hard it took it a second to remember what it was saying. "I thought you looked familiar. I saw you in the movies at the discount drive-in. You was great."

"Thank you," Dwayne said graciously and bowed.

All the Cows were wildly impressed with Dwayne's fictional acting career. I rolled my eyes and tried not to laugh.

"Seeing as we have a celebrity on the property, we'd like to invite you in and serve you up some milk," Francis said.

"Do we got any?" Jamie asked doubtfully.

"Hell to the yeah," Harley crowed proudly. "I shifted earlier and Lee yanked on my teats for a good two hours. We got plenty of milk."

97

"Come on in, y'all. Harley's milk's so good it will make you wanna slap your mamma!" Francis and the crew began to lumber over to the trailers.

We stood frozen to our spots. Were they for real? I didn't feel an ounce of fear and I could tell Hank, Granny and Dwayne didn't either. The Cows were either really good or really stupid.

"Hey, Dracula," Pat grunted as it and several others came up behind us to usher us to the trailer. "You happen to know a Vampyre named Dwayne?"

"Um, possibly," Dwayne, aka Dracula, mumbled as he glanced over at me with huge eyes.

"Hey," Pat shouted to the rest of the bovines as they moved en masse down the road. "Dracula knows Dwayne."

They all turned abruptly and ogled Dwayne. My hand went back to my gun and Hank's magic began to spark a bit. Granny took hold of Dwayne and kept him from levitating.

"I didn't say I knew him. I just know *of* him," Dwayne corrected Pat quickly.

"That's too bad." Francis' hands balled into fists and the others followed suit. "A poop patty told us to find him."

Hank pulled me and Granny towards him and moved Dwayne to the center of our tight triangle.

"What else did the poo pile tell you?" Granny asked.

Granny's fangs had dropped and popped through her colorful scarf. Thankfully the Cows didn't seem to notice.

"First of all, it's a poop patty. A poo pile doesn't speak to us. Poo piles are useless," Francis explained in a very serious tone.

"Good to know," Dwayne murmured tactfully. "Do the poop patties actually speak?"

"No," Harley said as they all laughed heartily. "They show us pictures and words."

"That makes more sense," Dwayne said with a sigh of relief. "Talking feces would just be alarming."

"'Nuff said, Dracula," Lee agreed.

"Well, if you wanna know the rest of the story, you're gonna have to come on in and set a spell," Pat said as she herded us forward.

"It's a real fine story," Francis said. "The poop don't lie."

"But Dracula does," I whispered under my breath.

"We going in?" I asked Hank.

"Don't see that we have much of a choice," he said quietly as the Cows behind us pushed us along with gentle nudges.

"Just don't get behind them," Granny hissed. "If the milk doesn't kill us the gas surely will."

"This may have been a tremendously shitty idea," Dwayne said nervously.

"No pun intended." Granny giggled.

"Actually it was," Dwayne corrected her.

"Oh. Then that was a good one," Granny congratulated him.

"Thank you."

"Nope, not a bad idea," Hank disagreed with Dwayne while completely ignoring the punny talk. "We'll find out what they want with Dwayne. If they want him—you—dead, we kill them."

"Well, there's a plan," I snapped.

"You have a better one, sexy?" he asked with a raised brow.

I thought for a brief moment and shrugged. "Nope. Works for me, love of my life."

"Let's go drink some milk," Hank said. "No one is going to believe this."

Truer words had never been said.

Chapter 8

The inside of the trailer completely belied the rest of the property. It was immaculate and huge. It was furnished comfortably in a style that hadn't advanced past the 1950's. It was actually kind of cool retro. Everything was mint green and white with a dash of yellow thrown in here and there.

Glass milk jugs sat neatly on a series of bright yellow shelves that lined the entirety of the mobile home. There were several closed doors that I assumed were bedrooms.

"What the hell?" Granny said as she admired the plastic slipcovered floral couches.

She glanced over at me as I gaped and gave me a sharp look.

"Close your mouth, Essie, you'll catch flies. Literally," she whispered. "Poop?"

I closed my mouth on a gag that I faked as a cough when the Cows looked over at me, concerned.

"Sit your cracks down," Francis demanded as she began pulling glasses out of a cabinet. "We're about to blow your minds."

That statement could go so many ways... All four of us wedged ourselves down on the couch as the Cows grinned and gave each other covert looks.

"We don't get much company," Pat said. "Humans used to come out here, but Jamie was having a bad day about three years ago and ate one. We don't see 'em much anymore."

"I can see how that might affect business," I choked out.

Hank was correct. No one was going to believe this.

"How are you feeling today, Jamie?" Hank inquired politely.

"I'm fine. Thank you," Jamie said.

"Thank k.d. lang for that," Dwayne mumbled.

Pat, Lee and Morgan served us tall glasses of milk. They sat them carefully on the mint green Elvis themed coffee table.

"Aren't you going to join us?" Granny asked as she eyed the milk distrustfully.

"Oh, hell no," Harley bellowed. "No way I'd drink something I spewed out of my body a couple hours ago."

The Cows all nodded in agreement. Holy hell, there was no way I'd be able to swallow the milk without projectile vomiting. However, Hank and Granny had no such issue. Dwayne was excused since he was a Vamp and only drank blood. Lucky bastard.

"Sweet baby Moses in a thong bikini," Granny gushed as she took another sip. "This is magnificent."

The Cows grinned and high-fived like they'd won a medal at the Olympics. No matter how much Granny liked it, I couldn't do it. Granny also liked lima beans...

"Ain't ya gonna try it, skinny girl?" Pat inquired with narrowed eyes.

"The whole spew out of the teats thing kind of put me off," I explained to Pat honestly. "I'll try it in a minute."

It took everything I had not to snap at Pat about the skinny comment. It certainly wouldn't help matters if I called it a fat ass.

All the Cows nodded in understanding and I heaved a sigh of relief.

"Do you shift much?" Hank asked as he put his barely touched glass down on the table with a slight gag.

"You want me to top that off?" Francis asked pleasantly.

"No, I'm good," he replied with a smile that resembled a grimace.

"I want more. That really is slap your mamma good," Granny complimented the Cows, holding out her empty glass.

Harley gave a whoop of delight and poured Granny another round.

"As to the shiftin'," Francis told us, "we don't do it much."

"No siree," Lee chimed in. "After Jamie ate that human we figured we should only shift to yank teat."

"Amen," Pat said with arms raised to the Heavens. "But because of Jamie's little snafu, the humans don't come round much no more so we got a milk overload."

"And since we don't drink the shit, we don't have much reason to shift no more," Morgan spoke up for the first time.

"Two or three of us shift every other week or so. If we don't we'll pop like a tick. Milk explosions are loud and ugly. They can cause deafness in your left ear," Pat shuddered and made a loud popping noise that created the picture vividly.

"I've exploded at least twelve times this year. It sucks growing back limbs," Jamie explained.

We all sat in somewhat awkward silence as Jamie shed a few tears over the *snafu* and the lost appendages. The Cows patted it on the back then grunted and swayed.

I accidently picked up my glass and took a sip in my panic to think of something to say. It tasted like warm butt, not that I knew what butt tasted like... but it sure as hell smelled like it. Swallowing my bile as not to upset the Cows was more difficult than beheading a Dragon, but I did it.

With tears in my eyes and my stomach roiling I decided to talk—it was either that or I'd puke. "So dude, um... ettes or not, I was wondering if you're related in any way."

"Yep," Francis said with a wrinkled brow, trying to figure out the first part of my sentence. "We're all Dungs."

Dwayne's gasp and girlie shriek was alarmingly audible. He stood up with fluttering hands and next thing I knew he was plastered to the ceiling.

"Shit fire," Granny muttered as she grabbed his leg, pulled him down and sat on him.

The Cows clapped wildly and begged him to do it again. Hank put his head in his hands and sighed heavily.

"So, um... about this Vampyre Dwayne..." Dwayne said from beneath Granny as he removed his scarf from his nose and tied it into a do rag on his head. "Why is it you want to see him?"

"The poop patty told us to wait here for him," Lee said.

"It told us he would come and save us," Pat added.

"From what?" Hank asked.

"The poop didn't tell us that part," Francis said sadly. "We stay here because we know he'll come."

Granny wisely placed her hand over Dwayne's mouth before he could say anything that would turn our strange social visit into a bloodbath. "Your poop lies," she said.

"Don't you be talking smack on the poop, old lady," Harley grunted as the others paced in agitation. "The poop clearly lies," Granny persisted. "You are not the only Were species in the world."

The grumbling was turning ugly. Hank quickly stood and put himself between us and the Cows.

I shot Granny a *shut the hell up* look and tried to diplomatically take over. "Wait," I shouted over the unhappy grunts, violent fist clenching and chest thumping. I was *not* going to die in a trailer in Indiana after accidently ingesting butt juice. "Is it possible you might have misread the poop? Could it have meant that you are the only Cow species left in the world?"

That stopped everyone.

"Hell and damnation," Jamie gasped out. "That bag of bones might be on to something."

The Cows all sprinted to the wall shelves and began taking down the empty milk jugs—that weren't empty. In the glass bottom of each bottle was a poop patty. Thankfully they were sealed shut. The Cows examined them with excitement and purpose. I pinched myself to make sure I wasn't dreaming this whole insane evening up. Nope, I was wide awake. This was a living nightmare.

"I found it," Terry yelled triumphantly. "That girl could be right!"

"The girl has a name," I muttered.

"There you go," Francis said, giving Granny a dirty look. "The poop don't lie."

"Okay, clearly the... poop is onto something," Hank said as he bit down on his lip to keep from laughing and inciting the Cows. "There has to be more in the poop about this Dwayne fellow."

"Not in the poop," Pat said with narrowed eyes and a flushed face. "In our history there are many stories of the Vampyre known as Dwayne."

"Oh shit," I whispered. This was going to be good... or really bad. If we were going to die I wanted to know something. "Do you people ever use pronouns to describe yourselves?" Everyone stared at me blankly. It was worth a try. "Never mind," I said in defeat. "Tell us the Dwayne story."

"Our mamma and daddy were married by the holy priest, Gay Vampyre Dwayne," Pat began.

All the Cows plopped down on the floor like children expecting a bedtime story. With clasped hands and wide eyes they waited for Pat to regale us. It was kind of cute in a nightmare- inducing sort of way. The mention of Dwayne's sexuality was interesting and weird.

"It was a beautiful ceremony with over a thousand in attendance," she went on. "Mamma wore a gown made by hogs and Daddy was nekkid. That's our tradition. Vampyre Dwayne... "

"Gay Vampyre Dwayne," Francis corrected Pat.

"Yes, Gay Vampyre Dwayne preached and stood on his head for three days. He wore a pink robe with no underpants."

"Was it the robe or the lack of undergarments that gave away he was gay?" Dwayne inquired, somewhat insulted.

Granny slapped his head and took another swig off of her milk. "Hush boy, I wanna hear about Gay Vampyre Dwayne."

Hank was looking a bit shell-shocked and said nothing, but kept his body between us and the sadly misinformed Cows.

"Now, normally Mamma would have eaten Daddy on their honeymoon, but Gay Vampyre

105

Dwayne inspired our parents to let go of their normal sexual eating patterns."

"How did he do that?" I asked, worried about what I would hear but too curious not to know.

"Not quite sure," Pat said with a shrug. "But if I had to guess I'd say it was the three hour performance of "Hey Diddle Diddle" done to a tribal drum beat."

I glanced over at Dwayne who was preening. I pulled his do rag down over his face. With no real clue where the tale was going, we didn't need Dracula to reveal his true identity yet.

"It also might have been the explanation of *eating* someone in a way more pleasurable than the kind ending in death," Morgan added with a blush to end all blushes.

I felt heat crawl up my own neck and land on my appalled face. I glanced around the room. Everyone was a varying shade of red except for Dwayne. Vamps couldn't blush. He was looking quite pleased with himself.

"So anyhoo," Pat went on, trying to ignore the icky sexual elephant in the room. "Mamma spared Daddy's life and they had ninety-two kids. We became pacifiers and started a dairy farm."

"Pacifists," Hank corrected.

"That's what I said," Pat shot back.

"Nope," Granny cut in. "You said you were a piece of rubber babies like to suck on."

"Well, I'll be damned," Pat sputtered. "That's completely screwed up."

"Happens to the best of us. So then what happened?" Dwayne asked as he rolled out from underneath Granny and stood next to Hank. "Where are all your siblings and your mamma and daddy?"

Pat's head dropped forward and its shoulders sagged pitifully. All the Cows on the floor closed in and moaned quietly. They looked like a clump before a rainstorm. "They're all gone. The Fire Breathers came and burned most of our family while we slept about fifty years ago. Mamma and Daddy were so sad they took their own lives."

"They ate each other?" I gasped out.

"Hell, no," Francis snapped with huge tears rolling down its face. "They both consumed three hundred packs of Pop Rocks and blew up like fireworks on the Fourth of July."

"It was awful," Harley sniffed.

"And messy," Morgan added.

Never in my life had I heard anything so bizarre and unsettling. I frantically searched for an appropriate condolence, but none came that weren't offensive or backed up by massively inappropriate laughter.

"Wait," I said, giving up on any compassionate response about the freakish demise of their parents. "Fire Breathers?"

"Yep. Never saw 'em, but we know they was fire breathers. Everything and everyone except us and Mamma and Daddy was burned to a crisp," Jamie said in a hushed and tear-clogged voice. "We didn't do nothing to nobody. Don't know why something wanted us dead."

"After Mamma and Daddy combusted we ran away. We was in Iowa at the time and we hoofed it down here and staked our claim to this land and tried to make a go of it," Pat told us. "Them Fire Breathers never came back, but we'll run if they do."

"Why wouldn't you fight back?" I asked.

"Don't know how," Morgan said.

"You are COWS," Dwayne shouted in frustration as he began to float skyward. "You are some of the most deadly predators in the world. You could kick the Dragons' asses."

"We could?" Francis asked, completely confused.

"Son of a bitch," Dwayne screeched as his head slammed into the ceiling. "This is all my fault."

"Not following you, Dracula," Pat said as it tried to help him down. "Dragons really exist?"

"Unfortunately, yes," I said as I helped pulled Dwayne off the ceiling. "They are very bad people and probably tried to eliminate you because of your power. My guess would be they know nothing of the eight of you or they would have come after you."

"That's just mean," Lee huffed. "We don't harm no one."

"It was an accident when I ate that human a couple years back," Jamie wailed pitifully. "I was havin' a real bad day."

"No one blames you for that," Francis consoled Jamie with a hug. "It could happen to anyone."

It gave us the evil eyeball and we all murmured our dubious assent.

"I can't take this," Dwayne bellowed and smacked himself in the head several times. "This is all my fault. I screwed with the intercourse food chain and destroyed an entire species."

The Cows were baffled at his outburst, but Granny, Hank and I were not. Hank's hand went to his concealed weapon as did mine and Granny's. Dracula was about to drop a bomb and there was no stopping him.

"My name is not Dracula," he continued at a decibel that was going to cause hearing damage. The Cows cowered and huddled. "My name is Vampyre Dwayne. I am your new father. I will be adopting you and raising you as my own since I'm dead and can't actually reproduce. Not to mention I'm gay. While I adore women and love playing them on stage, I am simply grossed out at the thought of playing hide the salami with a vagina. I shall endeavor to be a good yet profane and somewhat violent example for you.

You will live with me and I will shred the shit out anything that ever tries to harm you again. I will take you shopping for clothes that minimize your girth and you will learn why bath products are your friends. And just so you know, most of the wedding story is correct except the part about how many people were there."

The Cows were mute and stared at him like he had three heads. I held my breath and kept my hand on my gun. My wolf wanted to come out, but I pushed her back. Dwayne's farked up *Star Wars* speech had the potential of going very wrong.

"Daddy?" Harley whimpered as it stepped forward and fell to its knees at Dwayne's feet.

The other Cows followed suit until there was a sobbing, keening clusterhump at Dwayne's feet. Never, never in my life had I seen anything so odd. It was emotionally wrenching, heart warming, and appalling at the same time. Gay Vampyre Dwayne boohooed along with his new family and patted their dirty heads lovingly. Again, no one was going to believe this.

"I have an enormous compound in southern Illinois that does not smell like ass. There's a large house with fourteen bathrooms and ten bedrooms. It also has a pool, a pond and a sprinkler system, so I will brook no bull crap about staying clean. The lawns are manicured so there will be no pooping on them. Are we clear?" he asked as he squatted down to their eye level.

"Yes, Daddy," Francis blubbered. "We will not poop on your lawn."

"Are there any woods around there?" Morgan asked.

Dwayne thought for a long moment and then smiled. "I'll buy the adjoining two hundred acres so you'll have an outside defecation area."

The Cows giggled and nodded gratefully.

"You can each pick your own bedroom and I'll have a Were Possum designer I know come in and redecorate it how ever you would like. You'll each get a new car for your birthday. However, it will be taken away for bad behavior, poor table manners or consuming humans. We will go to the toy store and each of you can pick three things to play with. This will potentially help me figure out what you are without having to ask. Everyone will do online college classes until we can determine that you can follow simple hygiene rules and not eat anyone."

It was nice to know someone else was curious about their gender too.

"The poop patty has come true," Jamie yelled and hugged Dwayne so hard I thought he might snap. However, anything they accidentally ripped off Dwayne would grow back immediately. He was in Seventh Heaven.

Hank gave me a dazed look that captured what I was feeling. I bit back my laugh and grabbed his hand. Granny squeezed in between us and we all watched in wonder.

"If someone had told me how this would have gone down I would have thought they were insane," Hank muttered as he tucked a stray strand of hair behind my ear and kissed my forehead.

"That Pop Rock thing still has me scratching my head," Granny admitted. "Dwayne's gonna have his hands full with them."

A truer statement had never been uttered... pun intended.

Chapter 9

"They're not all going to fit in the Hummer," I said as I stared at the eight Cows now lined up ready to leave with us and their daddy. Dwayne stood proudly with his new children. The visual was redonkulous as each cow stood well over six feet tall and had to weigh in at a conservative three hundred pounds. Each had stuffed a backpack full of worldly possessions. They'd done their best to clean up for Gay Vampyre Dwayne's approval. The excitement was palpable and my heart felt light. These sexually ambiguous Cows just wanted to fit in somewhere and be loved. Dwayne wanted to be needed and he was a good man. I suspected he would spoil them rotten, but they'd had a hellish life so far.

"Not a problem," Francis assured me. "We ride hogs."

"Oh my god." I sighed in dismay and groaned. "Another Were species I didn't know about?"

"Um, no," Hank said with a lopsided grin and twinkling eyes. "Motorcycles."

I wanted to laugh and I wanted to slap him. He had enjoyed that one too much. However, I was relieved to realize a herd or gaggle of pigs would not be running behind the Hummer.

"Where are we going?" Pat yelled as it pulled up on the largest motorcycle I'd ever seen.

"I think we should drop my children off at the compound and get them settled in before we go after the Dragons," Dwayne suggested like any good parent would.

"That sounds like a plan," Hank agreed as he grabbed a can of gasoline and poured it around the trailers. "We need to burn this place down. No trace of the Cows can be left," he instructed.

"You don't have to do that," Pat told Hank.

He stopped patiently and waited for Pat to explain. God, he was going to be a good dad...

"We can blow the farm up in less than a minute."

Granny started running like Satan was on her heels and put her hands over her hair. Oh my sweet hell, I joined her as I realized what was about to happen. Hank was quick to follow, but Dwayne stood proudly with his children as they bent over and aimed their asses at the dilapidated farm behind them.

"Run," Hank shouted as he yanked Granny and me along. "This is gonna be bad."

"We're all gonna die," Granny shrieked as we tried desperately to put more distance between us and the eight Cow gastric inferno that was about to occur.

Hank picked both of us up as we sprinted and dove behind the Hummer. We were a good half-mile away now. Thank god we hadn't pulled the Hummer up to the trailers. The roads were so pitted we left it down the road when we'd picked it up an hour ago. It would suck having to share a hog with a Cow.

The sound was deafening, but the stench was like one I'd never known. Death didn't seem like such a bad option at the moment. The farm blew up in an explosion that could be seen for miles. The Cows jumped on their bikes and dragged an asphyxiated and paler than normal Dwayne with them.

We piled into the Hummer as they threw Dwayne in the back.

"Go, go, go," Francis shouted to Hank. "That there fire's gonna get worse before it gets better."

I was certain we'd all lost brain cells or at least our olfactory senses in the blast—but more shockingly, we were alive to tell the story no one in their right mind would believe.

As we floored it out of the property with the Cows behind us I started to laugh. Hank and Granny joined me until tears ran from our eyes. Dwayne just sat sprawled in the back and grinned.

"My children, are something else," he gagged out proudly.

"That they are," Hank said with a grimace and a cough.

***

"Something is very wrong here," Dwayne snapped with a wrinkled brow as we stood in front of his massive mansion in southern Illinois.

It was white and had an antebellum feel—elegant and symmetrical with a grand entryway flanked by columns. The porch wrapped the entire front of the home and balconies peppered the upper level. It was breathtaking and I had a hard time imagining it as the Cows' new home.

The grounds were manicured within an inch of their lives. Blossoming trees and beds of blood red flowers blanketed the area.

"This place is beautiful," Granny said and punctuated it with an appreciative whistle.

She was correct, but so was Dwayne. Something was off. I felt it in my gut. Hank did too.

Nothing looked amiss—it was in the air. A malevolent, almost undetectable mist hung on the breeze. The Cows stood quivering behind us.

"What the hell is it?" Hank asked as we scanned the area.

"Is the phone you used to call Junior secure?" I asked, wracking my brain to try and figure out how something had found us.

"It's a burner," he said tightly as the power that rolled off him made me back away. "Can't be traced."

"Sweet Dolly Parton in a jog bra," Dwayne hissed. "I texted the Were Possum designer and told her everything about my children and my house. I forgot I could be traced."

"Who in the hell would know to trace Dwayne?" I snapped as I pulled my Glock with my right hand and directed the Cows to get low with my left. "Me and Hank I get... but Dwayne?"

"Only one person I'm aware of knows Dwayne and I are working with you," Granny said in such a vicious tone of voice that the Cows started to cry.

"She wouldn't," I shot back with more conviction than I felt. Angela wouldn't set us up to die. She was my friend... kind of. I knew I annoyed her, but I certainly didn't think that she'd kill me over it.

"Can you explain this?" Granny demanded.

"No more than I can tell you the gender of Dwayne's children," I snapped angrily. I did not want to believe Angela would ambush us.

"We're girls," Pat whispered in a frightened voice.

"I'm sorry," I apologized sincerely and wanted to crawl into a hole. "That was extremely rude of me."

"No worries," she said kindly. "We know we're unattractive."

Now I felt like an ass, but at least I knew what they were before I died.

"You're all beautiful," Dwayne insisted. "You just need a bath, some blonde highlights, a little lipo and a new wardrobe. I have that all covered and if any of your eventual boyfriends make you feel unworthy, I will kill them dead after a marathon torture session."

"Thank you, Daddy," they all said in unison.

"You're welcome."

"Um, Daddy?" Jamie raised her hand to speak.

"Yes, dear?" Dwayne replied.

"It smells like Fire Starters to me."

Crap balls. She was right. I detected a faint Dragon scent. This was bad. Hank and I had experience with Dragons. Dwayne had destroyed two with a disastrous and messy mind meld, but as far as I knew Granny was a Dragon fighting virgin... and the Cows were probably useless.

"She's correct," Hank said grimly. "I can't tell if they're still here."

"I can feel them. They're still here," Granny whispered in a strangled voice.

"How and where?" I demanded wildly as I sprinted to the back of the Hummer and pulled out the liquid that prohibited the Dragon shift. Junior had created a compound that when ingested by a Dragon would keep them from shifting. A brilliant invention, considering a shifted Dragon was roughly the size of a football field.

I tossed loaded squirt guns full of the solution to the Cows, Hank, and Dwayne. Granny was frozen to her spot and had apparently lost her damn voice.

"You aim for the mouth," I informed the terrified Cows in a clipped tone. "The eyes or ears might help, but the mouth is a sure fire win—pun intended. Do not under any circumstance get it in your own mouth. You won't be able to shift if you do."

"What is this stuff?" Francis asked shakily.

"It's stuff that will keep us all from burning to a crisp if we aim correctly," I explained tersely. "Can any of you shoot?"

"Hell to the yeah," Pat said with pride. "We might be pacifiers, but all of us can shoot a single testicle off a bull from three hundred yards. Squirting some shit in a mouth won't be no problem."

Deciding not to correct her about claiming to be a rubber nipple, I narrowed my eyes and slapped my hands on my hips. "Are you bullshitting me?" I demanded. "One nut? The other one is totally intact?" I wasn't sure even I could shoot so accurately. Nuts were pretty close together.

"Yes siree," Jamie jumped in, defending her sister's boast. "One nard completely obliterated and the other one left in perfect acorn status."

"Jesus," Hank grunted as he leaned forward. "Harsh."

"Yep," I said, impressed. "But effective."

"My girls are amazing," Dwayne added as he too bent forward in phantom pain.

"I hate to break up the party," Granny whispered in a tone that made every hair on my body rise, "but there are approximately twelve Dragons on the roof."

I glanced up slowly and my blood turned to ice. They hadn't shifted yet which was to our advantage. Twelve of them. Twelve of us... kind of. I had a horrifying feeling the Cows might bolt. Dwayne removed his shirt, grabbed Granny's head and shoved it into his neck.

"This is another fantastically shitty idea," he ground out as Granny titty twisted him to break his hold. "Granny, drop fang and drink. There is no way in hell we're coming out of this alive unless we can all actually fight Dragons. I don't think I can mind meld twelve at once."

"Will I be able to fly?" Granny asked as she let go of her death grip on Dwayne's nipple.

"No," he said.

"Well, that doesn't really seem fair," she whined.

"Life is not fair and then you die," he hissed. "OR NOT if you drink my blood. Do it, damn it. Now."

Granny bit down without another complaint. My stomach churned at the thought she might end up having the same effects I did. However, Dwayne was right. We were staring at dismal odds at the moment. We stood a far better chance of coming out alive if we had his dark and scary Vampyre blood in our systems.

"Hurry," Dwayne insisted to Granny as he zeroed in on Hank. "You're next, big boy."

"I've already killed a Dragon," Hank said as he scanned the area surrounding us for movement on the ground.

I let myself go into my mind and pull up my Vampyre part that scared the living daylights out of me. Glancing up at the roof again I gasped in fury and dismay. The Dragons had disappeared. "Son of a bitch, they're gone. What's in the back of the house?"

"A pool in the center. Cabana to the left. Tennis courts to the right," Dwayne laid the landscape out succinctly. "You killed one Dragon," he told Hank. "How'd that work out for you?"

"I'm sporting a new arm and leg other than the ones I was born with," Hank ground out through clenched teeth.

"Drink," Dwayne shouted at him. "We don't have time to argue and you won't be any help if you are missing body parts."

"Point," Hank said as he let his fangs drop and sunk them into Dwayne's neck.

Granny was shaking with the new and deadly power that coursed through her small body. Her eyes

117

were dilated and her hands bunched into tight little fists at her side. However, the person I really worried about was Hank. His power was enormous without the Vampyre blood. What in the hell would this turn him into?

I needed to focus on the positive even though I wanted to rail at the Heavens.

"Are any of you able to fight?" I asked the Cows.

They stood in mute terror and my stomach dropped to my toes. This was a clusterhump waiting to happen. I pushed the ugly thought from my mind that Angela was responsible for this and focused on the matter at hand.

"Essie, you and four Cows will come with me around the right side of the house. Granny and Dwayne, you take the others and go left."

Hanks eyes blazed and the power that shimmered around him was mind-boggling, sexy as hell and completely unnerving. Dwayne was no slouch either. His skin glowed and his eyes were frightening slits. I held up my end as I felt the rush of unstable Vampyre voodoo fill my body. My hair flew wildly around my head and there was no breeze. Granny seemed to be the one a little off. Grabbing her, I shook her and made her look at me.

"Can you do this?" I demanded. "Are you okay?"

She nodded, winked and literally levitated off the ground.

"Okay," I muttered as I whipped around to Dwayne who was watching her in shock. "That is totally not fair. How the hell can she fly?"

"No clue, doll… and no time to figure it out," he said as he took Granny's hands and pulled her back to earth. "Plan?"

"Not really," Hank said. "Weapons won't work. We need to get the solution in as many mouths as we can or today will be our last. Remove the heart or head—neither is easy."

"Cows, you cannot run under any circumstances," I barked. "If you can't shift and fight, you need to aim and shoot the liquid."

"Should we fart at them?" Pat asked timidly.

To die of asphyxiation or by Dragon... that apparently was the question. Why Shakespeare came to mind every time I was facing death lately was a mystery, but it was an apt inquiry. We'd made it through the farts before; perhaps we could live through them twice.

Hank rubbed his jaw and blew out a long breath. "You will use your, um... gas bombs only if we tell you to. They may be a good distraction, but they could also debilitate us."

"Our ass-fire aim is pretty accurate," Harley said. "It does permeate the air, but the main damage goes where we shoot it."

"Good to know," Hank said with a wince and shudder. "You will fart on them only on command. We clear?"

Everyone nodded.

"I honestly can't believe I just said that." Hank laughed and ran his hands through his hair. "Essie, come here."

Hank grabbed me by the waist and kissed me hard and fast. My toes curled and my lady bits clenched in desire. I knew the kiss could be our last, but I refused to believe it. I would not believe it.

"I expect you to finish what you started here after we're done playing with the Dragons," I told him as my eyes turned icy blue.

"I plan on it," he told me with a smirk that despite all the danger we were in made me want to throw him to the ground. God, I was wild about him.

119

"That was hot," Francis said with a giggle and a thumbs up.

"I thought so." I grinned at her and gave Hank a quick squeeze.

"Maybe you can give us some flirting lessons if we're still alive after tonight," Pat suggested timidly. "We've never had boyfriends before."

"Um, sure," I said, wondering how in the hell I could help them.

"Essie is a fabulous flirt," Dwayne told his girls. "She could hit on a dead man and he would get it up."

"Dwayne," Hank barked. "One more sentence about my mate and you won't have to worry about the Dragons."

"Roger that," Dwayne answered with a salute.

"Let's go," Hank said. "Eyes open and squirt guns in front of you. It would be helpful if we kept at least one alive, but not necessary. Fight to kill because that is exactly what they will be doing."

Chapter 10

I imagined many different scenarios as we made our way to the back of the house. The one that greeted us stopped me dead in my tracks. On the near side of the pool twelve Dragons sat casually on cushions of hunter green and cream stripes that adorned the teak pool furniture. Behind them on the far side stood nine shifted wolves. Their scent was barely familiar as a shifter. The human side of the wolves was almost missing. Their eyes were an alarming shade of red that I'd never seen. All nine foamed at the mouth as they pawed the ground in agitation.

"What the hell?" I muttered as I froze and took in the horrifying scene.

Dwayne, Granny and his four Cows stood about a hundred feet to our left and gaped in confusion at the array of enemies before us.

"What's wrong with them?" I whispered to Hank.

"Don't know, but I'm sure we're about to find out," he muttered and stepped forward. "You're trespassing on private property," he said to the Dragons in a tone that belied the fury I felt building inside him.

"Is that so?" the Dragon in the front asked with a slick smile that made me uncomfortable, and my wolf claw at my insides for release.

They were a beautiful species—dark, mysterious and deadly. All of the Dragons I'd come upon thus far had black hair, sky-high cheekbones, full lips and gorgeous bodies. They stood over six feet tall and had eyes that appeared to switch from green to yellow with their moods. Right now they were a mixture of both.

"Yes, it *is* so," Hank shot back, equally as slick. "I'd suggest you leave on your own accord before you're forced. Violently."

"Now there's an irony," the Dragon said as he stood and casually stepped closer.

My body tensed and my fingers itched to wrap themselves around his very pretty neck. Hank, feeling my aggression, moved in front of me to stop me from throwing down the gauntlet first. He was correct. It was far wiser to let them make the initial move. I didn't for a second think we'd leave here without a battle, but stranger things had happened.

The other Dragons chuckled as the leader continued. It made me want to grind my teeth. Not helping matters—I could literally smell the fear from the Cows behind me.

"Yes, we were warned to leave by the staff. As you can see, that counsel fell on deaf ears," he purred and grinned, revealing a set of razor sharp fangs.

"And full stomachs," another added with a slimy smirk as he joined his comrade.

"I'm sorry," I said as I stepped out from behind Hank. "Could you clarify what you just implied?" I was fairly sure I understood, but desperately wanted to believe I was mistaken.

"You are quite daft for being so alluring," the Dragon said as he leered at me.

"Not daft at all," I shot back with a tight smile. "Just wanted to make sure you're as revolting as you seem before I remove your head."

He threw his head back and laughed. He patted his stomach and smacked his lips together. "They were delicious—screamed and fought the entire time we ate them. Quite a challenging meal."

Dwayne's cry of anguish was stupidly ignored by the Dragons as they kept their focus on Hank and me. I knew without looking the terrified Cows were backing away. Not good. It would be much easier for the Dragons to have them for dessert if they were far from us. Reaching down into the bag of Vampyre tricks I had no clue how to use, I willed the Cows to come closer. I felt them fight it, but it worked. They were now at our backs and shaking like leaves in a storm.

"You killed innocents," Hank ground out. "They had no part in your game."

"We were hungry," a third Dragon said sulkily as he and the rest rose and formed a semi-circle around their leader. "And they were rude."

The rabid looking wolves held their ground on the far side of the pool. staring with hatred at both the Dragons and us. Hell, were they in charge here?

"They were humans. They had no way to defend themselves," Dwayne hissed furiously. His skin was now iridescent and his eyes glowed. Granny held his arm as she struggled to keep from floating away. The Cows behind him looked close to fainting.

Again the Dragons ignored him as if he wasn't there. Were they stupid or did their arrogance make them careless?

"We've come for you," the Dragon said as he pointed at Hank and me. "There are some who wish to meet you before your untimely death. I really don't understand the curiosity about you two. You're just lowly wolves."

The laughter from the rest of the Dragons went all through me. My fangs dropped and my claws exploded from my fingertips. I held back the rest of my shift with great effort. I'd have a better chance in my Vampyre-laced human form than I would as a wolf.

"Actually, I'm in the mood for some steak," the one to the left of the talkative asshole added as he zeroed in on the Cows.

"Yes, that is very interesting. I thought we had eliminated the Were Cow species years ago. Looks like we missed a few," the head Dragon said with disgust. "Easily remedied."

"Actually, not so easy," Dwayne shouted in a voice which finally caught the attention of the Dragons.

Never in my life had I seen Dwayne look so frighteningly inhuman. His anger flew off of him in waves of purple crackling light. The beams were visible and clearly blistering as his daughters backed away, slapping out the small fires igniting their clothes. Granny stayed with him. She took in his magic and added a pink flame of her own to the violet electricity flowing out of Dwayne.

"You. Ate. My. Staff. Do you have any idea how hard it is to find humans who will work for Vampyres? Not to mention, *I liked them*," he bellowed so loudly we all winced.

He was literally on fire now and the Dragons had the wherewithal to finally look alarmed. However, it was too late…

"You remember Dwayne's party trick you never wanted to witness?" Hank whispered as he stealthily moved the Cows and me away from Dwayne and back toward the house.

124

"Oh shit," I gasped as I quickened my pace as much as I could without being obvious. "You're joking."

"Nope, I'm not. Duck and cover when they blow," he instructed under his breath.

"What in tarnation do you mean blow?" Francis choked out in a trembling voice.

Before we could answer Dwayne let out a sound so shrill I slapped my hands over my ears. The ground shifted beneath us and the six Dragons in the front sprinted towards my BFF in an effort to stop the noise. Bad move... or more accurately, last move.

Dwayne's voice rose to a pitch so high it shattered all the windows on the entire back of the mansion. Shards and chunks of glass rained down on us, glittering like deadly confetti in the mid-morning sun. The six Dragons closest to him inflated like ticks. The screaming was horrifying but I couldn't turn away. It was akin to watching the most ridiculous and gory horror flick ever imagined. Their skin turned a mottled purple and they blew up like bombs.

Guts and body parts flew like projectiles as we ducked and covered. The Cows forced Hank and I beneath them and took the brunt of the disgusting mess. My gag reflex kicked in with a vengeance and I was grateful my stomach was empty. Green gooey bile floated on top of the water in the pool and we were all covered in unidentifiable remains.

Dwayne and Granny had collapsed to the ground. The other four Cows surrounding them covered their passed out bodies. There were six Dragons left and they were pissed. They stood drenched in the goop that used to be their brothers. The shock had numbed them and they stood with mouths agape and eyes flaming. Tendrils of smoke wafted from each of their noses and dangerous fangs ripped from their gums.

"We have about thirty seconds before those psychos shift and cook us," I grunted as I pushed Francis and Pat off of me and went for my squirt gun. "Shoot. Now," I shouted as I aimed and fired into the open mouths of the Dragons.

It was either the shock of the catastrophe we had just witnessed or the bovines had bigger balls than I had thought. Without any prodding, pun intended... the Cows jumped to their feet and fired the solution directly into the kissers of the Dragons. Their aim was so accurate I paused to appreciate it. The gals could shoot—possibly better than me. In that glorious moment I decided to cut a deal with the girls. I would teach them how to flirt and they would give me their shooting secrets. My end of the bargain was probably impossible, but I would give it my all.

"Take that, you mother humper," Pat shrieked as she shot the disgusting fluid at the Dragons.

As we hit our bulls-eyes the Dragons coughed and gagged.

"What have you done?" a Dragon screamed as he spit the vile liquid from his mouth.

"I can't shift," another growled in fury as his arms flew wildly over his head.

The confusion and slippery debris had turned the monster movie into a macabre comedy as the Dragons collided into each other in their efforts to get to us and kill. Thankfully the battle would be in human form. I loved Junior so much at that moment it made my teeth hurt.

"You ready, baby?" Hank yelled over the chaos.

Sparks of color I'd never seen from him rolled off his huge frame. His power was massive and the Dragons took notice immediately. For a brief moment Hank even frightened me. He was like an avenging angel from Hell, but he was my angel, and I was going to fight right beside him.

"I'm ready."

I quickly glanced to my left to see if Dwayne and Granny would be available for back up. They were slowly rising to their feet with help from the Cows. They were disoriented and unstable on their feet. Hank and I were on our own.

"It's just you and me," I told him as I rolled my neck and prepared to rip off some Dragon head.

The enormous burst of green and yellow smoke took me by surprise. I couldn't even see my hand in front of me. I closed my eyes and tried to go by scent, but it was impossible—too many odors permeated the air. How the hell could we fight blind? More importantly, could the Dragons fight blind?

I reached for Hank but he was gone. My gut clenched and I dropped to the ground to see if the smoke was rising. If I could find feet I could find a Dragon. The whimpering of the Cows made me stop. They were going to be filet mignon for the enemy if they didn't shut up.

"Quiet," I hissed as I felt for them. "Don't lead them to us."

It seemed like an eternity, but it couldn't have been more than a minute or two before the smoke began to clear. I spotted Hank by the pool crouched low. Granny and Dwayne were huddled with their Cows and I was with the remaining girls. However, the Dragons were gone.

"Where in the hell did they go?" I got to my feet and cautiously walked toward Hank.

Could they render themselves invisible? Had the solution failed? Did they shift and fly to the roof?

"They're gone," Harley said as she sniffed the air. "I was really hoping to fart off those bastards."

"Are you sure?" Hank asked tersely as he scanned the area.

"Yes siree, they're gone," Pat added. "I really wanted to pinch a stinky off and aim at one of them bastard's mouths."

"Actually," I said with an inappropriate laugh as I tried to wipe some goop off, "I'm sorry you didn't get to do that too."

"Next time," Pat grunted. "Next time I'm gonna singe every hair on one of them goobers right off. Then when they're screaming I'm gonna drop a load on their head."

"Alrighty then," I gagged out, knowing the visual would stick. "We need to clean this mess up and… "

The growl from the far side of the pool halted my speech. The Dragons were gone, but the rabid looking Wolves were not. So much for getting out injury free…

"Shift," Hank shouted at the Wolves, who ignored him and paced in agitation.

"Were they with the Dragons or are they here on their own?" I asked Hank as I stood with him and stared at the Wolves on the far side of the pool.

"I believe they came with them, but they certainly weren't on their team," he said quietly.

"Doesn't look like they're on our team either," I mumbled as unease skittered up my spine.

"Nope, I'd have to agree with you." Hank spoke, but his gaze stayed trained on the Wolves.

"Why won't they shift?" Dwayne asked as he fell into line with us.

He and Granny looked pretty bad, but at least they were standing.

"I didn't think you could mind meld six Dragons," I said as I kept watch on the Wolves.

"I can't," he said. "It was Granny pouring power into me."

"That is some farked up stuff you have in your blood, Vampyre," Granny grunted as she shook her head and chuckled. "I feel like I did after twelve hours straight of shopping on Black Friday last year."

"Sorry, doll," Dwayne said as he ruffled her hair. "But thank you."

"You're welcome, bloodsucker. You've become the undead grandson I never knew I wanted."

"Oh my Donna Summer," Dwayne babbled as he hugged her tight. "As shittastic as this day is going, I'd repeat the whole damn thing to hear you say those words again."

"I love you, you high maintenance undead girly boy," she said affectionately.

"I love you too. I love you so very much," Dwayne replied so sweetly my eyes filled.

"Love-fest over?" Hank asked in a clipped tone.

"Yep," Granny said. "Those Wolves are trapped. Heard about this but never believed it."

"What are you talking about?" I asked.

"If you stay in wolf form for too long without shifting back there comes a time you can't anymore," she explained. "The red eyes and the foaming at the mouth are the giveaways."

"That's a myth." Hank ran his hands through his hair and then groaned in disgust as they came out covered in guts. "I need a shower," he muttered.

Amazingly, he still looked hotter than Hades. I needed my head examined.

"I always thought so too, but not anymore," she said sadly.

"Why would a Wolf not shift back? It makes no sense," I said as I watched their frustration grow. They were now snapping and the aggressive growls came from deep in their chests. We'd gotten off easy with the Dragons. I wasn't so sure about the Wolves.

"Has to be some dark magic at work here," Dwayne surmised as he surveyed the pack. "I have a difficult time believing a Wolf would give up shifting voluntarily."

"Did the Dragons make them?" I asked.

"Don't think so," Hank replied with a shrug. "I'd guess Witches are involved here."

"Might be why they didn't defend the Dragons." Granny sighed, hopped up and down and did a few jumping jacks. "Gotta get the blood flowing if I'm gonna take out some of my own no matter how screwed up they are," she told us as we watched her curiously.

"Do we have to kill them?" I really didn't want to. If they'd been forced by dark Witch magic to stay shifted to Wolf form for eternity, it felt wrong for them to die by the hand of their own species.

"That's up to them," Hank said tightly. "Entirely up to them."

Chapter 11

"If you can shift, do it now," Hank yelled to the Wolves as we waited. They took him in as if they understood, but didn't shift. If anything they got more agitated and angry. I debated shifting myself, but wanted to wait to see what they would do. I could shift in a second if need be. Glancing down at my claws, I realized I was partially shifted anyway.

"Send the Cows away," Granny said softly. "There's nothing they can do here."

"Will the solution help?" Lee asked as she held her squirt gun at the ready.

"No," I told her. "It stops a shift from happening. They're already shifted."

"How about a flaming butt bomb?" Morgan inquired hopefully.

"Wait a minute," I said, confused and completely grossed out. "You can blow a flaming fart?"

"Yep," Jamie chimed in proudly. "It burns like Hell in July, but it can be done. All we gotta do is put our right leg in front of our left about three inches apart, bend over, grunt real loud and then rap."

ROBYN PETERMAN

"I thought it was the left," Pat said with pursed lips.
"Nope. Right," Francis informed her. "We also need to visualize jalapeno peppers and an assload of wasabi."
"No pun intended," I mumbled.
"What?" Francis asked, bewildered.
"Nothing," I said.
"It helps too if we're completely nekkid," Harley stated as she began to remove her shirt.
Sweet hell, this was getting out of hand.
"Just your pants, Harley," Terry chided as she dropped trou.
"You girls can rap?" Dwayne asked as his daughters removed their pants.
"We sure as heck can," Francis said with pride as she began to beat box to a rhythm in her head that should have stayed there.
"Stop," Hank commanded as he tried desperately to avoid seeing the half-clad Cows while still watching the Wolves. "I'm not real sure where it's safe to look right now, but the Cows have to go. Gas will not kill the Wolves, it will just infuriate them and we don't need them more agitated."
"I agree," I said as I handed Francis her pants, keeping my eyes on her face. "Go in the house and lock it down. If any of the staff survived the Dragons tend to them. Do not come out here—no matter what happens."
"But," Francis started to protest.
"No buts... pun intended." I grinned at my own joke and halted any other suggestion which required smelly bodily functions before she could offer it. "Hank, do you still have the burner phone?"
He handed it to me quickly. "Good thinking. Junior is speed dial one," he muttered.

132

Hank was wound as tight as a drum and staccato sparks of magic bounced in the air around him.

"If we die out here you will call a man named Junior. Explain what happened and he will come for you," I told them.

"Will he think we harmed you?" Pat asked, ashen-faced.

"No," Hank promised the terrified Cows. "He already knows about you. He will protect you the same as we would."

"We just got our new daddy," Lee sniffled as she grabbed Dwayne's hand and help on tight. "I don't want to lose him."

"Your daddy's not going anywhere," I assured his frightened daughters. "He's a wedding consultant, a semi-famous drag queen, and he owns a Hummer which enables him to use the word freely without repercussion. Now he has a family. His life is practically perfect. You just get your overactive butts into the house. Go—or I will kick them into next year."

"Yes, ma'am," they all mumbled as they hauled tail to the house.

"I love my girls," Dwayne said as he heaved a huge dramatic sigh.

"Dude, what are you doing? You don't breathe," I pointed out.

"True," he agreed. "I just thought I would try something new in case we bite it out here. It's kind of fun."

"Can you mind meld again?" I asked, feeling ill that I was even considering blowing up some of my own kind.

"Doubtful," Dwayne said with a regretful shake of his head. "The last effort took it out of me."

"Me too," Granny added with a shudder.

The Wolves had not advanced yet and it was unnerving. What did they want?

"We don't want to harm you," Hank called to them. "I'm going to shift so we can communicate. It's not an act of aggression."

"Are you certain that's the best thing to do?" I asked him, worried. "You can't shoot if you shift."

"No, but you can," he said as he removed his clothes. "You got silver bullets in your gun?"

"Of course," I replied as I very inappropriately admired his beautiful muscular body. Even pending death didn't mute my attraction to him.

"Shoot for the brain to slow them and then go for the heart. Shift only if you have to heal yourself or if you run out of bullets," he instructed as he fluidly shifted to his Wolf.

I grabbed his guns and strapped them on. I had enough ammo on me to take out a small army. Hopefully I wouldn't have to use it.

"Granny and Dwayne, you ready?"

"I am," Granny said as she pulled her weapons and stood tall.

"Dwayne is always ready," my Vampyre BFF informed me cockily.

"You enjoy talking about yourself in third person." I pointed out with an eye roll.

"Yes," he agreed. "Yes, I do."

The Wolves seemed displeased Hank had shifted. The growling increased and my stomach roiled. This did not look good.

"*We mean you no harm,*" Hank told the Wolves. "*We would like to help you if we can.*"

Hank's Wolf shook his head and tried again. Thankfully Dwayne and I could communicate with Hank even though we couldn't hear the Wolves. Granny was the only one we'd have to interpret for.

"*We mean no harm. What do you want?*"

The Wolves gathered close to each other and bared their fangs as they howled and pawed at the ground.

"What did they say?" I asked Hank.

"*It's garbled—almost as if they're speaking another language.*"

"Make sense. They've probably created their own language," Dwayne said with an impressed nod. "Enables them to speak without any other Wolf understanding."

"Brilliant," Granny whispered as she watched the Wolves with an odd and unsettling expression.

"What's wrong, Granny?" I asked. Why in the hell was she staring like that?

"Hank, tell then I'm coming over," Granny said, ignoring me as she began to walk around the pool. "I need to see something."

"No," I shouted at her. "You can see fine right here."

"*Tell her to stay put,*" Hank demanded as he growled furiously. "*What in the hell is she doing?*"

"Granny, stop. Now," I yelled. "You're going to get killed."

"I have to see," she said desperately as she increased her pace.

"Oh my God," I gasped as I went to follow her.

"No," Dwayne bellowed as he levitated and began to glow. "Cover her with the gun. I'm going over. She's lost her ever lovin' mind and I am going to whale on her ass after this is over."

"*Stay here, Essie,*" Hank barked. "*Dwayne is right. Get ready to shoot. I'm going around the other side.*"

I'd never been so frustrated, scared and pissed off in my life. If Granny didn't die by stupidity in the next five minutes I was going to kill her dead myself. She was putting us all in grave danger by going in alone. Nine to four were horrific odds. Granny had been a WTF agent; she should know better than making the first move. It was a weak position and we couldn't afford it.

"*Essie, stop thinking and aim,*" Hank snapped in my head. "*I have no clue what Granny is doing, but it's done. Focus and forget she's your granny. Use your training and go for the kill.*"

He was right. I pushed my personal feelings and anger back, narrowed my gaze and kept my gun aimed about a foot in front of Granny as she moved. I prayed I could hit whatever came at her. Please don't let them all come at her at once.

"Bobby Sue," Dwayne yelled over the growling and gnashing of teeth as Granny approached the Wolves. "You stop right now."

He was clearly using some kind of Vampyre voodoo on her as her gait slowed. She moved as if she was underwater but she didn't stop. Her determination sickened me and I watched in horror, ready to shoot anything that jumped her.

The snapping of jaws increased. It sounded like a disjointed melody punctuated by hisses and yips of rage. My instinct to shift was almost debilitating but I stayed in human form. I refused to let my inner turmoil and fear for my clearly insane grandmother unhinge my focus. My training was top notch and I was about to put it to a test like I never had.

Granny was headed toward two silver Wolves at the back of the Pack. Hank was coming up with speed around the other side of the pool and Dwayne hovered over Granny as she blindly ran. The clusterhump was seconds away and I quickly pulled another gun from my belt. I was ambidextrous as far as shooting went, but I could only aim one gun at a time. Shit shit shit.

It happened like a slow motion B movie with a plot that gave you nightmares for the rest of your life.

The two wolves she was headed for backed away hissing and snarling as the rest of the Pack went for my Granny. I aimed and fired repeatedly, missing most of my targets because they were too close to her. Hank attacked the two biggest wolves on the outer edge and was in a fight for his life. I continued to shoot and mortally wounded three.

Dwayne was a tornado of fire as he ripped through several who were trying somewhat successfully to tear him apart. However, Granny wasn't defending herself. She was intent on the two who refused to fight. What in the hell was she doing?

The bullets were useless. I tossed the guns and shifted. I backed up about ten feet from the pool and took a running leap over it into the fray. My back paws caught the edge and I went tumbling into the bloodbath. Power surged through me as I ripped and tore at anything that came near. I lost sight of Granny and prayed like hell she would have the wherewithal to shift and fight.

A vicious burn shot up my back left leg as a large brown Wolf clamped his massive jaws down on me. Something unfamiliar roared through my blood and came out of my mouth—a sound so chilling it made me ill. I embraced it, flipped backwards and tore the Wolf attached to my leg to shreds. The blood ran hot down my throat as I clamped down on his neck and ruptured every major artery. His gurgled snarl as he bled out was beautiful and horrifying. The thing living inside of me wasn't satisfied though. It wanted more. It wanted to kill more. The thing was me, I realized with shock... and I needed to kill more.

It was so fast and so violent I was unsure where to focus next. Fur and bodies were flying. My coat was matted with blood and a deep laceration over my left eye made seeing difficult. I went by scent and continued to maim, mutilate, and kill. Part of my soul had taken a leave and I felt like an atrocity on autopilot.

Not knowing if we were winning or losing, I kept going. As I plowed through the rabid Wolves I searched desperately for Granny and Hank. Dwayne was still flying above even though it was clear he'd lost a few parts.

"*Speak to me*," I demanded of Hank and Granny. "*Where are you? Are you okay?*"

"*Never better*," Hank grunted. "*Five down. Four left. By the tennis courts. Go, go, go.*"

He didn't have to ask twice. I leapt over the dead and bounded to the tennis courts. What I saw was stupefying and I didn't know what to do. I skidded to a halt and tried to make sense of the scene in front of me.

Two jet black Wolves had Granny pinned to the ground. I howled with agony when I saw how damaged she was. She was unconscious and I was unsure if she was still alive. There was so much blood. Why hadn't she shifted?

Hank halted as he realized the same thing I did. The other two Wolves, the ones Granny had been trying to reach, were challenging the ones that had her down. They were silver gray and huge. Foam and blood dripped from their fangs as they advanced on the black Wolves. Granny's limp body was tossed behind the black Wolves as they dove at the ones trying to get to her. Was it a fight for the kill or were they trying to stop the black ones?

"*What's happening?*" I asked Hank as he inched closer, only to get thrown violently back by the larger of the silver Wolves.

"*It looks like they're trying to defend Granny*," he grunted as he struggled to his feet. "*It makes no sense.*"

"*Is she food?*" I asked, horrified at the thought.

"*Normally I'd say no. Wolves don't eat each other, but today I'm not sure,*" he said as he approached again. "*I'll distract them. You try to get to Granny.*" I'd seen Wolves fight. I'd seen Wolves fight to the death, but I'd never seen anything as vicious as the battle raging over Granny. The Vampyre blood coursing through my system made me an unstable monstrous killing machine, but these Wolves were downright barbaric. They were going for eyes and jaws, not directly for the kill. The damage they were inflicting was meant to cause humiliation and physical misery. My stomach churned as I attempted to circle the perimeter and get to Granny. How had I killed any of them? Had I fought with that kind of depravity just moments ago?

I pushed the thoughts away and tried to close in. If I could get to her I could drag her to relative safety as the blacks and silvers destroyed each other.

"*Hank, stay back. None of them need our help. They're doing fine on their own with annihilating each other. Circle around and meet me at Granny.*"

"*On it,*" Hank said gruffly as he inched along the far side of the assault.

The sounds of death mixed with eerie howls suspended my forward motion briefly. The silver grays had won. The black Wolves lay torn and mangled on the ground. Blood flowed and the silver Wolves appeared pretty torn up. As they made their way to Granny I increased my trot to a sprint. There was no way in hell they were going to eat her. It would be over my dead body.

I reached her very still body before they did and turned and growled. My teeth gnashed and I felt a blast of surreal and deadly rage rush through me. I stared straight into their red eyes with aggression and hatred. If they took one more step they would die. I might die with them, but I would not go out alone.

Hank's shoulder touched mine and the snarls and blinding sparks that swirled around his body were mesmerizing. They gray Wolves halted and watched with eyes narrowed to slits.

"I don't know if you can understand me, but if you take one step closer to my granny it will be the last thing you ever do," I hissed savagely. I held my bleeding head high and kept eye contact. *"I don't know if you can understand the concept of love or family, but she is mine. She is all the family I have left in the world. If you go for her I will crucify you and send you straight to hell."*

Time felt suspended as we stared at each other, waiting for one pair to make the first move.

"She's dying," the larger of the gray Wolves said in a deep and melodic voice. *"Go to her. We are leaving."*

With that they turned and walked away. Several times they glanced back. Hank and I stood our ground and didn't move a muscle until they had reached the far edge of the property and disappeared.

"What was that?" Hank whispered.

"They understand our language and they can speak it," I said as I scanned the tree line for proof they were truly gone.

"That makes no sense. Why would they leave?"

"I don't know. Are they definitely gone?" I asked. I saw no movement in the tree line, but I didn't trust they had left. These Wolves were far different than any I'd ever dealt with.

Hank lifted his muzzle to the wind and sniffed. *"They're gone, but we don't know if they're coming back. We need to get Granny inside. Shift."*

As I shifted and turned, my stomach dropped to my toes. Dwayne's agonized screams bounced in my head and I closed my eyes hoping when I opened them the horror before me would be different.

It wasn't.

Dwayne held a lifeless looking Granny in his mangled arms and rocked her while he wailed. This was not happening. She was going to walk me down the aisle. Granny was going to babysit my children some day and teach them bad words and how to play paintball without safety gear. She was going to feed them ice cream for dinner and they would tell her secrets Hank and I would never be privy to. She was supposed to ground me when she realized I got Hank's name tattooed on my ass. I hadn't even had time to get inked so she could be pissed and tackle me. This was wrong. This was not supposed to happen.

Speech left me as I dropped to the ground and felt for a pulse. It was a whisper, but it was there.

"Shift, damn it," I screamed at her unconscious body. "You have to shift to heal."

I grabbed her from Dwayne and shook her. She simply had to wake up and shift. "Wake up," I cried out as my own blood and tears rolled down my face.

"She has to wake up," I shouted at Dwayne. "Make her wake up. Please God, please God, please God," I muttered hysterically as I continued to shake her.

"Essie, stop," Hank said in a raw and pained voice as he squatted down next to me and tried to take Granny out of my arms.

"No," I hissed and slapped him away. "Can't you see? I just have to wake her up. Then she can shift and she'll be okay. Just let me wake her up. You'll see. She'll be just fine," I sobbed as I buried my face in her bloody hair. "She has to be fine. I need her."

"Essie, she's dying," Hank said grimly. "Let's bring her inside and make her comfortable."

"She's not dying," I insisted angrily. "She still has a pulse. She just has to… "

I couldn't finish. It hurt too much. I felt her slipping away as I gripped her body tightly to mine.

141

"I love you so much. My world will be so wrong without you in it," I murmured in her ear. "I forgot to tell you I was going to wear a purple dress to get married in, but now I have to wear that buttass awful one of Mrs. Wilson's. You would have been so pissed if I wore purple... please wake up, Granny. Please."

"She has a pulse?" Dwayne asked as her took her wrist and pressed on it.

I nodded and gently pushed the bloody hair off of her beautiful face.

"Why did she do this?" I asked through my tears as I tried to make sense of her behavior. "She didn't even try to defend herself."

Dwayne stood up and stared up at the setting sun for a long moment. "I'll need your permission," he said in a hollow voice.

"For what?" Hank asked as he wrapped Granny and me in his strong arms.

"I don't know if it will work since she's so damaged, but I want to try."

"Try what?" Hank asked tersely.

"She has a slight pulse and she's taken my blood," he said slowly as if he were piecing a plan together as he spoke.

"Yes. And?" I asked in frustrated confusion.

He looked straight at me and was more serious than I'd ever seen him. My head began to spin and my body trembled.

"Get to the point," Hank ground out.

"I want to turn Granny. I want to turn her into a Vampyre."

Chapter 12

"Absolutely not," Hank growled forcefully as he rose to his feet and placed himself between Dwayne and us.

"Why?" Dwayne asked as he paced tight small circles and wrung his quickly regenerating hands. "She's dying. Why wouldn't you give her another chance?"

"What in the hell would she even become?" Hank demanded harshly.

"I don't know," Dwayne admitted slowly. "I just don't know."

I sat silently and absorbed what was playing out. Would Granny want to be a Vampyre? Would I? Would her Wolf die if she was turned? Was I horrifically selfish to want to yell yes?

Glancing down at the precious woman in my arms I wished I could ask her. I shook her gently again trying one last time to wake her so she could shift and this whole conversation would be moot. I didn't want to make the decision, but I was very cognizant it was my decision to make. What would she choose for me if the tables were turned?

"Will she make it through the transition?" I asked quietly.

Hank's head jerked to me in surprise and I met his confused stare head on.

"I'm not sure if she'll survive it," Dwayne answered honestly. "It's difficult even if she's in top form. Plus, I've never turned a Were before."

"This is insane," Hank muttered angrily. "It's unnatural and could go more wrong than we could ever conceive."

"Why?" Dwayne shot back viciously. "Because I'm a Vampyre? She will be less because she will become a blood-drinking abomination of the night? Is that your issue, Wolf?"

"That's not what I said," Hank ground out in fury as he went toe-to-toe with Dwayne.

"Maybe not in words," Dwayne hissed and began to glow.

"Stop it," I cried out as they circled each other aggressively.

Gone was my silly gay Vampyre BFF and gone was my compassionate loving mate. They were two supernatural creatures about to kill each other.

"This is unacceptable," I yelled as they both stopped and struggled to regain their composures. "Granny would have both of your butts in a sling for this kind of behavior. I'm about to stand up and open a can of whoop ass on you two right now. We just survived Dragons and some whacked-out Wolves. We did this together. You will not harm each other. I can't take it."

Both men had the grace to look shamed.

I stood up carefully and held the limp, almost lifeless form of my beloved grandmother in my arms. I was hoping for some divine intervention as to what to do, but there was none. It was my call and I would make it.

"Hank," I said softly as I waited for him to look at me. After a moment of gathering himself and releasing his anger, his beautiful eyes rose to mine. "If it were me dying in your arms and you had the chance to keep me with you... what would your choice be?"

I already knew what my choice was, but I needed him to understand. I wanted him on board with me because I had no idea how it would all go down. I needed him like I needed to breathe and I was certain I couldn't do this alone. If I had to, I would—but I didn't want to.

He turned away and paced like a caged animal. Running his hands through his hair, his shoulders slumped forward and a shudder wracked his body. With slow methodical steps he walked back and stood in front of me. The pain in his eyes stole my breath and I moved toward him with Granny still in my arms.

"You are my reason for living," he said as he reverently ran his thumb along my bruised and battered cheek. "My existence is hollow and meaningless without you. I would kill for you and die for you. So yes, I would make the choice for you to be with me, no matter what the consequences."

My eyes filled with tears as he gently pressed his lips to mine and then to Granny's forehead. I loved him more with each day and minute that passed. I was not an easy person and he was as complicated as they came, but we fit together perfectly.

"Dwayne," I said as I moved away from Hank and approached him. "I love you and thank you for this gift. I want you to turn Granny."

"Essie," he began.

"I know she might not make it," I cut him off before he explained the dangers. "However, it will give her a chance. She'll be thrilled she can fly all the

145

time. And just think... you and she can keep the drag-strip act together for eternity."

My small giggle belied my fear, but the chance Granny could survive gave me strength and hope. I didn't want to hear what she would have to go through to live, but I was going to man up and ask.

"Will it..." I stuttered.

"Yes, it will hurt," Dwayne said in a business-like tone that I understood. This was difficult for him. He adored my granny like she was his own.

"How long?" Hank asked.

"A week or so," he answered. "I will drain the rest of her blood and then I'll slash my wrist and feed her hourly for three days."

"She'll know what's happening?" I paled at the thought of what I had agreed to, but knew it was right.

"No," he said tersely. "I don't think she will understand until she rises. She'll feel the pain but won't know why."

"Oh my god," I muttered as I held her tight. My stomach clenched and my throat felt raw. What if I put her through this and she didn't make it? Her last days on this earth would be excruciating. "Am I being selfish?' I whispered.

"Only you can answer that," Dwayne replied. "But if it makes you feel better I would do the same for you, even knowing what the risks were. I wouldn't do this if I didn't think she had a chance to survive. I love her too much to put her through what she's about to endure."

I knew he did and I did too. Her pulse was barely there now and I worried we might be too late if I asked more questions.

"Do it. Now," I said as I handed her over to Dwayne. "What can we do to help?"

"Leave," Dwayne said, carefully knowing it was not what I wanted to hear.

"What?" Hank demanded. "You can't think we're going to leave her here."

"Not here," Dwayne told us. "The Dragons and the psycho Wolves know where we are. I will take her to another compound I own in Michigan while she's in Death Sleep."

"How many compounds do you own?" I asked, even though it had nothing to do with what was important at the moment. Focusing on something mundane was going to save me from losing my mind.

"Too many to count," he replied. "Real estate is a very good investment."

Why didn't I know this? How many other secrets did Dwayne have?

"The Cows?" Hank asked as we made our back to the mansion, avoiding the piles of dead that littered the grounds.

"They will come with me. Granny will have blood lust when she rises. It's not safe for any human or Were to be around her for a while."

"But the Cows can?" I asked, confused.

"Ironically, yes," Dwayne said with a smile. "Their blood regenerates at a speed that is beyond very rare. They'll be able to feed her and their size is a bonus. If we have four of them with her at all times after she wakes they'll be able to calm and restrain her."

"She'll be violent?" Hank asked as he banged at the locked doors on the back of the house.

"For a bit," Dwayne answered truthfully. "Mostly just hungry. Once she gets a hold on the blood lust she'll be fine."

The Cows greeted us with ashen tear-streaked faces. They also had robes for Hank and me. In all that had transpired, I'd completely forgotten we were

147

naked after our shift back. I gratefully slid into my soft robe as Hank did his.

"Is she dead?" Francis asked quietly. She rocked back and forth in sorrow and her sisters joined her.

"Almost," Dwayne said as he lightly kissed his daughter's cheek. "I am going to turn her. You all will protect and feed her when she wakes."

"We'll do it with pleasure," Pat insisted as she ran her huge hand sweetly over Granny's lacerated face. "We've fed newbie Vamps before."

"A long, long time ago—going on eighty years now," Harley added. "But I enjoyed it. It tickled."

"Granny had her some pretty big balls as a Wolf," Morgan said appreciatively. "She's gonna be one wild mofo when she goes undead."

My stomach roiled a little at the thought and I prayed Granny wouldn't hate me when she realized what I had done. Of course there was the chance she would never know what I had done…

"When will we know if she made it through?" I asked as I clasped her hand, not wanting to let go.

"When she wakes," Dwayne said with a tension in his voice that sliced through me.

"If she wakes," I added almost inaudibly.

"Don't you worry your skinny little butt about nothin'," Harley consoled me. "Your granny is one tough nut and my daddy knows his shit. She's gonna be one fine undead bloodsucker slash wolf slash I have no idea what the tarnation she'll be."

I nodded, unsure whether to laugh or cry and I decided to skip the skinny comment, considering the source. There were no guarantees, but without trying there would be no Granny.

"Keep the burner phone," Hank instructed, referring to the phone we'd given the Cows earlier. "I have ten more in the glove box of the Hummer. The numbers are already set in your phone as speed dial two, three and four etcetera. If one doesn't work or if we aren't the ones to answer it, delete the number immediately and get rid of all other traceable electronics you have."

"Junior is speed dial one?" Dwayne asked as he laid Granny on an ornate couch and covered her small body with a blanket.

"He is," I said as I placed another kiss on her cheek.

"Um... we already called him," Pat volunteered sheepishly. "It looked real damn bad out there and we wanted some backup for you."

"Pretty sure he's on his way," Lee added with a shrug and a chuckle. "He has some salty language, that one."

"I'll call him and tell him the new plan," Hank said as he glanced down at himself. "Can you get our clothes from the car?"

"I'll do you one better," Dwayne said with an evil little smirk. "You two go upstairs and shower. I'll lay some outfits out for you."

"Why does that unnerve me worse than fighting Dragons?" Hank asked sardonically as he grabbed my hand and led me to the grand staircase.

"Because you are a very smart boy," I said with a laugh.

***

We were clean, ready to leave, and unfortunately dressed in clothing that made me belly laugh and Hank groan in dismay. We'd be stopping at the first rest stop we came to. We had clothes in the car but Dwayne refused to retrieve them, innocently explaining he couldn't leave Granny alone in the house. He also insisted we take the Hummer. He had a fleet of cars in the underground garage of the house including several high tech vans. They would use

those to transport Granny to Michigan in the next day
or two. He did manage to say the word hummer at
least twelve times before Hank threatened to remove
his vocal chords.

None of his staff had made it and Dwayne was
heartbroken. The Cows were composing letters with
information on the massive life insurance policies
Dwayne had given all his employees. He knew it
wouldn't bring them back, but he felt it was the very
least he could do for their families.

"You look fabu in gauchos, Hank," Dwayne
complimented him with glee and a whistle.

"You do realize I will get you back for this," Hank
groused as he pulled at the tight sky blue starched
wife beater that Dwayne had paired with a pair of
black and white hounds tooth gauchos. Thankfully
Hank's feet were too large for any of Dwayne's
pumps, so he'd wedged his size thirteens into a pair
of size seven red sequined flip-flops.

Luckily my Vampyre had picked out a lovely
strapless Stella McCartney sundress with wedge heels
for me. I looked great and my man looked like a
circus reject. However, I still wanted him with a
vengeance.

"Wait," I said as I glanced around the room.
"Where is everyone?"

The Great Room was empty. Pieces of glass from
the mind meld were sprinkled around the massive
space, but everything else was pristine.

"In lockdown in the basement," Dwayne explained
as he adjusted the waistline on Hank's gauchos. He
stopped immediately when Hank clocked him in the
head.

"Hank, be nice," I said with a giggle as Dwayne
staggered and fell to the couch with a thud.

"Trust me, that *was* me being nice," Hank
responded.

SOME WERE IN TIME

"Why are they in lockdown?" I asked. I wanted to see Granny one more time before we left.

"I've drained her and given her the first blood. It's no longer safe for you to be around her."

I held my tongue as Dwayne covertly snapped a picture of Hank in his gaucho glory with a conveniently stashed camera.

"How did she do?" Hank asked the question I was too scared to ask.

"She did well," Dwayne replied cautiously as he sat on the camera. "It's a good sign, but we have a long way to go."

"Little victories will work right now," I said. "Thank you."

"You're welcome, doll. I promise to take good care of her and I'll keep you informed."

I nodded, too afraid if I spoke I would cry.

"Now about Chicago," Dwayne said briskly, changing the subject. "I have a home under one of my aliases in Lincolnshire. It's not traceable and you will use that. I forbid you to go back to your apartments—too dangerous."

"Outstanding." Hank nodded with approval.

Dwayne handed us an address and keys. He also handed us our fully reloaded and cleaned guns along with all the unused squirt guns.

"Memorize it and then eat the paper," Dwayne advised.

"Dude, I am not eating paper," I said as I quickly committed the address to memory.

"Fine," Dwayne said with a sniff. "The Cows will eat it. It's good fiber."

"You're going to need a few parenting books." God only knew what he was going to feed his new daughters since he didn't eat.

"Dwayne does not need any help," he said with a grin. "Most of what I do will send them to therapy anyway. I do not need a human book to help me with that."

"Point," I caved and laughed. "How did you do all this while we showered?" I asked as I strapped the squeaky clean weapons to my body.

"My girls did it," he answered proudly. "They're also bathing Granny and doing her hair. They kicked me out because I'm a man. I tried to explain that I'm gay and swore I wouldn't be ogling Granny's lady bits, but they were having none of it."

I couldn't love those Cows anymore if I tried. The Universe was working in bizarre ways and I decided to embrace it willingly.

"When she wakes," I said, refusing to add an *if*. "You need to find out why she didn't shift and defend herself. There's something missing here and we need to know what happened."

"I will," Dwayne assured me. "But she might not remember everything. It can be hazy for a bit."

"Will she know me?" The bile rose in my throat at the thought that Granny might not recognize me.

"She should," he said as he gave me a quick hug. "Most likely her brain will block the trauma that led to her death. I won't know until she wakes."

The need to move consumed me. Scenarios ran wildly through my head—good, bad and ugly. I dislodged myself from Dwayne's embrace and jogged around the perimeter of the large room. Moving and planning would keep me sane. Jumping Hank and making him see Jesus would help, but I didn't think Dwayne would appreciate it. Or possibly he might appreciate it too much. Hank and Dwayne's eyes followed me with concern. I knew they were worried I was close to losing it. Their concern was well warranted. Lists. I needed to make mental lists.

"We will go to Chicago and settle in at Dwayne's house. We'll contact Angela and her Dragon and arrange to meet them on neutral territory. If she had anything to do with this ambush I will kill her. And Hank, *I* will kill her. I want no help. Moral support will be welcome, but if she ratted us out she's mine."

"I'm good with that," Hank said with a curt nod and a feral grin.

"Holy Phyllis Diller," Dwayne sang as his skin took on a slight glow. "I'd really like to see that."

"Trust me," I told him with a smile that came nowhere near reaching my eyes. "You wouldn't. Now about the mess here... "

"No worries," Dwayne assured us. "Before we leave I'll alert the local Hyena Pack. Place will be spotless in an hour or less. Those bastards will eat anything."

"Um... I got nothing," I choked out. I had to close my eyes against the picture now resting in my brain.

"On that unappetizing note," Hank said with a barely concealed gag, "we're out."

"Wait," I yelled, alarming both men. "I need to lay out the plan a little more."

"Do it, babe," Dwayne said as he patted my back. "Get organized. It will calm you."

Hank nodded and sat back down. My men knew me well and I was humbled at how much my need to hang on to my sanity meant to them. Or more likely, my prior breakdowns had taught them a healthy fear for their lives.

"The Dragons are our first priority. They will lead us to the leak. I need to know the connection between them and the Wolves. Finding out who cursed the Wolves has to go at the bottom of the to-do list, but that's something I want to know too. The Council needs to be aware of rogue Wolf Packs running around."

"The Council stays in the dark until we have all the information we need to get out alive," Hank stated firmly.

I knew he was referring to the fact some on the Council wanted me dead. Agreeing with him was a no-brainer. The Council would be the last to know anything we found out. Any intel we compiled would be used as bargaining chips for my life and for information as to what really happened to my parents.

"Absolutely," I concurred with Hank. "I think the Wolves figure in more than we realize."

"You think they're involved with the crossbreeding of species?" Dwayne asked as he mulled the prospect over.

"No," I answered thoughtfully. "I don't. I'm not even sure the Dragons are pushing the cross species thing. It might have been an isolated incident with the three imbeciles that came to Georgia. They're wildly secretive and I'd place a bet they were trying to raise their own status in the Dragon world."

"How much?" Dwayne asked as he pulled his wallet from his pants.

"You'd bet against me?" I gaped at him.

"Wait, I just heard the word bet and got excited. What are we actually wagering on?"

I rolled my eyes. "Angela thinks some of the Council may be in cahoots with the Dragons. My guess is the crossbreeding debacle was a cover for something much bigger," I said, finally beginning to calm.

"Don't discount the fracture in the Council about revealing the Wolves to the humans," Hank added with an expression that looked like he'd swallowed a lemon.

"All super natural species?" Dwayne asked with a bewildered shake of his head.

"Nope," I said. "As far as I know the Wolves would be the only reveal."

"That is the stupidest thing I have ever heard," Dwayne yelled. He shoved his wallet back in his pants so violently he accidently ripped the pocket right off. "Dang it, I loved these capris."

"Without the pocket I can see the shape of your ass better," I said, hoping to derail the fit I knew he was about to throw.

"Really?" he asked as he looked over his shoulder and examined his rear end. "I think you're right. Maybe I'll take the pockets off of all my pants."

"You do that," Hank said with an exasperated sigh. "We need to go, Essie. You ready?"

"Nope, but I'm coming anyway," I said with a grin.

"That's my girl." Hank grabbed my hand and gave Dwayne one more slap to the head.

"What the hell was that for?" Dwayne griped as he tried to swat Hank back.

"The gauchos and the photograph, asshole," Hank said with a smirk as he successfully avoided Dwayne's counterattack.

"We're out of here." I pulled Hank to the front door before one of them lost a limb. We simply did not have the time to regrow anything. "Call me every few hours about Granny and let me know how she's doing."

"Will do, doll."

"Do you need extra protection in Michigan?" Hank asked as he paused at the door. "I can send some of the Pack from Georgia for reinforcements."

"Got it covered," Dwayne mumbled and began to frantically straighten the pillows on the couch.

Crapcrapcrap. Dwayne only straightened things when Armageddon was approaching.

"Spill it," I said as I marched back over to him.

"Fine. I called a few Vamps to help guard the compound in Michigan. Too dangerous for anything but dead people and Cows to be around for a while."

"I thought you told me Vampyre get-togethers end in decapitation?"

"Occasionally," he hedged. "However, I made some deals."

"They owe you?" Hank asked.

"Um... not exactly. I kind of sort of might owe them now."

The story just kept getting worse...

"We. We owe them now," I stated firmly.

"Sweet Jessica Simpson on a skinny-ish day, I will not allow you to owe a Vampyre anything. Ever," Dwayne said so loudly even he winced.

Hank's sharp intake of breath and audible groan shook my confidence a little, but the was no freakin' way in hell Dwayne was going to bear the brunt of the consequences for taking care of my granny.

"I'm serious," I said loudly. Loud was good. Loud sounded confident—or certifiable. I was going with confident. "How bad can it be?"

"Um..." Dwayne started.

"Stop," I shouted and slapped my hand over his mouth. "I don't want to know. I feel it would be better if I use avoidance on this one until it's in my face. We clear?"

"Yep," Dwayne said with wide eyes and a small scream.

"Alright, Hank, don't say anything and don't look at me for five minutes until I'm past imagining what owing a Vampyre a favor means. You got that, big guy?"

Hank inhaled deeply and blew the air out of his mouth. He held onto his anger by a thread. It made my brain run wild with thoughts of being chained to a coffin in a dank basement for a decade and performing blood slave duties for a pale-skinned, stinky Vamp with long fingernails, putrid breath and a weird bun head. I really needed to stop watching TV.

Hank nodded curtly and picked up the camera Dwayne had hidden on the couch and crushed it. Dwayne's shriek of dismay made me grin and forget for a moment that I might be beholden to a Vampyre who wasn't my beautiful, gay best friend.

Thank god for senseless destruction of property... it really did take your mind off of your problems.

"Well, have a good time and don't die," Dwayne said in a cheery voice as he snapped another shot of Hank with a second camera and hustled us out of the front door.

"You take care of Granny," I said as I hugged him tight.

"With my life," Dwayne promised and kissed my cheek. "With my life."

Chapter 13

"I need to do something life affirming," I said as I searched for a song on the radio I could deal with. Meditating was out. I couldn't find my center in a moving vehicle. "Do you want a blow job?"

"Oh my god, Essie," Hank groaned with a pained laugh. "You have just made a long drive much longer." He shifted uncomfortably in his seat and gripped the steering wheel like it was going to fly away.

"Does that mean no?"

"Yes."

"Wait," I said as I settled on a top forty station that would make Dwayne proud. "I'm confused. You *do* want a blow job or you *don't*?"

"I always want a blow job," he said tightly. "I just don't want a life endangering blow job."

"Are you saying that because I'm so good at blow jobs or because any blow job would make you wreck the Hummer? Pun completely and totally intended."

"The only person I want a blow job from is you," he said as he tried to readjust his now tight pants.

"Because I'm so awesome at them?"

After a brief pause and a chuckle he said, "Yes. Yes, you are."

"Thank you."

"You're welcome."

"How about a hand job?" I tried again.

His grunt of agony was music to my ears.

"How about we wait until we get to Chicago and go for broke?" he suggested with a sexy half-smirk that melted my panties.

"Works for me."

"And I just want to thank you for still being attracted to me in gauchos," he added with a shudder.

"Hank, I would be attracted to you in a strapless beaded gown and a boa. You're all kinds of hot and all kinds of mine no matter what you're wearing."

"Back at ya, baby."

Indiana was flat and kind of mind-numbing. However, the miles of windmills kept me busy as I tried to count them, much to Hank's amusement. The outskirts of Chicago were industrial and stinky. We bypassed the city, got on 94, and arrived in Lincolnshire just as the sun was setting. Apparently Dwayne kept this particular abode because there was an in-the-round dinner theater he enjoyed performing at. The thought was alarming and yet also strangely comforting. His biggest credit was playing the king in *The King and I*. I'd lay money it was due to the fact he was bald and hotter than Hades, because his voice was more suited to Lady Gaga than Rogers and Hammerstein. Plus most Vamps preferred big cities and he was relatively safe from friendly decapitation in the 'burbs.

"I say we call Angela and her Dragon in the morning," Hank said as he pulled the Hummer into the garage.

159

It was a four-car garage and Dwayne had a hot little silver-blue Mustang that had my name on it. I prayed the keys were in the house.

"Sounds like a plan," I agreed. "What do you want to do now?"

"Hmmm, I suppose we could think of something if we tried hard enough," he said with a sexy lopsided smile.

"Pun intended?" I asked suggestively.

"One hundred percent."

***

"Oh my god," I hissed. "Do that again."

Round three of going for broke was going to turn either my mind or my legs to mush. Honestly, I didn't care. I was having way too much fun losing all my brain cells as I rode Hank like I was at a rodeo.

"Bend over the couch and pull up your dress," Hank ordered as he steered me toward the leather couch facing the fireplace.

Dwayne's house in Lincolnshire was far more modest than his mansion in southern Illinois, but it was clear the Vamp had money and good taste. The two-story brick Colonial home was in an upper middle class neighborhood. Not in a million years would I have guessed a Vampyre lived amidst the perfectly coiffed and properly dressed families of the affluent suburb. The furniture was all in neutral tones with lots of leather and overstuffed comfy chenille chairs. He had overdone it a tad with the crystal chandeliers hanging in every room, but it made me happy because it was very Dwayne.

"Shouldn't I be naked?" I asked as I flopped over the arm of the couch with my dress over my head.

"Nope," Hank said in a husky voice as he gripped my hips and ground himself against my delighted body.

We'd been so intent on getting down to business neither of us had removed any of our clothing. Thankfully Hank had exchanged the gauchos for jeans and a t-shirt back in Indiana. Even though he was hotter than asphalt in August, it might have been a bit unsettling to have sex with him looking like a metrosexual, gay Vampyre fashionista. The jeans were around his ankles and his shirt was shredded from round one when it had gotten a little out of hand and my claws had come out. It was all kinds of sexy and all kinds of out of control.

"I am so in love with you," he whispered in my ear as he slid into my body and began to pound me like there was no tomorrow.

I arched my back and met his wild thrusts with screams of pleasure. I sure as hell hoped Dwayne's neighbors weren't home.

"How does this keep getting better?" I cried out as I felt the familiar tingle begin to coil in my body.

"Don't know. Don't care," he ground out as his thrusts became frenzied.

"I'm close," I gasped as I clawed at the couch and gripped him within my body like a vise.

"Come," Hank demanded as I felt him grow larger inside me. "Now."

I came with a shriek as I closed my eyes and brilliant color ripped across my vision. I gasped for air as every nerve ending in my body shuddered with pleasure. Hank's breathing was labored as he planted kisses all over my shoulders and neck.

"Love you… love you so much," he muttered as he pulled out and gently cradled my still quivering body in his strong arms. "Never gonna let you go."

"I'm not going anywhere, big guy," I whispered as I pressed my kiss-swollen lips to his cheek. "You're stuck with me forever."

"Damn right," he said as his head fell back on the couch.

We cuddled in silence. In this moment my world was perfect. My worry for Granny was still there, but I felt safe, loved, and cherished.

"Hank, can I ask you something?" I asked as I reluctantly crawled off his lap and straightened the dress I'd never removed.

"Anything."

"Did the Vampyre blood affect you? Do you feel different?" I asked as he followed me to the kitchen and watched me rummage through the cabinets for something to eat. We'd used up an enormous amount of calories and I was starving.

After a long pause he sighed. "I do feel strange. The murderous streak I felt in the battle was disconcerting. I couldn't quite control it—it felt like it was controlling me. My need to kill verged on psychotic."

"How does Dwayne handle that?" I asked as I gave up on finding anything edible in a Vampyre's kitchen.

"He's three hundred years old," Hank reminded me. "He's had time to rein it in... or he has some secret serial killer life we don't know about."

I considered the possibility for a moment. It was a surprise to me how much property he owned. However, the thought of Dwayne going out on pleasure murders was ludicrous. Was Dwayne just different from other Vamps? The thought of owing a favor to a bloodsucker who didn't have his shit together like Dwayne did give me pause.

"I couldn't let Dwayne take all the responsibility for Granny's safety," I said quietly. The ramifications of what I'd done by taking on the responsibility of the debt to the Vamps was starting to really sink in.

"You were correct. As much as I don't like owing Vamps, we take care of our own."

"Maybe it won't be too bad," I said in a cheery tone that didn't fool either of us.

"Uh huh," Hank shot back with a small shudder. "Let's just go with that one until we find out differently."

"Deal. Wanna go find food?" I asked, happy to change the subject.

"Drive thru or sit down?" he asked as he played with my post sex messy curls.

"I don't know," I said. "Either. Why?"

"Sit down—we have to change." He smirked like a dude who'd gotten majorly laid as he glanced down at his shredded shirt. "Drive thru—we can go looking like we've just had sex for several hours."

Looking down at my wrinkled and torn dress, I grinned. "I'm hungry. I'm not changing."

"Then drive thru it is." He chuckled as he grabbed my hand and we ran out of the front door.

***

"I'm having a hard time dealing with the fact I just ate ten tacos. I'm pretty sure I have a food baby," I muttered as I patted my full stomach.

"That's nothing," Hank bragged. "I ate seventeen. I have food quadruplets."

I giggled as I slurped on my soda and tried to keep my eyes open. It had been a long couple of days and sleep hadn't been a priority. We were parked outside a local taco joint because neither of us could wait to eat until we got home. The fabulous Mustang we'd found the keys for got a few envious glances, but I didn't care. It drove like a dream. I scented only humans and was relieved we were probably safe from danger at least for the evening.

"So do we have a plan for tomorrow?" I asked as I tried to tamp down my gluttonous need for more cheap Mexican food. Thank god Werewolf metabolism was fast.

"We call on the burner phone and we meet up."

"Let's do it in a public place. How about on Clark by Wrigley Field?"

"I was thinking the Lincoln Park Zoo in case we have to shift," he countered.

"Damn, you're good. The Dragon drinks the serum before we get into any logistics." I looked away from the mound of empty taco wrappers so I could pretend I hadn't eaten quite as much as I had.

"Excellent. We'll say we'll meet by the Red Wolf area, but we'll stay in the shadows until we know they're alone," Hank suggested.

"We call and give them eight minutes to get there. That's enough time from the office if they run. Leave a note at the Wolf cage and then tell them to proceed to the monkeys. At the monkey cage, leave a note to send them to the reptiles, and if we think they're clean by then—we talk. If we think they're being followed or they brought anyone else to the party, we disappear."

"God, you're hot when you go all agent," Hank said with a whistle and a quick peck to my lips.

"Wait, one more twist. Have them start at Wrigley and then we call them with the burner and start the maze at the zoo."

"Just when I thought you couldn't get any hotter…"

"I'm good like that," I said with a giggle.

We sat back in our seats and basked in our smart plan and full stomachs.

"If you put a pin in me I'd pop," Hank said with a groan.

"Good thing we had sex before we ate our own weight in tacos," I said as I seriously contemplated going through the drive thru one more time.

"True," Hank agreed and then laughed. "You wanna get a few more?"

"Oh my god, you are so the man for me."

And we went back through the drive thru... two more times.

Chapter 14

"You armed and ready?" Hank asked quietly as we walked into the zoo.

"Yep. Locked and loaded."

The morning had dawned sunny and beautiful—not a cloud in the sky. The breeze floated playfully through the trees in the park. Sadly, I felt anything but playful. It was early and not many people were in the zoo. I was thankful for that. There was the potential for things to go very wrong with a Dragon involved. I still didn't trust my boss for pairing us with a species that had tried to kill me twice in the last month alone. Whatever. I was sure she had her reasons.

We'd placed the notes where they were certain to find them and we found an excellent hiding spot in the bushes outside the reptile house. Our greenish brown fatigues blended right in. My adrenaline was pumping and the Vampyre blood in my system itched for a bloody fight. Not to mention my inner wolf was rattling her cage like a crazy person. Tamping both instincts down took effort, but I succeeded. I was only going Rambo if I had to.

"You wanna make the call?" Hank asked with a grin that belied the tension I could feel coming off of him.

"I most certainly do," I answered as I rolled my neck and popped my sternum.

"Doesn't that hurt?" Hank asked as he winced at the sound of my bones popping.

"Dude, we turn into Wolves. How can my popping my sternum freak you out?"

"Point," he conceded with a chuckle.

I stared at the phone for a long moment. The same one I had talked to Dwayne on only an hour ago. They were in the process of moving Granny to Michigan and so far things were going as expected. Dwayne was cautiously optimistic. However, the Cows were downright ecstatic at the thought of feeding and coddling Granny. The girls had no doubt whatsoever that she would wake up in a week. I wasn't as sure, but I wanted to believe it so badly my heart hurt.

"What are you waiting for?" Hank asked as he watched me closely. "Do you want me to make the call?"

"Nope," I said with a sigh. "It's just when I make the call there's no turning back. The ball will start rolling and there is no way in hell to stop it."

"The ball is already rolling," Hank said logically and without emotion. "We're going to stop it and obliterate it. The call is just a small piece of a puzzle already halfway put together. Lose the feelings you have for everyone but me. Use your training and let instinct guide you."

"My instinct says to let my Wolf and Vamp out and kill shit," I told him with a rueful smile.

"Well, then… listen."

He was correct. The time for introspective thought was over. It was time to trust no one but Hank and myself. I would proceed with caution and with my eyes and ears wide open. I felt for my Glock and the knives and squirt gun filled with the solution Dima would have to drink. It would prohibit her shift and potentially elongate my life and Hank's.

Everything was in place as much as Hank or I could manage. It was time to call my boss.

I dialed and held my breath.

"Angela... dude, how's it hanging?" I said breezily as she picked up her phone and grunted what barely passed for a greeting.

"Where in the hell have you been?" she shouted as I yanked the phone away from my ear. *"And what phone number are you calling from?"*

"Had to get a new phone plan since I haven't seen my paycheck this month," I explained with a touch of sarcasm in my tone. "You sound like you ran out of whiskey."

"It's in your mailbox at the apartment you haven't been back to," she snapped. *"And for your information, I've been through several bottles in the last few days, thinking you were dead."*

"Now why on earth would you think I was dead?" I asked coldly. I most certainly could have been dead if the Dragons or the Wolves had succeeded, but did she know that?

"Because you're two days late and I haven't heard from you or Hank or Dwayne or Bobby Sue," she screeched. *"I have no more hair on the right side of my head. I could skin you alive right now, Essie."*

"Yeah, well, get in line," I muttered.

Her demeanor was the same as it always was. She'd threatened to kill me at least three times a week for the past year and never made good on it. The maddest I ever saw her was when she realized I'd used the company card for a spa day and dinner at Ruth Chris. The front row seats to a Coldplay concert for Dwayne and me also hadn't helped. I had been fairly sure that day was going to be my last on earth, but I was still kicking. I needed to be careful not to read too much into anything.

"Get your ass down to headquarters. We have situations in the making and I have no more time for lazy agents who can't make deadlines," she grumbled.

There was that word again... dead. Why it kept popping out at me was an irony. Angela was no different than she always had been.

"No can do, hot mamma. I'm in no mood for a clusterhump today," I replied calmly.

Her silence was unexpected. Was it the "no can do" or the "hot mamma" or the "clusterhump" that threw her off her yelling game? My lack of respect for authority was nothing new.

"I do believe my statement was a direct order," she ground out.

I heard a rustling in the background and I was positive she was searching for her booze.

"I *do believe* we are off the grid and you are not giving the orders," I countered in a tone I rarely used. "Is the Dragon with you?"

"Um, yes," she stuttered, not quite as sure of herself.

"That's wonderfully sucktastic," I yelled. Her yelp of pain amused me and I decided to yell the rest of the conversation. "You have exactly eight minutes from the time we hang up to get the Dragon and your half-bald Wolf ass to the front entrance of Wrigley Field. If you fail your mission we'll be gone."

"What the hell? There's too much traffic to make it there in eight minutes. This is ridiculous."

She was pissed.

"Nope, not ridiculous at all. You're correct about the traffic. I'd suggest running. If you sprint you can make it. If you need a hit I'd suggest a flask. A bottle would be messy if you dropped it on your run. No flunkies or we disappear."

"*I should fire your ass,*" she muttered angrily.

"Is that a threat or a promise?" I shot back.

"*Neither,*" she snapped. "*If you weren't so damned valuable I wouldn't put up with this shit.*"

"That's the nicest thing you've ever said to me," I cooed.

I could hear her breathing and I felt her blood pressure rise through the phone. I knew I was treading on thin ice if I wanted to actually keep my job, but being a WTF agent had become extremely unappealing in the last month. Defending my life on a semi-daily basis was not what I had signed up for. My dream had been to defend my entire race... not just myself.

"Does the Dragon know she'll be drinking the formula?" I asked.

Angela's ginormous pause answered the question. "*Not exactly,*" she hedged.

"Well, I'd suggest you get the fire breather up to speed on your run. She doesn't drink—we have nothing to say or do with her... or you," I said tightly.

Hank tensed beside me. I knew he wanted to rip the phone from my hand and let Angela have it. Out of respect for me he stayed still.

"*You really want to leave her defenseless?*" she asked with disgust.

"After my week—yes. Yes, I do."

"*What the hell does that mean?*" she demanded, completely exasperated.

"If you don't already know, I might let you in on it when I see you," I informed her cryptically. "You have eight minutes. Starting now."

As I hung up the phone I heard her screaming a string of obscenities that made me cringe. To say she was pissed was an understatement, but I didn't care. I wasn't sure who the bad guy was anymore and I was taking no chances.

"I think that went well," I said to Hank with an evil grin.

"The half-bald Wolf ass comment was inspired," he said, congratulating me.

"Yep, I thought it was a nice touch," I agreed with a real smile. "Dima doesn't know about the solution."

"I gathered as much," he replied as he ran his hands through his hair. "She won't want to drink it."

"Do you know her?" I asked. I didn't like the idea he had possibly interacted with the Dragon.

"I've met her."

"And?"

"And she's a Dragon."

"Pretty?" I inquired casually as my pea green jealous side roared to the surface.

"Aren't they all?" he said.

"You could say she was fugly and smelled bad," I said as my eyes narrowed.

"If I lie and she shows up looking like she does, you'll want to castrate me and wonder what else I'm being untruthful about. Correct?"

"Um... maybe," I mumbled. God, sometimes it annoyed me that he knew me so well.

"She's gorgeous and she leaves me cold. There is no one in this world for me except you. We clear on that?" he asked with a raised brow and a hint of a smile on his lips.

"Yes," I said sheepishly. I had a possessive streak a mile long, but Hank's was worse.

"Six more minutes till the second call," he said with a feral grin.

"Are you enjoying this?" I asked as I punched his arm.

"Aren't you?" he countered.

171

I paused and considered my answer. I didn't want to enjoy it, but if I were being truthful... I was. The adrenaline pumping through my blood made me feel alive. The threat of danger appealed to my inner wolf and the desire to win consumed me. It alarmed me how I felt most alive in a battle or in Hank's arms. However, denying what I was could be deadly. I was a predator and I had enemies. It would be helpful to know a concrete list of who my enemies actually were, but living on the edge was invigorating... and possibly stupid in a deadly way.

"I do enjoy it," I admitted. "Will we ever be able to live a normal life?"

"Normal is a relative word," Hank said. "One person's normal is another person's hell."

"That didn't actually answer my question."

"Point," he conceded with a slight shrug. "But our normal or abnormal will always be fine as long as we're together."

"Okay, so I'm guessing no white picket fence with two point five children and a minivan," I said sadly.

"I was thinking more like six children," he replied with a sexy smirk.

"Clearly you've been smoking crack," I shot back with a laugh and an eye roll. There was no way I planned to blow out six pups.

"Nope—just wishful thinking. I want little girls who look just like you."

My heart melted and I wanted to get started on baby making immediately. However, the public zoo was not the most romantic or legal place to start a family. We weren't even married yet.

"Enough of the family planning," I admonished him sternly with a barely concealed smile. "I can't be thinking about you naked while I'm at work. Is Junior on his way up?"

"I really don't like *Junior* and *naked* being used in the same sentence by you," Hank snapped.

"Oh. My. God. First of all, they were two separate sentences and the thought of Junior naked is so wrong it's laughable."

His jealous streak was so hot...

"Oh. Well, alright then. He's going to the house to wait for us. I left him a note about what was going down today."

"You wrote out our plans out and left them lying on a table?" I was shocked.

"It's all in code. No one can read it except Junior and myself," he said, calming me. "If I don't contact him in a half hour he'll come after us."

Hank's brilliance constantly amazed me. "Can I learn the code?" I asked.

"It'll cost you," he said with a suggestive grin.

"Will I enjoy the terms?"

"I believe you'll find the conditions to your liking."

"Deal," I said as I checked my watch. "Three minutes."

"You want the second phone call?" he asked.

"Yes. Yes, I do."

We stared at the phone and waited.

"Do you think you can raise the bar on *half-bald Wolf ass*?"

I paused for a brief moment and decided to take the dare. "Yes. Yes, I believe I can."

"Go for it," Hank said with a grin that made me laugh. "Thirty seconds."

I dialed and bit back my grin. My sexy man could even make impending bloodshed and possible death fun. He was a total keeper.

"Asscrackada, did you make it?" I bellowed into the phone.

"*Yes*," she huffed like she was about to drop. "*Where the hell are you and what the hell did you just call me?*"

"I called you Angela."

"*No, you didn't,*" she wheezed. "*It sounded like asscaca.*"

"Sweet fecal hell," I laughed. "You need your ears checked, Anaconda."

"*Whatever. Where are you?*" she demanded.

"We're not there, Angina," I told her evenly. "There's been a slight change in venue. You have exactly seven minutes to get to the Lincoln Park Zoo and go to the Red Wolf cages."

"*You've got to be shitting me,*" she coughed out.

"Um, nope. Not shitting you at all, Ammonia."

"*What in god's name did you just call me?*" she shouted as I tried not to laugh.

I did feel a little bad about making her run. She was wildly out of shape for a Werewolf. Most of me liked her the way one likes a cranky teacher who has to put up with you because she has no choice.

"I called you by your name… Alfalfa."

"*That is not my…*"

"You have seven minutes." I cut her tirade off. "Starting now."

I tossed the phone to Hank, who was laughing.

"God, my world would suck without you in it."

"I rose to the challenge and then some," I said proudly. "Alfalfa was my crowning moment."

"I'm partial to Asscrackada," he said.

"Happy to oblige."

"When they get here we pat them down and put the solution in Dima's mouth. Then we let them talk their way into a hole… or not," he said as he checked his weapons.

"I'll pat down Dima," I said, not making eye contact. There was no way I wanted to watch him put his hands on her if she was as hot as I imagined.

"Fine by me," he agreed, clearly understanding and politely ignoring my jealousy.

"They have three minutes to reach the wolves and then I'd say approximately two to the monkeys and then two to the reptiles," I said as the tension and excitement in my body coiled tightly.

"Seven minutes till show time," Hank whispered.

"Do you think Angela is playing us?" I asked.

"Don't know, but we'll find out soon enough."

I prayed to all the angels and saints and threw in Dolce and Gabbana in honor of Hank's mom. If Angela wasn't involved with the ambush, she sure as hell was going to help us find out who was.

Chapter 15

We stood as they approached. Dima was every bit as stunning as I'd assumed and Angela looked like she'd been hit by a truck. The Dragon had long flaming red hair and a body to die for. Her boobs looked fake to me, but Were bodies rejected plastic surgery so the monsters had to be real. I hated her on sight. Not because she was a Dragon and had ginormous perky knockers... because she was ogling Hank like he was dessert. Setting her straight would be fun and hopefully a little bloody.

The coast was clear and I scented no other Weres in the area. That relieved me more than I wanted to admit. The thought that Angela had betrayed me didn't sit well at all. Hopefully the Dragon would drink and the meeting would be filled with facts instead of death and fire. However, if she touched Hank she'd lose a hand.

As we stepped away from the bushes Angela's eyes narrowed to slits. It took all I had not to burst out laughing. She hadn't been exaggerating when she said she'd pulled half of her hair out. I felt bad for a moment, but her nervous tics were not my problem. However, I was delighted to realize the burner phone had photograph ability. This would come in handy if I stayed on with the WTF. I captured a fond and unattractive memory of my boss as we stopped and stood about six feet from them.

"I'd say it's nice to see you again, but it's not," I said calmly. "Has the Dragon agreed to drink?"

"The Dragon has a name," Dima countered smoothly as she glanced at me briefly before her eyes landed back on Hank and stayed there.

She was very short-sighted not to talk to the woman. Just like a typical car salesman—she thought the man was in charge. She had another thing coming.

"The Dragon drinks now or the meeting is over," I said tightly.

Hank stood quietly beside me with a vicious expression on his beautiful face. His eyes were on Angela and he ignored the Dragon completely.

"*You're in charge here,*" he said in my head. "*Let the Dragon know you mean business or we'll have trouble.*"

"*Can I punch her in the head?*" I asked.

"*Will that make you feel better?*"

"*I think it would,*" I answered honestly.

"*Then by all means—punch away.*"

"Drop all your weapons and slide them over. I want your phones too. Now," I demanded.

"What are you doing?" Angela snapped. "We are not the bad guys."

"That remains to be seen, boss lady," I replied coldly. "We've had a few little unexplainable issues on the way up and it's a bit difficult not to connect them back to you."

"Care to explain?" Angela asked as she reluctantly removed her weapons and dropped them and her phone to the ground.

"Not particularly," I said with a smile that didn't reach my eyes. "Suffice it to say we won and they lost."

That wasn't exactly true since Granny's life still hung in the balance, but there was no way in hell I was turning over that piece of intel. The Council would destroy a Wolf-Vampyre hybrid faster than I could blink.

"Who lost?" she bellowed. "What in god's name are you babbling about? Where the hell are Dwayne and Bobby Sue?"

"Michigan," I said.

"What the hell is in Michigan?" she demanded.

Ignoring her, I focused on the Dragon, who was taking her sweet time unburdening herself of her firearms, knives, and whatever else she had hidden under her ridiculously tight pants and t-shirt. God, her boobs were distracting.

"So… Wolf," she purred with distaste as a thin tendril of purple smoke wafted from her nose. "You're going to take my weapons and make me drink something to prohibit my shift?"

"Yep. Them's the rules," I said, pulling out my best Southern accent with a vengeance.

"Do you think I'm stupid?" she asked, putting her hands on her hips.

Finally I had her full attention.

"I have no idea if you're stupid and I don't actually care. What I do know is this—if you can shift I can't kill you if the need arises. If you stay human, I can rip your head off of your body with my bare hands. I've done it before and trust me, if you cross me… I will happily do it again."

"That was you?" she asked as she paled and gaped at me. She shot a quick and angry look at Angela, who shrugged noncommittally.

Clearly Angela hadn't kept the Dragon entirely up to speed. This was good to know.

The Dragon was both impressed and appalled. Interestingly, she had completely forgotten Hank was anywhere in the vicinity. However, I was still going to punch her in the head.

"You going to drink voluntarily or do we get to fight a little first?" I inquired casually.

"*Careful, Essie,*" Hank warned. "*She can still shift.*"

"*She won't fight,*" I assured him. "*She has an agenda. There's got to be something larger than money at stake for her to be doing this.*"

"*True,*" he agreed, "*but she's still a Dragon.*"

"*Good point, well made. However, I will bet you three backrubs with oil and sex afterward that I'm right.*"

"*That's a win-win for me,*" he growled. "*I shall take those odds and raise you twelve tacos post sex,*" he countered.

"*I can live with that,*" I said with glee. "*I'm still going to punch her in the head.*"

"*I expect no less.*"

"It's unfair and ludicrous to expect me to give into all your demands. You clearly have issues with Dragons. Am I to believe you will defend me if the *need arises*?" Dima hissed angrily.

"Yep. You've got it right. You can earn back your weapons, but not drinking the solution is a deal breaker," I told her as I crossed my arms over my chest and waited.

"This is not smart," she muttered. "I could defend all of us."

"Possibly," I agreed. "But you are a Dragon. You're also a double agent. I have no clue whose side you're actually on. Your words and promises mean less than nothing to me at the moment."

"It'll be your funeral," Dima snapped as she slid her weapons over.

"Speaking of my demise," I said as my gaze zeroed in on Angela. "Who else knows Dwayne and my granny are working with me?"

"That sentence made no sense," Angela grumped as she kicked her phone and guns over.

"Trust me," I shot back as I crunched her phone beneath my rockin' cool combat boot, much to her dismay. "It makes plenty of sense. Answer the question."

"I know. You all know. And some of the Council knows," she told me.

I was speechless. Why in the hell did anyone on the Council know? I could tell it took everything Hank had not to take three steps forward and end Angela's life.

"Explain," I said tersely as I put a hand on Hank's arm.

Dima watched the drama unfolding with curiosity.

"It's protocol," Angela griped.

"*I need to kill her,*" Hank said with a coldness that made me shiver.

"*Nope. If she dies, I get the honors,*" I told him.

"*She put a target on our head. Is she stupid or just totally by the book?*" he demanded.

I couldn't answer that one.

"Nothing about this mission is protocol," I hissed viciously as Angela took several tentative steps backwards. "You wanted us to find out if the Dragons were crossbreeding and then ascertain if the Council was in cahoots with the Dragons. I fail to see how reporting the inner workings of the mission to the Council benefits anyone."

I knew my hair was blowing around my head. Angela and Dima watched me with both fascination and fear. My Vampyre was showing...

"The Dragons are working with the Council?" Dima asked, surprised as she kept her eyes glued to me.

"Holy shit," I groused. "Why in the hell are you on this mission? Do you not have any of the intel?"

"My intel seems to differ from yours," she said, glancing over at Angela with suspicion. "I'm here to take out the alpha Dragon and you're supposed to help me."

I stared up at the clear blue sky for a long moment. My need to tear something from limb to limb was dangerously close to the surface. The sparks flying off of Hank didn't bode well for anyone. The smoke wafting from the Dragon's nose was a clear indication all hell could break loose any moment.

"Listen," Angela said reasonably. "The goals all match up. There was no reason to brief all of you on every little piece of the puzzle. The Alpha is apparently the mastermind behind the crossbreeding. He needs to go. We also think he's the one funding the part of the Council that is fighting for the reveal of the Wolves to the humans. If we take him out we can go into his financials and figure out who he's paying. We stop the crossbreeding and we nail the Council. The Weres stay hidden and everyone wins."

"Angela, the whiskey has finally eaten your brain. Why in the hell would the alpha Dragon's financials be available to us if we off him?"

"Because I'm his daughter and I'm next in line for alpha," Dima said with eyes as dead as I'd ever seen.

"It's lovely you want to kill your dad and all—I'd expect no less from a Dragon. However, this plan is sucktastic and is a death trap waiting to happen," I said as I pulled the squirt gun from my belt.

"You know nothing of me or my family, Wolf," Dima snarled.

"Enlighten me," I said sarcastically.

ROBYN PETERMAN

"My father killed my mother and my five brothers
brutally—in front of me. He tried to kill me
throughout my entire childhood, but failed because
my mother always outwitted him. He leads our
people as a dictator and he's stayed entirely too long
at the fair. I plan to find him and kill him. It will hurt
and he will suffer just like my mother did. I have no
plans to fail. You are wanted by the Dragons... both
of you," she said, referring to Hank and me. "They
can't understand your power—and quite honestly,
neither can I. But I don't care what you are so long as
you help me kill him."

Her story shut me up for a moment. Dima's life
had sucked, but it was not my problem to fix. I had no
intention of letting anyone in on my Vampyre blood
secret. Ever. However, I did have a few pertinent
questions.

"What's with the crossbreeding?" I asked.

"The crossbreeding thing is utter bullshit. A few
rogue idiots trying to take over. From what I
understand they were taken out..." Her look to me
was questioning. "It was you?"

I nodded curtly and she smiled with satisfaction.

"Outstanding. You will be very helpful."

"Let's get something straight here, Dragon. We are
not working for you. If you behave and drink your
medicine we might let you tag along," I informed her
coldly.

"Does he speak?" she asked, referring to Hank.

"He's a man of few words," I replied.

"Nice," she purred as she looked him over from
head to toe. "I like a man of action."

"While that's incredibly awesome to know," I said
in a voice that drew her startled eyes right back to me,
"he's taken. His mate is wildly jealous and
occasionally unstable. If you so much as touch him
you'll lose a body part... starting with your hand,

182

followed by your overly inflated left boob. Afterwards his mate would probably rip out your entrails and shove them down your throat. She wouldn't kill you... she'd play with you. Once a limb or knocker started to grow back she rip off three more body parts to compensate. You understanding where I'm going with this?" I inquired politely.

"Got it," Dima choked out and avoided Hank completely.

"That was appetizing," Angela said with a chuckle and a gag. "Back to business."

"You actually think we're going to take directives from you?" I asked as I gathered up all the weapons and handed half to Hank.

"Um... yes?" she answered hesitantly.

"Wrong," I snapped as Dima laughed and Hank grinned. "You are not in charge here. I need the names of the Council members who know the details of this mission."

"That's not protocol," she said indignantly.

"I can assure you that you don't want to know what Essie will tell you to do with your protocol. Certainly after her description of what touching me results in... I'd think twice about making her unhappy," Hank said with a deadly smirk on his face. "Spit out the names or I'm quite sure you'll be choking on your protocol for days."

"Months," I added. "And your throat is not the only place I plan to shove them."

"Aramini, Gades, Weterman and Dahn," Angela offered quickly.

"Breakdown on how they side on the reveal?" Hank demanded.

"Aramini and Gades want the reveal. Weterman and Dahn do not."

"Was that so hard?" I asked sarcastically.

She shook her head in defeat, reached into her pocket and retrieved a piece of paper. "I'd suggest you memorize this and then eat it," she advised as she held it out to me.

"What the hell is it with people wanting me to eat paper lately?" I asked as I took it from her slightly shaking hands. "What is this?"

"I'll eat it," Dima volunteered.

"Um... okay," I said as I scanned the typed information.

It was names, addresses and habits of the alpha Dragon's homes and businesses. I handed it to Hank.

"Isn't this information Dima already knows?" I asked my boss.

"Well, yes... but since she can't defend herself I'm not sure how long she'll be around. And I wasn't sure if she would willingly give you the correct intel," Angela explained.

"Well, isn't that special," Dima ground out through clenched teeth.

"And yet you thought it was a brilliant idea to pair someone you clearly don't trust with us," I said so quietly Angela had to lean forward to hear.

"Well, when you put it that way, it sounds awful," Angela groused and yanked on the little bit of hair she had left.

"Look, it's a bad idea all around," Dima stated the obvious. "But you need me and I need you."

"Who did I screw over in a former life to deserve this?" I muttered as I committed the information to memory.

"The sun god?" Angela suggested.

We all gaped at her. She simply shrugged, pulled her flask from her cleavage, and took a healthy swig.

"Open up, Dragon," I instructed as I aimed the squirt gun at her very full and redonkulously pouty lips.

"You're really going to do this?" Dima asked with narrowed eyes and a disgusted shake of her head.

"I am really going to do this," I replied with a wink.

She had no clue what my experience with Dragons had been thus far and I wasn't keen on informing her. I was slightly uncomfortable leaving her completely defenseless, but she could earn her weapons back as she earned our trust.

"Where are you staying?" I asked the Dragon as she choked down the vile solution.

"Wherever you are," she replied with an evil little grin and a very unladylike burp.

The burp almost made me like her, but her words... not so much.

"How about no freakin' way?" I yelled. "You are not going to... "

"Oh thank god, are you guys Wolves?" a stressed out female voice called to us.

"Um..." I stammered as she and her husband and about fifteen large children approached us like a freight train that had run off the tracks.

It was a family of Werewolves and they were a mess. They were dressed loudly and sloppy. The kids were smacking each other and had remnants of popsicle and chocolate all over them. The husband appeared bored and was trying to pretend he wasn't part of the motley crew. He stood slightly off to the left and stared at his fingernails.

The overly made-up and exhausted woman sniffed the air and sighed with relief.

"I knew it," she sang out and slapped two of the more unruly kids in the head. "I knew there were Wolves here. We're visiting from out of town and we got our credit cards stolen. Do you have any money we could borrow for a taxi back to our hotel and possibly a little extra for a bottle of Jack?"

"Is she for real?" Hank asked.

"Um... I think so. Do I give her money?"

"Normally I'd say no, but we need her and her brood to leave. Give her a hundred."

"Those kids are damn big," I mumbled as I reached into my pocket and pulled out a wad of cash.

As the woman reached greedily for the money, my instincts kicked in and a horrid feeling of dread shot up my spine.

"That's because they're not kids." Hank yelled as he pulled his weapons.

It happened so fast I was unsure if I was seeing it correctly. All hell had broken loose as the ragtag little family from out of town drew baseball bats and knives and syringes. What the hell?

"Duck," I hissed at Dima and Angela as I took aim and prepared to fire.

Dima was close enough to pull behind me, but Angela got swallowed up in the melee.

I had expected trouble from the Dragon or my boss, not from a group of garishly dressed Werewolves from out of town. We couldn't catch a break lately if it bit us in the ass.

"Do you know these freaks?" Dima hissed as she grabbed one of her knives and planted it in the head of a Wolf that was beating on Angela with a bat.

"Hell to the no," I snapped as I picked off two who were running at us with syringes held high.

Syringes? Who were these people? And what in the hell was in the syringes?

Hank used his fists. Dima hurled knives and I vacillated between throwing stars and daggers. A gun would draw entirely too much attention. I was shocked and grateful we hadn't attracted an audience.

As fast as it started it was over. In all the confusion and screaming not one of us realized several of the *children* had come up behind us. I felt a horrific burning as a large needle pierced my spine. My knees buckled and I saw Hank falling forward as the poison entered his system. Turning my head with inhuman effort, I realized Hank and I might have gotten off easy. The sound of the bat connecting to Dima's head was something I would have a difficult time forgetting. It caved the back of her skull in and she dropped to the ground like lead. Thankfully the blow wouldn't kill her, but it was awful to see. Bright red blood saturated her red locks and her eyes remained open. She looked dead.

"What's happening?" I whispered Hank as I tried to move.

"They injected us with something that paralyzed us," he grunted. *"I think the Vampyre blood is the only reason we're not completely knocked out."*

Dwayne comes through again...

"Who in the hell are they?"

"Don't know. Essie, even if you can move, stay still. The Vamp blood might negate the crap they shot us up with. We don't want them to know," Hank instructed.

I did as told and searched the thinning crowd for Angela. Had she been injected? Was she dead?

"Hank, I can't move at all. Can you?"

"Nope, not yet."

The *family* backed away and formed a circle around us effectively blocking out anyone who passed by. Angela lay on the far side and was a bloody mess. My gut clenched in disgust with myself. I never should have taken her weapons. She looked half dead. She could have killed a couple of the bastards if she'd been armed. What the hell had I been thinking?

"Essie, do not second guess yourself," Hank reprimanded harshly.

"How did you know I was?" I asked, surprised. Son of a bitch, could he read my mind too?

"*I know how you think,*" he said. "*Angela will live. A beating will not kill her.*"

"*Well, at least we know she's not the bad guy.*"

Nope, she was not the bad guy and the *family* was only the hors d'oeuvre for the bad guy. The bad guys had finally arrived. There were four of them and they were huge.

"*God damn it,*" Hank growled. "*I should have known.*"

"*It's some of the Council, isn't it?*"

"*Yep. It's the top guards for the Council members themselves,*" he said as he watched them closely. "*Can you move yet?*"

"*No.*"

Ignoring us completely, the guards went directly to Angela and continued the beating—her body flailed about like a rag doll. My stomach roiled and my heart was beating so hard I was certain it would burst from my chest. Was she being punished for communicating with us off the grid? Did the Council not know about Dima? Were they planning on killing her in front of us? Were we next?

"*I need to move,*" I grunted as I tried desperately to make my useless muscles work. "*I have to kill them. They can't do that to her. It's my fault she's unarmed. I have to protect her.*"

Hank's fury and frustration flowed off of him in waves. The utter insanity of what we were watching made no sense. How was this happening?

"*Little bro bro? Essie?*" Junior's voice boomed through our heads. "*I'm in the zoo. Where in hell and tarnation are you?*"

"*Junior,*" Hank gasped with relief in his voice. "*We're at the reptiles. Totally surrounded by Council— four major dangerous guards and around twelve to fifteen lesser targets. We've been injected and paralyzed. You alone?*"

"*At the moment, yes, but I can have a posse in about six seconds. Hang tight, Baby Bro, I'm on my way.*"

"*Move it, big Bro. It's ugly here and getting uglier.*"

"*Be there in ten,*" he said.

"*Minutes?*" I shouted. Angela would be dead in ten minutes.

"*Seconds, little girlie. Ten seconds,*" Junior promised with a grunt of laughter.

"*Thank god,*" I groused in relief.

"*Any humans around you?*" Junior asked.

"*Negative,*" Hank answered. "*Only Were.*"

"It's going to be okay, Essie," Hank whispered as Angela's violent beating continued in the background.

"Do you swear?" I demanded in a harsh voice as I forced myself to watch my boss's blood run red over the pavement.

"I do. I swear. Junior might be off his damn rocker, but he's one of the smartest and deadliest sons of bitches I know."

"I hope to hell you're right," I muttered as Dima moaned in pain beside me.

"I know I am, baby. I know I am."

Chapter 16

"Holy sheeeot on a stick in a hula skirt! Is that Brad Pitt shootin' a fight scene for a movie?" Junior bellowed as he and about forty Were Pigeons in both human and bird form came barreling toward the circle from hell we were trapped in.

I knew Were Pigeons existed, but I'd never seen them until now. There were only three known Packs of Pigeons in the world—Chicago, New York and London. In their Were form they looked like Pigeons on steroids—about four times the size of a normal pigeon. However, the razor sharp and unnaturally long fangs were a dead giveaway that they were not typical birds.

Half of the group was in bird form and the other half in human, but with fangs and claws flying. Holy shit, it was an Alfred Hitchcock nightmare on crack.

"*Jesus H Christ*," Hank gasped as he took in the deadly circus descending on us.

"*And then some*," I muttered. "*Wait. What does the H stand for?*"

"*What?*"

"*I mean, I've always wondered. It must stand for something because everyone uses the same initial.*"

"*Um... Henry?*" Hank guessed.

"*Nice try, Henry James Wilson.*" I laughed. "*I was thinking it might stand for Hesus.*"

"*So his name is Jesus Hesus?*" Hank asked, confused.

"*I suppose it is a little weird and rhymey,*" I admitted.

"*Gross. I think I just got pooped on.*"

"*It's good luck,*" Hank explained as he tried to move his still useless body. "*I just sure as hell hope Junior was clear on who the bad guys were when he briefed the flying, crapping time bombs.*"

"*I'll second that,*" I mumbled as I watched the drama unfold.

"I love Brad Pitt," an adorable female Pigeon screamed at a decibel that made every Were within a surrounding mile wince in pain.

She tore through the circle along with two dozen others and jumped on the back of the largest, most violent Council guard. He tried to throw her off, but her sharp little claws were embedded tight.

"It *is* BRAD PITT," she wailed, and then triple-winked at her delighted bloodthirsty friends. The guard was still trying to shake her off when she began pecking a rhythm in his neck that made my teeth hurt and the guard swear in fury and pain.

The *family* glanced wildly around in confusion. I swear to Jesus Hesus some of them were actually looking for Brad Pitt. The IQ level of these particular Wolves was very low... With a shrill whistle and a quick chorus of yipping, the Pigeons went ballistic on the Wolves. The lupines were screaming and running for their lives as the birds dove and attacked. Their human counterparts pecked the living hell out of the bastards.

Junior was beating the crap out of anything that came close to us. Dima was slowly waking up, but Hank and I were still frozen and useless.

"Junior," I shouted above the din. "Find Angela. She's across the circle. She needs our help."

"I'm on it," he yelled as he placed several Pigeons in front of us for protection.

Never in a million years would I have guessed how freakin' violent Pigeons were. They were tearing the *family* to shreds and enjoying the hell out of it, if the laughing and backslapping were any indication.

"How did he find forty Pigeons?" I muttered to Hank as I watched in horror.

"Junior can find a needle in a haystack. Finding forty Pigeons would be a no-brainer for him. Plus, I'm pretty sure he does online gaming with Pigeons," Hank explained.

Of course he did.

The crowd thinned dramatically as the death toll of the Wolves rose. The battle was basically over and the Pigeons had definitely won. The birds were as quick as they were violent. Dead bodies disappeared faster than they had fallen to the ground. How were they doing that? That's when I noticed what they were wearing—uniforms. They all had safari uniforms on. The Pigeons worked at the zoo. They were the grounds people, ticket takers, animal caretakers and security.

Freakin' brilliant.

This was the first time I'd come across a Were Pigeon and I was kind of hoping it would be the last. These suckers had ridden the bus in from Crazytown and stayed.

"She's gone," Junior huffed as he wiped his brow in frustration. "Three of the guards got away and they took Angela."

"Son of a bitch," Hank roared in frustration. "We have to get her back. Of course it would help if I could freakin' move."

"Ease up, Bro," Junior said as he gave a hand signal to the Pigeons.

They drove a golf cart over and proceeded to dump Hank, Dima and myself in the back.

"Should we cover them up?" a male Pigeon inquired as he patted my head sweetly and gently pushed the bloody hair out of Dima's face.

"Yep," Junior said. "Keep 'em covered until we get them out to my SUV in the parking lot. And let me tell you something... you sons of bitches were goddamned incredible. I have never seen such focused and direct violent bloodshed—very little wasted movement. I'd like to bring a few of you down to Georgia to do some combat training with my Pack if that might interest you."

"It most certainly does," the gal who started the whole Brad Pitt scream-peck-fest said with pride. "Most Weres discount us as beneath them because we're birds. We would be honored to visit you in Georgia."

"Anyone who discounts you is a dumbass," I muttered as the golf cart jerked forward.

"And are you a dumbass?" the Pigeon inquired as she peeked under the tarp.

"Absolutely not," I told her with a grin as the feeling in my legs slowly began to come back. "I'm a smartass."

Her laugh was musical and I decided maybe I was wrong about never wanting to see a Were Pigeon again. I certainly never wanted to be on their bad side, but their fighting technique was outstanding. I could learn something from them.

"Do you shoot?" I asked the Pigeon as her giggles died down.

"Name's Birdie," she said as she shoved her hand under the tarp, grabbed my still limp one in a firm grip and shook it.

"Essie," I said as I bit back a laugh at her moniker.

"You can laugh," she said with a put upon sigh. "Everyone else does. My Mamma was a little out there and very literal—hence the name."

"I actually like it," I told her.

It was adorable, just like her. Of course, she was also one of the most violent Weres I'd ever come across, but she was cute.

"As for shooting..." Birdie said thoughtfully. "Not really. I'd sure like to learn."

"How about I trade you some shooting lessons for some lessons on whatever the hell you just did to those Wolves?"

"Take her up on it," Junior advised my new friend as he jogged alongside the golf cart. "Essie can shoot the teats off a cow three counties over... blindfolded."

"Deal," Birdie said. "I'm always here, so you just come find me when you're ready."

"You live here at the zoo?" I asked.

"Yep. Got everything we need right here."

"Do you guys own the zoo?"

"You could say that," she said with a wink and a grin. "Kinda depends on who's in office, but we own most of the real estate in the Midwest."

"For real?" I asked impressed.

I never knew Weres were such shrewd businesspeople.

"For real," Birdie said. "Now take care and don't get killed. I don't make new friends too often, so when I do I like to keep 'em."

"Will do," I promised with a grin.

"Thank you for defending us today," Hank said as he gingerly rolled up on his side. "We're indebted to you."

"Ahhh, it was fun. Haven't been in a smackdown in at least two weeks. Call it even," Birdie said as she slapped a wobbly Hank on the back.

"Much obliged," Junior said gratefully as he helped transfer us to his SUV. "I'll be in touch about Georgia."

"We'll be waiting!" Birdie yelled as we pulled away.

About a hundred or so Pigeons waved goodbye as we slowly rolled through the parking lot and onto Lakeshore Drive. I shook my head and grinned as Dima gaped at the Were Pigeons. She had missed the whole thing. She was never going to believe it, but that was not my problem. I was just happy to be alive.

Now we had to go after Angela.

***

"You have got to be kidding me," I shouted as Junior approached me with a needle the size of an arm.

"Goddamn it Junior, why did you have to show her the needle? You know how she feels about getting stabbed," Hank grumbled as he held me still.

Dima sat in silence on the far side of the room and watched in horror.

We'd made it back to Dwayne's in record time since Junior drove like a bat out of hell on speed. Junior had quickly created an anti-serum for the poison the Wolves had injected into our bodies. I'd wisely shut my eyes while Junior worked on Hank and stupidly opened them as he came to work on me.

"Wait," Dima said with a confused shake of her head and the beginnings of a smile on her lips. "You can rip the head off of a Dragon, but you're a weenie when it comes to getting a shot?"

"Dude," I shouted. "That is not a shot. That is a freakin' pole with a point. And I am not a weenie."

"Actually, you are," Junior said logically.

"No, I'm not."

"Are," he said with a smirk.

"Do you want your nuts lodged in your esophagus?" I inquired politely as Hank swallowed a bark of laughter.

"Is that a trick question?" Junior asked with narrowed eyes.

"Nope."

"Since I plan to father ten to twenty-four kids with Sandy Moongie, I'd like to keep my nuts in my underpants," Junior said as he took three steps closer to me. "Essie, shut your damn eyes."

"I can't," I whispered. "I already saw the needle."

"Do you want to stay partially paralyzed?" Hank asked reasonably.

"Jesus Hesus, of course not," I snapped.

"Oh my God," Dima yelled. "Is that what the H stands for?"

I turned to her and an evil little grin spread across my lying lips... "Yes. Yes, it is. OUCH," I squealed as Junior stabbed me and Hank held me still. "You people suck."

"All better. The paralysis should be completely out of your systems in the next half hour. It was a fairly complicated compound for those Wolves to have used. They didn't seem that smart."

"They weren't smart at all," Hank said as he stretched his legs and walked around the room. "It had to be the Council directing the entire show."

"How would they have known to even be ready?" I asked as I felt the full use of my arms and legs coming back.

"They clearly have someone on Angela," Hank said. He turned to Dima. "Did she make any calls on the way to meet up?"

"No, but I think she was texting," Dima said as she shook the dried blood out of her hair. Suddenly she looked like a freakin' supermodel again. "Or maybe she was drinking... Honestly, I couldn't tell. I was wrapped up in my own hell when I realized I'd have to swallow your farked up shift prohibiting juice. Angela and her weirdness were the least of my problems."

"Sounds pretty simple to me," Junior volunteered as he put all of his potions back into his bag.

"Can't wait to hear this," I mumbled as I massaged the hole Junior had made in my arm with his version of a shot.

"Council caught Angela going behind their backs by working with you three. Council no likey agents playing both sides of the coin, so they followed her and busted on her. Literally."

"Why'd they leave us alone?" I asked as I tried to make sense of the most recent bloodshed.

"Angela's beating was a warning," Hank surmised.

"To stop us," Dima said. "They want us to stop whatever we're doing or we'll end up like Angela."

"Clearly they don't know us very well," I said. "Wait, does this make you want out?"

"No, it doesn't," she said with an eye roll and a smirk. "I am not a weenie."

"Really?" I asked nicely.

"Yes," she answered hesitantly, clearly wondering why I was being so polite.

"Junior, do you have a vitamin concoction in that bag from hell?" I asked.

"Why yes, yes I do."

"Awesome! Dima would like a massive B-12 shot in her ass. Now," I told him as I watched my Dragon partner pale considerably. "Still not a weenie?" I asked her.

"You are a terrible bitch," she hissed and backed away from Junior as he prepared her shot.

"I've been called worse," I said with a grin.

"Fine," she huffed. "You're not a weenie. I'm not a weenie. I do not need any vitamins. Ever. And I am

197

not giving up. I want my father dead—he's an evil man. If that helps you accomplish what you need to get done, then that's freakin' fantastic. If you're going in a new direction, then we can split up now. No harm—no foul. Your call."

"We're staying the course," I said as I glanced over at Hank.

He gave me a quick nod and sat down at Junior's laptop.

"We can't just walk into the Council building and ask for Angela," I muttered as I paced the room and tried to come up with a plan.

"Nope, but I can," Junior said slowly.

"He's right," Hank said as he closed the computer and leaned back in his chair with a lopsided grin.

"Explain," I said.

"I can't ask for your boss, but I sure as hell can march into the building and register as the new Alpha of the Georgia Pack. I'll be able to tell if she's been in the Council chambers."

"I'll go with him," Dima volunteered.

"You're a Dragon. They'll smell you a mile away," I said.

Was she an idiot?

"I have a cream that blocks…" she started.

"Self-tanner?" I asked with narrowed eyes.

"As a matter of fact, yes," she said defensively. "How did you know?"

"Because your kin used that crap when they were hiding who they were and abducting female Werewolves," I snapped as I advanced on her. "Did you work with those bastards on that little project?"

"Back off," Dima snarled. She went into a defensive position as Hank and Junior moved to flank me on either side.

"Did. You. Work. With. Those. Now. Dead. Douchecanoes?" I ground out, very happy she had drunk the solution that kept her from shifting. It was going to be far easier to kill her in this form.

"I did not," she hissed. "My very missed and sadly murdered brother came up with the compound. It was stolen by his murderer."

"And that would be?"

"My father."

"Holy hell, you have whackjob of a family," Junior muttered.

"Tell me something I don't know," Dima snapped. "So if you want to go at it, let's go. If you want to get to the bottom of what's happening, I'd suggest you take three steps away from me. I might not be able to shift, but I can light this house on fire in about two seconds flat."

Slowly I backed away. I still didn't completely trust her, but I believed her story. Plus, we did need her. I wasn't even sure what we were looking for anymore, but the more heads the better at this point.

"You'll go with Junior and feel it out. Does anyone there know what you look like?" Hank asked.

"Nope, I've only ever been to the parking garage. Angela never let me in the building," she said with a shrug.

"That's rude," I muttered. "I suppose she was hiding you."

"Or hiding something," Hank said. "If you're not back within the hour we're coming in, which would be a very bad thing."

"Couldn't agree more," Junior said. "So Dima, do you have a mate?" he asked politely as they made their way to the front door.

"My dad killed him," she replied with very little emotion.

"Jesus Hesus," Junior shouted. "I'll kill your dad for you. Guy's an asshole."

199

With a curt and grateful nod, Dima stopped and turned back.

"Does the H really stand for Hesus?" she asked with a doubtful squint of her eyes.

"Um… no," I admitted. "But if we say it enough we could make it the new thing."

All four of us mulled it over for a bit. Were we damning ourselves to hell by lying about Jesus' middle name? Did Jesus even have a middle name? And if he didn't… was it wrong to give him one?

"I'm in," Hank said with a grin that made me giggle.

"Me too," Junior added.

"Me three," Dima said with a quiet chuckle.

"Awesome. I'd say it will take a week or two of constant usage, Twitter, Facebook and Instagram to get it to catch on. Junior, you ready to hack *Webster's Dictionary*?"

"Yep," he snorted. "And the religious ones."

"We really are going to hell," Hank said with a laugh and a groan.

"It's fine. I already have a suite reserved," I joked…kinda.

"Air conditioned?" Dima inquired.

"But of course," I said.

"Then we're good," Junior said as he pulled a laughing Dima out the door. "We need to get this shit done so I can get back to Georgia and convince Sandy Moongie she can't live without me."

"Oh my god," I gasped. "Do you think she'll get stolen away while you're here?"

"Hell to the no," Junior said with confidence. "I threatened to kill any male who even looks at her while I'm gone."

"Well, there's a novel way to earn the trust of your new Pack," Hank said with a disgusted shake of his head.

"Right?" Junior said proudly.

"I was being sarcastic," Hank explained to a now confused Junior.

"Well, it was better than locking her up in solitary confinement so no one could flirt with her... don't you think?" he asked, now not quite as confident with his choices.

"Yes," I said as I shoved him and Dima out of the front door. "It's very good not to lock your future mate up—especially since she still doesn't like you all that much. You did good. Now go find out what the hell we're dealing with so you can go home and screw something else up with Sandy."

"Good thinking," he said as I slammed the door shut and leaned on it.

"Oh. My. God," I said with a sigh. "Sandy is in for some trouble with that one."

"Agree," Hank said as he handed me the ringing burner phone. "It's Dwayne."

My stomach dropped as I took the vibrating phone from Hank's hands. I could only pray Granny was doing better than we were.

Chapter 17

I was pale when I hung up the phone. I was also exhausted.

"Just tell me Granny's all right and then you can get to the rest of the story," Hank said gruffly as he waited to know Granny's fate.

"She's the same," I said as I shook my head and tried to remember everything Dwayne had just told me. "She's still in Death Sleep, but she's alive—as much as a dead person can be."

"Okay, good," Hank said as he dropped down on the couch and waited for more. "You were on the phone for twenty minutes and said barely ten words. What in the hell was Dwayne rambling about?"

"Well, um… "

Where to start? I ran my hands through my hair and tried to find words that would make sense.

"Is it that bad?" Hank asked with a grimace.

"No… it's just that *weird*," I told him.

"Maybe I don't need to know."

"Nope, if I had to hear your redonkulous bullcrap all the time, you have to have what I just heard branded into your brain too," I informed him. "Let me just start by saying Dwayne is all over Jesus Hesus.

While we were talking he tweeted and emailed about six hundred people. He says it will only take three days of focused work for it to make national news that Jesus' middle name is Hesus."

"Speechless and scared," Hank said with a shudder.

"That's nothing," I deadpanned. "You know all the Vampyres we owe favors to?"

"The ones protecting Granny?"

"The very same. Apparently they are quite taken with the Cows and are trying to barter for marriage."

The sound that came out of my mate was alarming. I jumped up and slapped his back. Hard.

"I just choked on my own spit." Hank gagged and then doubled over in laughter. "Are they blind?"

"Hank, that is not nice," I reprimanded him sternly.

"Essie, it was driving you nuts when you couldn't figure out if they were male or female. I'm getting busted on because I'm asking if the Vamps are blind?"

"Okay, fine," I huffed and tried not to grin. "Clearly they must like the metrosexual ambiguous genitalia thing the Cows have going for them."

"So is Dwayne going to marry his daughters off?" Hank asked as he bit down on his tongue to stem the hysterics threatening to escape.

"Well, if I have this right and I think I do... I believe he's going to do a contest of sorts for their hands. Kind of like a Vampyre Olympics slash Gladiator thing. Whoever is alive at the end gets a Cow."

"Is that a joke?" Hank stuttered as he sat up and gaped at me.

"I wish," I mumbled. "Dwayne has always gone for the absurd and bloody."

"Understatement," Hank said as he stretched his arms over his head pulling his t-shirt tight across his perfectly muscled chest.

I actually forgot what I was talking about for a brief moment. He was so pretty it was just wrong. I considered jumping him since we were alone, but then I remembered the rest of the story...

"And the feral Wolves followed Dwayne to Michigan."

"*What?*" Hank yelled as he hopped up and closed the distance between us. "The feral Wolves are in Michigan?"

"Yes. That's what Dwayne said. They haven't caused much trouble. They're staying on the outskirts of his property, but they won't leave."

"Have they gotten into it with the Vamps?" Hank asked.

"Yep, and the Wolves won. The Vamps want to kill all of them, but it's not so simple. The Cows think the Wolves mean no harm. Since the Vamps are trying to woo the Cows they've refrained from killing the Wolves."

"The fact I even followed and understood what you're saying is frightening," Hank muttered.

"Right?" I agreed. "I can't believe I repeated it. Anyhoo, that's still not all... "

Hank turned to me and held his breath.

"Apparently the Dragons are skulking around too."

"Jesus Hesus," Hank shouted. "Is Michigan some kind of vortex for screwed-up paranormal activity?"

"Jesus Hesus really works, doesn't it?"

"It really does," he agreed with a surprised nod of his head.

"And to answer your question... I'd have to say yes," I told him. "Michigan seems to be the new armpit of magical hell."

"Fine. We do what we have to do in Chicago, and then we leave for Michigan," Hank said as he whipped open Junior's laptop and began scrolling for restaurants that delivered.

"Do you see any Mexican?" I asked, looking over his shoulder.

"Yep," he said. "Tacos?"

"Eight," I said.

Hank laughed.

"Fine," I grumbled and punched him in the shoulder. "Fourteen, and I'm not sharing so get enough for yourself, Junior, and Dima."

"Do Dragons eat Mexican?" Hank wondered out loud.

"Dude, they eat people. Mexican is a vast improvement over people."

"Good point," Hank agreed.

"How long do you think they'll be?" I asked.

"An hour—two hours, tops. Depends if the Council keeps them waiting."

"Will they be okay?" I asked, now more worried because it was our fault Dima couldn't shift.

After what I'd done to Angela I was beginning to question my judgment.

"Junior can kill almost anything and Dima took back all of her weapons and then some," he said.

"Holy shit," I stammered. "I didn't even see her. Did you?"

"Yep. I saw her. She was fast and she was good."

"I don't like her pulling one over on me, but I'm wildly relieved she can defend herself if she needs to," I said as I dug into my suitcase for something clean to wear. My clothing had gotten fairly destroyed during our visit to the zoo. "Dress or pants?"

"Dress. No panties," Hank said as he emailed our massive food order.

"Pervert," I said with a grin.

"Guilty," he answered with an unapologetic leer as he smacked my bottom.

I curled up on his lap and laid my head on his strong shoulder. The feeling of being loved would get me through all the crap that lay ahead. Hank was my rock and I was his. I had no clue how I got so lucky, but I was just grateful for my good fortune—very grateful.

***

"God damn, these tacos are good," Junior grunted as he shoved taco number ten down his throat.

"They are pretty awesome," Dima said as she shoved her own number seven down hers.

"Okay," I said with a mouthful. "We are all in agreement about the delicious cheap Mexican food. We need to get down to business."

"Do I need to call out for more?" Hank asked as he hoarded the remainder of tacos.

"I have to be out of town in an hour or my ass is grass," Junior said as he tackled his brother for his tacos. "Can they deliver fast?"

"Yep," Hank said as he backhanded Junior and threw him across the room. "They can be here in fifteen. How many you want?"

"I could probably eat about twenty more," Junior huffed as he got up and took a running dive at Hank.

"If you break the computer there will be no more tacos," Hank informed his brother with a precise punch to his head.

"What? Your phone doesn't work?" Junior grunted as he put Hank in a chokehold.

"Oh my god, you two. Stop it now. This house belongs to Dwayne and he will be pissed if you destroy all of his furniture," I yelled.

"Are they always like this?" Dima asked as she pilfered a few of Hank's tacos he'd left unguarded during the smackdown with his brother.

"Pretty much," I told her as I picked off the last three and ate them.

"I can't believe you split my lip over tacos," Hank grumbled as he took another swat at his also bleeding brother.

"Dude, you beat my ass for a hot dog last Fourth of July," Junior accused as he nursed his bloody nose.

"Forgot about that one." Hank grinned and tossed Junior a wad of napkins.

Junior promptly shoved some up his nose and mopped up the excess blood with the rest.

"Good thing this place belongs to a Vamp," Dima quipped as she looked around at all the random blood dripping off the walls and furniture.

"No. Dwayne will have their butts in a sling for this. Hopefully, he won't see it for a while." I rummaged through the kitchen cabinets looking for cleaning supplies to remove bloodstains.

"You're going to clean up after them?" Dima asked, surprised.

"Hell to the no." I laughed and dumped a bunch of rags and cleaners into a bucket. "Those dumbasses are going to clean up after themselves."

"Right, but don't forget Junior has to leave town very soon," Dima reminded me.

"Why?" I asked as I plopped the bucket down and marched back into the living room. "Why do you have to leave town?" I asked my soon to be brother-in-law.

"Not real sure," Junior admitted. "They had me sign some papers and then told me to basically haul ass back to Georgia or I'd be held in contempt."

"Contempt for what?" Hank asked as he shook his head in frustration. "That makes no sense."

"Agreed," Junior said. "However, I'm sure as hell not staying around to find out what some bogus trumped up definition of contempt means. I have a Pack to lead and a mate to boff."

"Sweet Jesus Hesus," I shouted. "Do not under any circumstances let Sandy hear you say you're gonna boff her."

"Is it not hot?" Junior asked with raised eyebrows and an honestly confused shrug.

"*NO*," Dima and I hissed in unison.

"It's not hot," I told him. "Stick to things like, um…"

I wracked my brain for something he could say that wouldn't get him into trouble. Nothing. I could think of nothing.

"Just don't say much. Be strong and silent where Sandy is concerned. Got it?"

"Yep. Strong and silent. Like throw her over my shoulder and take her home with me?" he asked with a hopeful smile.

"You can try that one after the tenth date," I explained and thought about warning Sandy.

Nope. Sandy liked Junior no matter how much she denied it. She had it as bad as he did. She was just gonna make him work for it—and rightly so.

"Anyway… something is off with our illustrious Council. Three or four of them slept right through my introduction. And half of them are apparently on their way to Michigan," Junior said.

"Are you serious?" I demanded as I felt a skitter of dread crawl up my spine. I quickly glanced at Hank who did not seem happy with this information either. Crap. "Michigan? You're sure those old bastards are going Michigan?"

"Yep, they said Michigan. I mean, what the hell is in Michigan?" Junior laughed and then froze. "Oh shit… "

SOME WERE IN TIME

"How bizarre," Dima commented as she sharpened her knives in a rhythm that made me uncomfortable and bizarrely happy at the same time. "I searched Angela's office while you were getting dissed by the Council. There was an open map of Michigan on her desk."

"Was she in there?" I asked, still worried that she might be dead.

"No, but she had been. There was fresh blood on the map. It was hers and I picked up the scent of several other wolf shifters who were more than likely with her."

"Could you tell by scent what kind of shape she was in?" I asked, wondering how far Dragon sniffing powers went.

"Not exactly," Dima said slowly. "But the scent of blood was heavy. Meant she was clearly bleeding a lot."

"Damn it," I muttered and began to pace.

The sound of the doorbell made me jump and pull my Glock. Why in hell was everyone headed to Michigan? There was no way they knew about Granny's potential half-wolf slash half-Vampyre status. Or at least I hoped not...

"Stand down," Hank instructed firmly as I re-holstered my gun. "It's the taco dude and I'm still hungry. Do not terrify the kid."

"Affirmative," I said as I snapped my gun in tight. Killing the innocent human delivery boy would put a real kink in the plans. Plus I was still hungry too.

"Alright," Dima said, all business. "Get the door and tip the taco dude well. You're still bleeding and you look kind of scary," she told Hank. "We divide the tacos evenly or I will bloody some of you myself and then we eat. Fast. Junior then goes back to Georgia and we leave for Michigan."

"Sounds like a plan." I nodded and got ready to fight for my tacos if needed. "We can drive to Michigan in about two hours. Dwayne's place is a little inland from Harbor Country."

"It's beautiful there," Dima said.

"Where'd you hear it was beautiful?" I asked as I grabbed the bag of tacos from Hank and divided them evenly so we could avoid bloodshed.

"It's where I was raised. My father's compound is also in the area."

"What the hell?" I grumbled. "There is no way this is all a seriously unlucky coincidence."

"Well," Junior surmised as he ate his pile, "it's either an unlucky coincidence or one shit-ton of good luck or bad luck—depends on how you wanna look at it."

"I'd say good luck at this point," Hank chimed in as he destroyed his own mound of Mexican food. "All the players are now in the same spot. Saves time. We can kill—*and I do mean kill*—an assload of birds with one stone."

"Something is very off about all this," Dima said. "However, I'm going with Hank. The more the merrier in one place."

"I'm sad those douchecanoes are making me go back to Georgia," Junior griped in frustration. "I'd like to go kick some Vampyre, Council, Dragon, feral Wolf ass."

"Don't you think you should get back to Sandy and your Pack?" I asked as I realized I was looking forward to a potential Council ass-kick.

"Yep," Junior said as he tried to steal two of my tacos. "Sandy needs me. She doesn't function well when I'm not around to make her life a living hell."

"It's good to know you're clear on where you stand with her," I said as I smacked his hand away.

"I might play a dumbass on a hit TV show, but in reality I'm freakin' brilliant," Junior stated.

"Wait," Dima said as she protected her tacos. "He's on TV?"

Everything stopped for a brief moment while we digested that Dima actually believed Junior. No one believed Junior and with good reason. He was so full of crap his eyes were brown... well, not really, but it sounded good.

"I'm gonna pretend you didn't say that," I told her with an eye roll and a laugh.

"You people are insane," she muttered.

"Correct," Hank told her. "And Junior is one of the most certifiable. Now everyone eat up. We're leaving in ten."

"Seconds?" Junior shouted as he shoved his food in his mouth so quickly he choked.

"Minutes," I said with a grin and a wallop to his back. "Slow down. Tacos are not worth dying for."

"These are," he said solemnly as he gently caressed his remaining Mexican feast.

"He might be right," Hank said reverently as he cuddled his own stash.

"Actually, I think he is," Dima added, not really hugging her tacos in a loving way—more of an *I will kill you if you touch my tacos* kind of way.

"Oh my god. Fine." I laughed and shook my head. "Eat. You all have exactly eight minutes and nineteen seconds till we're out of here."

Thankfully there was no more talking. We ate our *to die for tacos* and left. What lay ahead was anyone's guess, but we would face it on full stomachs.

Full stomachs and a hell of a lot of unanswered questions.

Chapter 18

"You two going to tell me what's really going on?"

Dima asked the question from the backseat of the Hummer as we sped along I-94 towards Michigan. I figured silence would answer her question sufficiently so I kept my lip zipped—as did Hank. The sun was setting and rush hour was over. We were making great time.

"Interesting," she said as she shuffled some papers around. "I should have guessed you'd keep me in the dark, considering you've taken my ability to shift away."

"You're on a need to know basis," I replied calmly. "You need us more than we need you. Killing your Pappy is not high on my priority list."

"It should be," she said with a polite smile and a shake of the stack of papers in her hand.

"I know you want me to ask you why." I texted Dwayne that we were on our way along with an unfortunately large portion of the Werewolf paranormal government on our heels. "But I have to pee and I can't concentrate on your potential bullshit at the moment."

"After you relieve yourself I'd suggest you ask me what the hell is written on the papers I'm about to eat," Dima shot back.

"You're really gonna eat paper?" I asked with a grimace.

"Yep. It insures my life for a bit."

"Eating paper?" I asked.

"Not the paper itself. The intel on the paper is what will keep me in the land of the living for a few more hours," Dima explained as she wadded up the papers and ingested them.

For such a gorgeous girl she was kind of gross.

I realized I'd possibly made a grave error in letting her eat the paper, but she was not one to screw with. If the Hummer caught fire it would blow up pretty fast.

"Okay, fine. What was on the paper?" I asked, realizing it was crap I probably needed to know.

"Your question should be—where did I get the papers?" she corrected me.

"I'll bite. Where did you get the papers?"

"Angela's desk—in a folder labeled *confidential*."

"Is she stupid?" I shouted. "Why would she leave a folder labeled confidential on her damn desk?"

"Maybe she's not stupid at all," Hank interjected reasonably. "Do you think she left it there so we would find it—and possibly find her?"

I was silent. I took some air in through my nose and blew it out through my mouth. There was a very good reason to have partners—especially when part of the mission was to protect your own family. My conflicts of interest were starting to screw with my ability to think rationally. Shitballs.

"That's all kinds of brilliant," I muttered, pissed I hadn't thought of it. "Angela's leaving us clues because she knew we'd come back for her."

"Jesus Hesus," Dima said with appreciation. "You Wolves are smarter than the rest of the Shifter world says you are."

"What in the hell is that supposed to mean?" I snapped and moved to take a piece out of the Dragon.

Thankfully Hank took one hand off the wheel and put it on my shoulder. "You can punch her in the head, but under no circumstances can you kill her or do anything that will take more than an hour to heal."

I nodded curtly and reined in every instinct I had to remove her head. "Tell me what was written on the papers," I insisted.

"Pee, then talk," she said guardedly. "I have to pee too."

"You'll remember what you just ate?" I asked with raised brows.

"Yep." She grinned and winked. "I have a photographic memory."

"Lovely," I said with a glee. "You'll also have constipation or god knows what considering you just ate ten pages of paper recycled from cow and horse poop."

The silence was deafening. I could literally see her brain working trying to figure out if I was screwing with her.

I wasn't.

It was all kinds of awesome.

"We need to pull over now," she screeched as she gagged. "Paper is not supposed to be made out of poop."

"Correct," I said with a casual shrug. "I refuse to even write on the shit—pun intended. However, those pesky Wolves are trying to save trees and have found new, innovative and stanky ways to make paper products."

"I did wonder about the brown flecks," Dima choked out.

"Did it taste like poop?" Hank inquired as he quickly pulled into a rest stop filled with church buses.

"Since I don't eat poop," Dima snapped, "I wouldn't know."

"But you do eat people?" Hank asked.

"I do not eat people," she yelled.

"But your people eat people?" I prodded nicely.

"Occasionally," she hissed. "And your people sniff each other's asses when in animal form..."

She had a point—and a foul one at that.

"I'm not into the ass sniffing thing," I said with a shudder.

"I did it a couple times in high school, but then the actual mechanics of what I was doing kicked in and I had to stop," Hank volunteered without an ounce of shame or embarrassment.

"Have you ever eaten a person?" I asked Dima, trying to level the playing field a bit after my mate's horrific admission.

"Well... yes, but it was a long time ago," she admitted.

"How long?"

"Um, about two hundred and fifty years ago— give or take a few years," she answered as she hopped out of the car and high tailed it to the bathroom.

How in the hell old was she?

The rest stop was typical—vending machines and bathrooms up against the backdrop of a scraggly forest. The parking lot was full of busses and cars sporting large full color photos of a guy who looked vaguely familiar. I just couldn't place him...

"You think she'll make it to the bathroom before she hurls?" Hank asked as he got out and stretched his long sexy legs.

"I'm gonna say yes. She's fast and apparently really old."

"The ruling Dragon family is older than dirt. I'd put her father at approximately a thousand or so, and Dima at around five hundred."

"Really?" I asked surprised. I knew she was probably older than us, but I didn't think she was older than Dwayne and everyone else I knew combined. Dragons clearly stopped aging at about thirty.

"Yep."

"Why hasn't she killed her father before now if he's so awful?" I asked as I meandered up the sidewalk toward the bathrooms.

"Don't know," he answered. "You'll have to ask her."

We both tried to avoid the throngs of talkative and pushy church-goers who were wearing *Jesus for President* t-shirts. I shook my head in confusion. Were they just stupid or were they *stupid*? And then it hit me. There had to be hundreds of them milling about. It was perfect—or perfectly awful.

I froze and Hank almost tripped over me.

"You okay?" he asked concerned.

"Yes... but I'm fairly sure I'm going to hell," I replied.

"Why are you going to hell?" Hank asked and then started to laugh.

"Should I tell them?" I asked with a scrunched nose.

"If you wanna make it a *thing* this is probably a very fine place to start."

"You think?" I asked as I screwed up my courage to lie like a rug.

"Yep. This is not just any church group—it's the group who does the live show with the pastor who's gone to prison a few times for tax evasion, among other things," he said with disgust.

"The one who has six wives and wants all gays and Buddhists deported to third world countries?" I asked with narrowed eyes, thinking of Dwayne—my wonderful *gay* Vampyre BFF. Now I knew why the guy plastered on the sides of the cars and busses looked familiar. He was shyster skank-hole Pastor Bob.

"Yep," Hank replied and watched me closely. "You cannot maim them. We don't have time. However, you do have enough time to screw with their heads."

"Jesus does not hate gays and Buddhists," I whispered viciously. "Jesus and God love everyone—including these imbeciles who hate everyone."

"Couldn't agree more," Hank said as he discreetly removed my weapons from me.

It was a smart move. It was not my job to erase hate with a bullet... even though it would have felt good. Two heinous wrongs would not make a right.

"Jesus Hesus Christ," I shouted and fell to my knees, much to the shock of the idiots around me.

"What did you say?" a large, red-faced, angry woman screeched.

"I just said Jesus' full name," I told her as I rose to my feet.

"His middle name is Hesus?" she demanded doubtfully.

"Um... yes. Yes, it is," I said without cracking a smile.

Hank stood stoically behind me, lending his silent support. His muffled laughter appeared to be a coughing fit to the throng around us.

"His middle name rhymes with his first name?" the woman queried still doubtful.

"Yes, it does," I told her.

"How did you learn this?" she demanded suspiciously. "Was it the gays or the Buddhists?"

"Nope, it was the IRS," I replied with barely contained ire. "And the American Civil Liberties Union."

"Well, your sources certainly sound official," she said with pursed lips and her hands on her hips.

"They are," I told her. "It was certified and proven true by the LGBT division of the Civil Liberties Union."

"Really?" she asked, impressed as a horde of idiots began to surround her. "Hey, I have learned the middle name of Jesus," she called out to the dummies.

It saddened me to realize none of them had a clue about what the Civil Liberties Union was or the fact I'd just told them the Lesbian, Gay, Bisexual and Transgender division had certified that Jesus indeed had a middle name which rhymed with his first. It was all kinds of appalling.

There was no time for me to straighten these people out, but making them look more like assjackets than they already did could help others see how awful these people's beliefs were.

"Can we guess?" a tiny little dude with a mullet and skinny jeans asked.

"Of course," the woman sneered condescendingly.

The names flew fast and furious. It was all I could do not to laugh. Why did these people have so much hate in them for others who were different? They would definitely lead the front line in trying to destroy Werewolves if we were to come out of the closet. I would represent an abomination from hell. Was it lack of education? Was it simply fear and stupidity?

"Jim Bob," a man guessed.

"Skooter," another yelled.

"Homer."

"Moses."

"Kevin."

"Herman."

"Kyle."

"Billy."

"Bubba."

"Nope!" the red-faced angry gal shouted above the excited voices of the dumbass crowd. "It's Hesus. Rhymes with Jesus!"

"Jesus Hesus Christ," an older pinched-faced lady said with bravado. "I already knew this. Everyone who is a true believer knows his middle name is Hesus."

"I knew it," several shouted.

"I knew it," the large gal snapped. "I was just testing the rest of you."

I bit down on the inside of my cheek and slunk away to the bathroom. I didn't need to hear any more. If it wasn't so sad it would have been funny.

"Did you just create the shit show out front?" a pale-faced but amused Dima asked as she walked out of the bathroom as I was walking in.

"Yes. Yes, I did. Did you just puke?"

"Yes, I did." She shook her head and sighed. "I will never eat paper again."

"What about people?" I asked, wondering if she wanted to rid the world of some intolerant hatemongers.

"Too chewy. I like tacos better," she said with a grin. "However, I do know a few Dragons who like to eat bigots and homophobes."

"This is good to know," I said as I did my business. After I washed my hands I gently pushed her back out to the Hummer. "We won't be needing social media in our quest to let the world know Jesus' middle name."

"Nope," Dima agreed. "These assholes will take care of it within the hour."

219

"Do you think Jesus is going to be mad at me?" I asked as I contemplated what I had just done.

Dima thoughtfully pondered my question. "No. No, I don't think he would be mad at you. I firmly believe he has a great sense of humor. He'd have to if he let imbeciles like those wankers be created," she said, referring to the churchgoers. "I'd like to believe he's more unhappy with what those horrible people preach than the fact we gave him a middle name."

"I didn't want to like you, Dima," I said honestly.

"But you do," she said with a smirk. "And I like you even though I wanted to hate your lupine guts."

"I suppose we're no better than the dummies we just duped."

"I don't know," she said quietly. "The simple fact we're capable of seeing we were wrong and changing goes a long way to our credit."

"I'm wrong about a lot of things," I muttered as I glanced over at the dorks trying to prove they had known all along Jesus's middle name was Hesus. "I couldn't have been more wrong about the Cows."

"The ones who pooped my paper out?" Dima asked.

"Nope. The sexually ambiguous ones with the awful haircuts and hearts bigger than anyone I've ever met who are feeding my granny," I stated, then slapped my hand over my mouth.

"Guessing that was a secret two seconds ago," Dima said with a grin.

"Um... yep," I replied.

"Well, I do believe this car ride is the setting for trading secrets. You went first—now it's my turn. The Dragons trained and house the feral Wolves."

I was stunned to silence. How was that possible? Did the Dragons practice the witchcraft that trapped the Wolves in their animal form?

"Why would you assume I know about the feral Wolves?" I asked her coldly.

"I never assume—makes an ass out of you and me," she replied smoothly, using one of my own lines. "One—it was on top of the pile of poop paper on Angela's desk. I would guess she might think you would come to her office so she left something to entice you on top. Two—on the car ride back to your Vampyre friend's house from the zoo, I heard feral Wolves mentioned as I came around."

"Did the Dragons trap the Wolves in their animal form?" I asked.

She'd been around for several hundred years... surely she knew some of what went on with the Dragons.

"That's a question for my father," she replied with barely contained hatred. "You may ask him before I rip his head from his body."

"You've got some big daddy issues," I said as I clicked my seatbelt and mulled over what I had learned so far.

"Don't you?" she asked.

"Nope," I said with conviction. "Never knew my dad. He was a WTF agent with my mom and they were both taken out when I was a baby."

"Did they find their killer?" she asked as she laid her head back on her headrest and shut her eyes.

"Nope," I said tersely. "Case was dropped—considered unsolved."

"Dude... um," Dima said slowly.

"Yes?"

"That's the strangest thing I've ever heard. No paranormal case is ever closed before it's solved. It's how we stay secret from the humans. We deal with everything in-house. Who closed the case?" she asked, now sitting forward in her seat.

"The Council closed the case," I said tightly.

"How much are you sharing?" Hank asked as he pulled back onto the highway.

"I don't know," I mumbled as I let my head drop into my hands. Decisions were getting harder and harder to make—at least good ones were.

Was Dima what she seemed to be? Was she going to turn around and kill us dead while we slept? Worse... if she knew about Granny, would she tell? There wasn't a species around who would be okay with a Vampyre-Werewolf hybrid. I didn't even know if that was what she would turn out to be. Hell, I didn't know if she would ever wake up again.

"We can tell her some, but nothing about Granny being turned," I told Hank.

"Affirmative. Careful about the Cows too. It was the Dragons who took them out all those years ago," he reminded me.

"I know you guys are talking," Dima said with a snort of frustration. "Look, trust me or don't—I don't care. I'm not sure how much I trust you either. Just tell me enough so that I'm not walking in blind. I don't want to get killed in the first five minutes."

"Fair enough," I said. "We're headed to my best friend Dwayne's home. He has a lot of them. He's a three hundred year old Vampyre. He's very recently adopted eight Were Cows and they are being courted by the Vampyres who are protecting Dwayne's property. Dwayne is going to have a gladiator-type competition to marry off his daughters to the bloodsuckers. Also, just as a heads up, Dwayne's mind meld is what killed a few of your less than stellar Dragon kinsmen. It's very messy and smells like hell. I'll make sure he knows you're on our side unless you do something shitty and then he has full permission to blow you to smithereens. I have no mother-humpin idea why the Council is headed to Michigan and I don't like it. I would assume they know we're headed there and are going to use Angela as bait."

"I'm kind of lost and grossed out here, so I'm just going to stick to the part which made a modicum of sense. Why would they use Angela as bait and for whom?" Dima asked as she massaged her temples in confusion.

"For Essie," Hank answered stiffly. "Some of the Council want her dead."

"Oooookay," Dima said. "I can see how some might find her annoying and want to slap her around a little, but wanting her dead? Don't get it."

"You do realize we can still put you out of the car," I snapped.

"P.S.," she whispered loudly. "I can fly."

"Whatever," I muttered. "If I tried hard enough I could fly too."

The silence was loud and Hank shot me a look of displeasure.

Crapcrapdamndamn. Me and my big braggy mouth.

"Werewolves can't fly," Dima said evenly as she crossed her arms over her chest and waited for more of an explanation.

She wasn't going to get one... at least not an accurate one.

"Just wishful thinking," I told her with a laugh that I prayed didn't sound as fake to her as it did to my own ears.

"Hmmm," she said. "Anything you want to share on why you're able to kill Dragons when very few others can?"

"Um... nope," I said with certainty.

"Of course not," she muttered with annoyance. "Anything else?"

"Let me synopsize... do not kill the Vamps or the Cows. Dwayne will be furious if any of them die—

well, maybe not the Vamps, but don't kill them. The Cows are sacred. Pretend we're in India. There are feral Wolves hanging out on the perimeter of the property and apparently some Dragons skulking around."

"That would be because of the Wolves," Dima guessed.

"Are they on the same team?" I asked.

"Nope. From what I understand the feral Wolves hate the Dragons and visa versa."

"Now there's an understatement," Hank said sarcastically.

"Meaning?" Dima asked.

"Meaning we had an unexplainable run in with the feral Wolves and Dragons and it wasn't exactly pleasant," I said.

"You lived through it?"

It was obvious by her tone that Dima was astounded by the news.

"Duh," I said with an eye roll. "Sitting in the car with you... which would lead me to deduce we're alive."

"You're an ass," Dima snapped.

"Occasionally," I agreed. "Tell me another secret."

Dima sat and deliberated what to tell me. I never should have let her eat the damn paper. I was driven by my juvenile need to tell her she'd eaten poop. What if she overlooked something important—or life threatening?

"There were dossiers," she said and then sat quietly.

"Cryptic much?" I huffed. "Who were the dossiers on?"

This was going to be a long car ride if we played the game like this. The only thing I had on her was helping with offing her dad.

"You, me, your grandmother, Hank, Dwayne and two who I assume are your parents."

"Assuming is dangerous..." Why in hell was Angela looking at my parent's dossiers?

"Annie and John McGee?"

I was silent. Those were my parent's names. Annie and John—the beautiful Annie and the handsome John. My dead parents.

Hank took my hand in his and squeezed. My emotions were riotous where my parents were concerned. Ever since I had learned their death had not been an accident it was hard to think about them without getting a feeling of panic. Granny had kept the truth from me and I honestly wished she hadn't.

"Okay," I said softly. "Go back to the feral Wolves being housed and trained by the Dragons. What else do you know about them?"

I needed to move on and get focused on what was going to be in front of me in the very near future.

"Are Annie and John your parents?" Dima asked.

I nodded and leveled her with a stare. She met it and gave me a small sad smile of condolence.

"Feral Wolves?" I reminded her, not wanting her sympathy.

I didn't know what to do with her sympathy because I didn't even know what to do with my own feelings about my parents.

"I don't know much about the Wolves directly," she said in a business-like tone. "I've lived on the fringes of my people for quite some time now so I could stay alive. That's neither here nor there," she said with a sigh I felt deep in my gut. "The Dragons often take over failed projects of other species... for money."

"Keep going," Hank said through clenched teeth.

"I'm guessing the Wolves were an experiment from within your own circles that went wrong," she said with a shrug.

"We did this to our own people?" I hissed. "We prohibited their shift back to human and left them stuck as animals? What kind of horrific *experiment* is that?"

"Can't answer," Dima said. "Sounds like it might have been a punishment of sorts. There are about thirty feral wolves under my father's rule."

I mulled the information over and tried to stop myself from shredding the interior of the car. I was furious anyone could be so vile and inhumane. What the hell was wrong with people—my people?

"Were," I corrected her. "There are now twenty-three."

"Oh my God," Dima whispered. "You killed feral Wolves?"

"Um… yes. It was them or us at the time. I'm getting married in a few months and in no mood to die." I turned to Hank and made a momentous decision. "This clusterhump has given me the confidence to tell your mom I'm not wearing her poofy wedding dress."

"Really?" he asked, abject fear clearly written on his gorgeous face.

"Well, um… maybe not," I whispered.

The car was quiet as we all pondered if it was worth it to die over a wedding dress. A large part of me felt it was very worth it.

"Is it really heinous?" Dima asked with a half suppressed grin.

"From what I understand it's huge with a train and poofy sleeves," I said as I bent over in pain thinking about it.

"I'm so sorry," Dima said. "I hurt for you."

"Thank you. I plan to beat the shit out of whoever takes a picture of me in the dress."

"Could you stage a separate set of pictures with just you and Hank in a different dress?" she suggested.

"Like how?" I asked, intrigued.

"It's risky, especially if you want to display it. You'll have to remember to remove the picture any time Hank's mother is going to visit," Dima recommended.

"Sounds dangerous," Hank said with a shudder. "And potentially bloody or life ending."

"He's right," I said dejectedly. "She'll remove body parts if I don't wear the damn thing. It's all Dwayne's fault. He'll be in some fabulous bridesmaid gown while I'll be the billowy, inflated white poofy thing from hell."

"Dwayne's a guy, right?" Dima asked, a little confused.

"Yes. Drag queen," I explained. "He's my man of honor and really wants to wear a dress."

"Make him wear Hank's mom's dress," she suggested.

The car went silent. My eyes grew wide and I almost screamed with joy.

"Ohmygodohmygodohmygod," I babbled and punched Hank in the shoulder. "Your mom likes Dwayne way better than she likes me... maybe she would be thrilled for Dwayne to wear her gown."

"Essie, I am so staying out of this," he said with a healthy fear of all women in his eyes.

"Probably smart," Dima chimed in. "Do you think she would go for it?"

"If Dwayne suggested it she would. She thinks he's the Second Coming," I said.

"Jesus Hesus number two?" Dima inquired with a silly grin.

"Yes," I said with a laugh. "Definitely Jesus Hesus number two."

With a hearty high five and a fit of giggles, Dima and I sat back in relief. Her being truly concerned that I didn't look like the Pillsbury Dough girl on my wedding day made me like her even more. It would be a challenge to get Dwayne to wear the fugly dress, but he loved me and I planned to beg… and beg… and beg… and beg.

"Are we there yet?" I asked an amused Hank.

"Are you serious?" he shot back with a raised brow.

"Yep."

Hank shook his head and chuckled. "In a half hour we'll be there."

"Half hour more of death-free existence," I said as I turned up the radio. "You like the Clash?" I asked Dima.

"Yes, I do. I also like AC/DC, Johnny Cash and Maroon 5," she added.

"You are my kind of girl," I said with a grin. "My kind of girl."

Chapter 19

"While the concept is interesting, the implementation is horrifying," Dwayne said as he mulled my proposition over and shuddered at the thought. "Dima, I am going to assume this was your suggestion."

"Um, well, I…you know… " Dima stuttered.

"While my Essie is quite brilliant, it would take a mind both devious and intellectual to come up with it," Dwayne explained to a very nervous Dragon.

Clearly she remembered Dwayne was a skilled mind melder and enjoyed blowing up Dragons.

"Wait," I cut in, a little put out. "Are you saying she's smarter than me?"

"I'd suggest zipping it, Ester," Dwayne advised as he bit back a smirk. "You might be winning at the moment."

I zipped it and gave Dima a nudge to continue.

"Well, I just thought since Essie was so incredibly devastated at having to wear a dress that wasn't the one of her dreams on her *special day*—a day which will only happen *once* in her lifetime—that you might find it in your heart to help a girl out. I heard you were wanting to wear a dress, which is delightfully brave and sexy. Soooo... I thought you could save Essie from a massive tantrum and the crying fit which would go hand in hand with her wearing Hank's mom's dress."

"You forgot the words butt-ass fugly," Dwayne said with a raised brow which would have reached his hairline if he'd had hair. "And you should have said *dead heart* since I'm a Vampyre and therefore technically dead."

"Sorry," she mumbled.

"No problemo," Dwayne assured her. "It was an impassioned plea. I'm quite impressed and slightly grossed out at the thought of wearing a poofy dress. With my pecs I should be in a strapless sheath, but I shall take it under consideration. I'm fairly sure with the right heels I could pull off pretty much anything. However, it would go a long way toward convincing me if I knew I was going to perform Lady Gaga in full drag at the reception."

"Done," I shouted as Hank winced and shook his head helplessly.

"Can I throw in a Cher and a Dolly Parton set?" Dwayne negotiated shrewdly.

I thought about it for only a brief second. He could have said he wanted to perform Miley Cyrus naked with a wrecking ball hanging from the ceiling and I would have said yes. Anything was fine so as long as I didn't have to wear the puffed out dress from hell.

"Deal. Shake on it," I demanded. "In front of witnesses."

"I have got to score an invite to this wedding," Dima said as she took in the grand decor of the Great Room of another of Dwayne's homes. She walked the room and ran her hands over the furniture and knickknacks. Dwayne watched her with an odd expression on his face.

"If you live, you're invited," I promised as I tried to figure out what was going on.

"Awesome. Yet another reason to kill my dad."

Dwayne fluffed some pillows and gave me a look indicating we needed to talk in private, but as always he was the polite host.

"So Dima, how old are you?" he asked.

Well, kind of polite...

She pursed her lips and gave him a look. "I'm assuming since you're asking you already know," she said.

"Possibly."

"I'm four hundred and ninety-nine years old. I'll be five hundred in nine months. If I don't find a mate, which by the way is very difficult to do considering my father has killed every male Dragon I have shown even the smallest amount of interest in, I'll die on my birthday."

"Dude, that's harsh," I said seriously.

"Yep," she agreed. "No male Dragon wants to be in the same room with me, so I'm gonna have to kill Pappy."

"It certainly won't be a loss if he's no longer in the world," Dwayne muttered. "Are you prepared to rule your people?"

"No, but is anyone ever prepared for that level of responsibility?" she shot back.

"I suppose not," he said as he eyed her with interest.

"Daddy," Pat yelled as she ran into the room. She tripped over and broke what I was positive was a priceless turn of the century antique coffee table. "Granny is convulsing and spitting up blood. Something is wrong."

"Oh shit," Dwayne hissed as he flew from the room at a speed that would have been impossible to follow.

231

"Where is she?" Hank ground out as Pat picked herself up off the floor and wiped her tears.

"Dungeon," she said and then saw the looks of shock and horror on our faces. "Oh my goodness," she sputtered. "It's lovely—not your typical dungeon at all. It has carpet and cable and air conditioning—very nice. But then again, my Daddy is not your typical Vampyre."

"I need to go to Granny," I insisted as I grabbed Pat and pulled her in the direction Dwayne had flown.

"Oh Essie, I don't know if it's a good idea yet," she said as she wrung her huge hands. "It might be too dangerous for you if she wakes and is hungry."

"I don't care," I yelled. "If she's dying I need to be with her."

"She's already dead," Pat corrected me. "We are hoping she stays that way."

"Wait. What?" Dima asked, completely not with the program.

"Semantics," I huffed, ignoring her as I pushed Pat out of the room. "Take me to her or I'll go all Vampy on your ass."

"Yes, ma'am," she sputtered as she led us to a door. Behind it were a series of halls and stairwells.

"I have so many questions I don't even know where to begin," Dima said as she followed close behind. "And you're smoking crack if you think I'm not coming."

"Hold it," I shouted and slammed the Dragon up against the wall. "You tell me something now that will get you killed if it gets out. If you don't, you're not going a step farther."

"How will you know I'm not lying?" she challenged with narrowed eyes as thin tendrils of blue-green smoke wafted out of her nose.

"I won't, but if I think you are I will kill you dead right here. Right now," I said so calmly she tried to back away. Walls weren't conducive for movement.

"I'll know if you're lying," Hank said softly in a hard voice that made me shiver and not in a good way.

He stood next to me as we boxed Dima in. We watched her closely. If her story to Dwayne was true, she probably wasn't long for this world and had little to lose. Lying to us would be small compared to what possibly lay ahead in her not too distant future. However, I liked her. I wanted her to be a good guy. I wanted her to come to my wedding. I wanted her to see Dwayne in the horrid poofy dress.

"The Dragon property butts up to this one. I've stayed in this house before. It's always empty—has been for about forty years. I knew a Vamp owned it, but this is the first time I've ever heard of him being here," she said carefully.

"More," I growled. "That's not enough. That info doesn't put your life in danger. Talk fast, Dragon, or you're out of here."

"If I tell you more, you will let me have the ability to shift. I can't kill my father or protect myself unless I can shift," she bargained.

Her demand wasn't unreasonable—at all. It made my stomach clench, but I wouldn't send any soldier into battle unarmed. She'd had plenty of opportunity to try and kill us, but she hadn't. Trusting my gut was a lot easier when the most complicated thing I was doing was playing Candy Crush. Real life had a way of making one second guess themselves.

"You can shift. We won't make you drink anymore," Hank told her.

I glanced over in surprise, but he just gave me a terse nod. If he trusted her not to enlarge to the size of a football field and roast us like marshmallows, then I would too. However, I needed more blackmail information first.

"Talk, Dragon," I snapped.

"I don't know if this will count, but the Dragons know every inch of this house."

"Why?" I asked, knowing it was probably not a good thing at all.

"Because it butts up to our land and Dragons are curious. It's full of expensive and shiny objects."

"So the whole Dragons hoarding treasure thing is true?" I asked.

"For some," Dima admitted grudgingly.

"What exactly does a hoard mean to a Dragon?" Hank questioned as he backed off a bit.

After a short pause, Dima exhaled and hung her head. "Everything. A Dragon's hoard means everything to them. Without it a Dragon is nothing."

My stomach roiled at what I was about to do. I didn't want to do it, but my granny's future existence was on the line.

"Where is it?" I asked quietly.

Dima's quick intake of breath and Hank's sharp exhale proved I'd hit a nerve—a big one.

"I don't know what you mean," she mumbled without making eye contact.

"Yes, Dima. Yes, you do. Tell me where your hoard is or I will have Pat kick your Dragon ass right out of this house and out of our lives. You can kill your daddy all by yourself or die trying. I don't care," I said harshly. I felt ill saying such things to her, but there was simply too much on the line to play nice.

"Something else," she begged brokenly. "Ask me for anything else."

"Their entire self worth is wrapped up in their hoard," Hank said in my head. *"It's a brilliant move to make her tell us where hers is hidden."*

"Why do I feel like such an asshole then?" I asked.

"Because you're a good person."
"With a nice ass?" I asked
"With a great ass," he assured me.
"Thank you."
"Welcome."

"You'll understand why I'm making you tell me this in a few minutes. What you'll see will convince you why I will never in my life share the location of your hoard. You just have to give me something worth dying for because what I'm about to show you—I would definitely give my life for," I told her.

Her stare came from miles away. I was cognizant this was costing her more than I was able to comprehend, but I didn't care. My granny's safety was worth more than any piece of gold.

"It's here," she ground out through clenched teeth. "It's under this house."

"Where?" Hank asked.

"In a tunnel off the dungeon. The third hallway. I'll show you."

"No. If I need to find it the information you gave me is enough," I said as I started moving again.

I could scent Granny. She smelled different, but I could still tell it was her.

"I'm coming," I whispered. "You'd better be the good kind of dead, Bobby Sue, or I'll kill you myself."

***

"Holy shit," Dima muttered as we stood on the far side of the room and watched.

Granny's body flailed violently and there was blood spattered everywhere. It looked like a bad B horror movie. She was tangled up in the sheets and moaning in agony. Dwayne gently pulled them away and tried to calm her. My heart was in my throat and my instinct to run to her was overwhelming. It was a very good thing Hank, Dima and Pat were strong.

235

Holding me back was not easy—evidenced by the grunting, sweating and swearing.

Pat had been correct, the dungeon was really just the basement of a very nice house without any windows. The room Granny was in was large and had been converted into a mini hospital. She looked tiny as she lay in the middle of the huge bed and thrashed. She was hooked up to monitors that were not beeping—a very good sign Pat assured me as I clenched and unclenched my fists in panic.

Bags of blood on ice were in containers on the counters that lined the room and a pile of restraints sat on a table next to the bed. It was somehow comforting that she wasn't tied down during her Death Sleep. The Cows hustled around and did all they could to make her comfortable.

I was so focused on my granny, I hadn't even noticed the Vampyres. At least a dozen of them floated around the room above eye level. They were inhumanly beautiful and clearly concerned about the shit show going on below. Their eyes were glued to the Cows with quick glances spared for Granny and Dwayne. My BFF was correct. The Vamps had it bad for the Cows and the Cows could care less. If life as I knew it wasn't about to detonate in my face, I would have giggled at the how ridiculous the situation was.

"She's not going to make it," I whispered as I watched the horrific scene play out before me.

"We don't know that yet," Hank replied tightly.

I'd made the wrong choice and my Granny's suffering would be on my head for as long as I lived. Hindsight was twenty-twenty. If I had it to do over, I would have let her die with the dignity she deserved. I had no idea how much it was possible to loath myself. I rocked forward and tried my best not to sob. Hank's arms around me were of little solace. I wanted to feel the same pain Granny was feeling. It was the very least I could do for her.

"Get up, girlie, but stay over there in case I do something weird—not quite feeling like myself. I could eat the entire spread at Burt's Buffet and Karaoke," a ragged and beloved voice called from the bed. "What in the hell am I wearing and where am I?"

My eyes filled and my voice caught in my throat. I stayed put, but it was difficult. She looked bad, but she was as alive as a dead person could be and she was talking. Good—this was very good.

"It's Prada," Dwayne said with so much relief in his melodic voice I calmed down. "Or it least it was before you destroyed it, old lady."

"Who you callin' old, you bald-headed bloodsucker," Granny grunted as she tried to sit up and fell backwards immediately. "You wanna tell me why I wanna bite you and feel like I've been put through a paper shredder?"

"You don't remember?" Hank asked as he took a tentative step toward my granny, only to be blocked by concerned Cows.

She looked over at us in confusion and my gut tightened. Did she recognize Hank? Or me?

"You're a fine-looking young man," she said as she squinted at him. "I know you, but I can't quite place you, sugar."

"What about me?" I asked louder than I intended. I stepped forward and pushed my way past the Cows. If she bit me and drained me, it would be no less than I deserved. "Do you know me?"

"I do, Essie," she said slowly as she ran her hands nervously through her hair. "Where are your mamma and daddy? Are they with you? Did you find them? They'll be so excited to see you."

I closed my eyes and forced a smile. She knew me, but it was all jumbled. She didn't remember my

237

parents were dead and I didn't think now was the right time to tell her. I was still unclear exactly what she was... a Wolf slash Vampyre—a Vampyre only? It didn't really matter as long as she was still here. Hopefully, she would remember everything. If she didn't, she didn't. I still wanted to know why she didn't defend herself from the feral Wolves, but I might never know the truth behind that one.

"I haven't seen them for a bit, but I'm looking for them," I told her. It wasn't even a lie. I was looking for what happened to my parents and I would make the person responsible for their death pay. "I want to hug you. Would that be okay?" I asked in a voice that sounded small and childlike to my own ears. Hank's hand on my back felt good this time. I needed him.

She looked to Dwayne for confirmation that she wouldn't hurt me. "What am I?" she asked.

Dwayne tilted his head to the side and grinned. "You're perfect. Not quite sure how we'll define you yet, but I can say with certainty you are one of a kind."

"I was always one of a kind," Granny informed the entire room. "Anyone wanna tell me why a gaggle of dead guys are flying over my head? And yes, Essie, I would very much like a hug from you. However, if I bite you please feel free to punch me in the head. Hard."

"Um... okay," I said as I carefully approached.

"Am I really okay to be near her?" Granny asked Dwayne. There was fear written on her face.

"Yes," he promised. "And I will be right here to deck your skinny old ass if you do anything out of the ordinary."

"Thank you," she said as she squeezed him lovingly. "Get over here, little girl, and bring your good lookin' lug with you. He looks like he's gonna have a heart attack if you leave his side."

"It's Hank, Granny. He's my mate," I told her as I crawled up on the bed and got close.

She put her hands to her temples and closed her eyes. "I remember. Alpha. Sheriff. Gave it all up because he loves my girl so much he can't live without her... Hank," she said with such relief in her voice I almost cried.

"That's right, Granny," I said as I took her very cold hand in mine.

Was this her new temperature? Whatever—cold hands, warm heart. Or dead heart... whatever.

"I died, didn't I? And Dwayne brought me back?" she asked as she held tight to my hand.

I nodded, not sure what I could say and not say. The last thing I wanted to do was upset her.

"I can't remember any more than that," she snapped, frustrated. "Why can't I remember?"

"Well," Dwayne said logically. "It's common to block out unpleasant things, like how you died. It will probably all come roaring back at a dinner party or the mall—someplace totally inconvenient and embarrassing. It's what happened to me and don't even ask Vlad what he experienced," Dwayne said as he pointed to a good-looking dead dude flying along the perimeter of the room.

"Oh dear god, it was awful. I'm still in therapy and it happened eight hundred years ago," Vlad told us with a shudder and a groan.

While curious about Vlad, it wasn't the time or the place to get into it. I just wanted Granny to be okay. If she needed therapy, I would get her therapy. I'd get her whatever she needed.

"Sweet Baby Jesus in a thong," she muttered as she squeezed my hand. "Maybe amnesia is the way to go. Essie, just hold my hand, baby. I'm a little nervous about being too close to your neck."

"Roger that," I said as I squeezed her hand back.

If I was honest, I was a little nervous too. I could feel Hank's freaked out emotions coming off of him in waves.

"Alrightyroo," Dwayne said as he hopped off the bed, dragging me with him. "I want my girls to feed Granny. Vamps, if it gets back to me that you have touched any of my daughters' asses again I will remove your hands. Literally."

"Daddy," Pat said sheepishly. "I told Vlad he could touch my butt."

Dwayne was at a loss. His girls were growing up fast. I watched him seriously consider having a hissy fit and then decide against it. "Well, fine then," he huffed, giving a gloating Vlad the evil eye. "If you want your bottom defiled by a Vampyre, so be it."

"Thank you," Pat said, missing all of the passive aggression Dwayne was throwing at the floating Vamps.

With an eye roll and a put upon sigh, Dwayne steered Hank, Dima and myself out of the room.

"Where are we going?" I asked as I waved bye to Granny.

"We're going to Dima's room. I've been curious about her room for forty years," Dwayne said.

"I'm sorry, what?" Dima gasped and almost fell to the ground.

"Don't be coy. It doesn't become you," Dwayne said dismissively. "I've never gone in. I have respect for other's property... unlike others I know."

"You know about my room?" She was positively flabbergasted.

"When you walked in I recognized your scent," he said as he led the way down a maze of hallways.

"But I've never seen you here."

"And I've never seen you, but I'm a Vamp. I know when someone has been in my home. Actually, quite a few of you have traipsed through, but you stayed. I wondered what you would look like. Your scent is lovely."

"I suppose I should say thank you and sorry at the same time," she mumbled as she continued to get paler and paler as we got closer to her hoard.

"You're welcome and no problem," Dwayne replied as we rounded a corner and Dima fell to her knees.

"You have to understand what's in the room is not evil. I know this is not my home, but I will kill any of you who try to harm my hoard," she said as she crawled to a wall, stood and plastered herself against it.

"What the hell is in there?" I muttered.

Dima eyed us warily and then slowly chanted a spell that opened the wall. I held my breath and waited to be attacked by something vicious, but I couldn't have been more surprised.

A baby boy, gold and silver Dragon flew out followed by three smiling female Dragons in human form. The baby was roughly the size of a large ape and was babbling up a storm as it flew with joyous abandon toward Dima.

"Mommy," the baby Dragon squealed. "Me love me mommy!"

It tackled Dima and covered her in wet sloppy baby Dragon kisses. My heart was in my mouth. Her hoard was her child—not jewels and money. She had hidden her child from danger. I now knew why killing her father was so imperative to her. She was going to possibly die in nine months, leaving her precious child without protection.

"This is what I would die for," she said as she stared hard at Dwayne, Hank and myself. "My own father killed my child's father. Now I am going to end the murderous bastard's life."

"I get it," I said as I reached out to touch the baby Dragon.

"Daniel, shift, my love. Shift back for Mommy and meet her friends," Dima said in a voice so filled with love I felt like I was watching something I shouldn't.

The baby Dragon shimmered as he went from Dragon form to the human body of a beautiful four-year-old boy. He was shyer in his human body. He ran behind his mother and peeked out.

"Heather, Kathleen and Melissa, these are my new friends. Meet Essie, Hank and Dwayne," Dima said as she introduced us to the women who were clearly looking after her child. "Dwayne is the owner of the house and our unintentional host."

"I am now your intentional host and I insist you not hide this child and his caretakers in a small room under a tunnel. You will have the run of the house, but you are probably safer staying in the dungeon area until you have dealt with your father," Dwayne told them.

The three caregivers bowed to him while Dima gave him a grateful nod.

"You are Wampyre," Daniel said as he pointed at Dwayne with a huge toothless grin.

"Yes, I am… and you are a Dragon. Do you think we can be friends?" he asked as he squatted down and addressed the child.

"Yes, me do," Daniel said as he put out a small hand to shake Dwayne's.

"You be Wolf, but you are diffwent," Daniel said as he pointed at Hank and me.

"How are we different, little man?" Hank asked as he got down next to Dwayne to talk to the boy.

"You no have red eyes. Me like the red eye Wolves. People be afraid, but not me," he explained in a very serious four-year-old way.

"The feral Wolves—he's talking about the feral Wolves," I said.

"Well, that makes sense," Hank said.

"How so?" I asked.

"They know the boy is here. He's why they won't leave the perimeter of Dwayne's property," he said.

"Dang it, you're smart," I said with a shake of my head. I knew Junior was MENSA, but I wondered now if Hank was too. Hell, if he was then our kids had a chance of being amazing...as long as they got all of his genes. My genes liked to skip classes.

"Sounds possible," Dima said thoughtfully, "but the Wolves wouldn't give away the location of Daniel."

"Do you know these Wolves personally?" I asked, wondering if she'd been straight with us earlier.

"No, most of them want nothing to do with Dragons. However, there are two who seem attracted to Daniel."

"Does your father know of Daniel's existence?" Hank asked as he picked the child up and put him on his shoulders, much to the small Dragon's delight.

"He suspects," Dima said darkly. "He's not sure. Hardly anyone has ever seen Daniel and no one will until it's safe."

"Okey dokey," Dwayne said as he took Daniel from Hank's shoulders and handed him back to his caretakers. "We need to get back upstairs and figure out a game plan for a game where we have no real clue who the players are, what the rules are, or what the end goal is."

"Sounds like my kind of plan," I said. "It's a weird one, but since I don't have anything better I'll go with it."

Dima kissed her child and sealed the wall with a reverse spell. We quickly made our way back to the

Great Room and sat down to figure out what the hell was going on.

Way easier said than done...

Chapter 20

We sat in the Great Room and mulled the possibilities.

"So you think the Council is out there somewhere and is going to use Angela, with the horrendous dress sense, as bait to get to you?" Dwayne asked, trying to clarify.

"Possibly," I said. "Is there any way they'd know about Granny's situation?"

"No, I don't think so," he said.

"Edward and Spike are friendly with the Dragons and the Council," Vlad called down from the rafters of the room as he tattled on his comrades.

"If you're going to speak, then get your dead ass down here," Dwayne reprimanded the Vamp.

"For enough money they'd talk to anyone," Vlad informed us as he floated down to the floor.

"I don't know," I said with a firm shake of my head. "This situation is stranger than that. It's been like one big elaborate set up for something. We've been attacked several times in the last week."

"You told Angela that Dwayne and your grandmother were in Michigan when we were at the zoo," Dima reminded me.

"Mother-humper... I did."

"I certainly hope you were paid well," Vlad said with distaste at my perceived faux pas.

"She's a good guy. She's on our side, Dead Dude," I snapped at him. "Oh my God, do you think they beat it out of her?"

"It's possible," Hank replied.

"Why does the Council want you dead?" Dima asked.

"We're not a hundred percent sure," Hank said as he touched my shoulder possessively, "but we think it's because they don't want her looking into the death of her parents."

"Which leads me to believe the Council was involved," I added with very little emotion.

I was going on autopilot. I needed to divorce myself from feelings to get the job done.

"So your granny is just confused about your folks being alive?" she asked.

"Looks that way," Dwayne confirmed. "Too many coincidences here—makes me uncomfortable. It's as if I was performing Madonna dressed as Donna Summer."

"God, that does sounds horrible," Vlad said as he flew around the room in agitation.

"Yes. Yes, it does," Dwayne whispered in horror.

"I do believe you might want to look out the window," Vlad informed us as he halted and floated in front of what had to be a fifteen-foot floor to ceiling sheet of glass.

"What the hell?" I muttered as I made my way over and tried to make sense of what I was staring at.

The compound was surrounded by Dragons and Wolves—not feral Wolves—Council Wolves. The feral Wolves were facing off against the Dragons and Council and stood squarely in front of Dwayne's house to defend it.

"Does anyone else think what those feral Wolves are doing is really weird?" I whispered as I made sure I was armed to the teeth.

Dima's quick intake of breath made my stomach drop.

"What?"

"My father is out there with the Dragons. Why in the hell is he out there? It's below him to be with commoners."

"Call me crazy, but my guess is he knows you're here and has come to kill you," I said.

"Okay, Crazy," Dima said with a grim look on her lovely face. "I think you are correct."

"Vlad, there are people trespassing on my property," Dwayne said casually. "What do you think we should do about them?"

"I think we should politely ask them to leave," Vlad answered with a smile so terrifying I got a little sick to my stomach.

"Yes," Dwayne said as he put on a boa which was conveniently laying on the couch. "I think that is a grand idea."

"Oh shit," Hank muttered under his breath.

"I second your shit and will raise you an oh my hell," I mumbled back.

***

"There were thirty," Hank said as he hung up the phone.

"Thirty what?" I asked as I checked my guns.

"Thirty unsolved deaths of WTF agents over the last thirty years, according to Junior."

"Thirty?" I asked, completely shocked. "The Council let thirty cases go unsolved? Thirty cases where their own agents were murdered?"

Like every other stinking epiphany about WTF, I would deal with the information Hank found later.

Right now I wanted to get Angela back if she was out there. I wanted to kill Dima's asshole dad and figure out why the Council was here in the first place.

Was it for me? Was it for Granny?

"Yep. Junior will call with more info as it comes in. He thinks he's on to something," Hank said as he put the burner back in his pocket.

"Why aren't the feral Wolves siding with the Dragons?" I asked.

I looked in dismay at the Cows who were preparing to fight alongside us. It was a tremendously bad idea since they were pacifists.

"Um... maybe you guys should..." I started, but the explosion that rocked the house shut me up quick.

"Half the Cows go to the back of the house and half to the front," Hank yelled as chaos ensued. "Just aim the serum at the mouths of the Dragons, same as we did the other day. We have to stop them from shifting. Vamps divide and cover the Cows. Everyone else go out front."

"Weapons won't work on the Dragons," I called out. "How many of you Vamps can mind meld?"

None of them raised their hands.

Shit.

"I'm the only one," Dwayne said. "I'm a bit drained from feeding Granny, but I'll try if the need arises."

"Good. Dima, you wait to go after your father until we've nailed him with the serum and we're with you. Understand?" I asked tersely.

"Yes," she replied in a clipped tone as pink and silver tendrils of smoke fanned out of her mouth and nose.

"Can you shift?" Hank asked her.

"I can."

"Um, Essie?" Pat called out, raising her hand.

"Yes, Pat?"

"Fart bombs?"

I grinned from ear to ear and bit down on the inside of my cheek to keep from laughing at such a serious time. "Yes, you can utilize fart bombs, but wait for us to give the go ahead."

The Cows all high-fived while the love-struck Vamps looked on in pride. Again, if it wasn't life or death staring us in the face I'd be on the floor in hysterics. Hank groaned and shook his head.

"We need to add nose plugs to our weapons arsenal," he mumbled.

"Is it that bad?" Dima asked as she checked her stash of knives and daggers and strapped on several more.

"Bad doesn't even begin to describe it," I said with a full body shudder. Simply thinking of it set off my gag reflex.

"Who's watching Granny?" I asked as we all made to go outside.

"Nobody," Granny announced from the doorway that went down to the dungeon. "I'm fine, and if any of them get too close there's a good chance I'll go all Wolfy-Vamp on them. God only knows what that means."

A quick glance at Dwayne confirmed my worst fears. He looked ready to have a fit—similar to the one he'd thrown when he realized Milli Vanilli wasn't really singing. However, this was much worse and far more serious. Granny was a danger to the bad guys, and very possibly the good guys. She needed to go back to the basement with a few of the Cows to protect her.

The second explosion put a stop to moving Granny anywhere.

"Go, go, go!" she yelled as we all broke and headed for the doors. Several of the Cows dove right out of the windows with the Vamps flying on their heels. Two of the Vampyres exploded out of

Dwayne's chimney, blowing fieldstone hundreds of feet into the air and the rest of us took the doors. It was a spectacular entrance.

And then there was silence.

Nothing was happening outside. I wasn't even sure who set off the explosions.

Was it the Council? The Dragons? The feral Wolves?

There were about ten or so of the feral Wolves standing guard. Where were the others? We'd killed seven—there should be twenty-three...

They completely ignored us and stayed focused on the quiet threat hovering in the hills surrounding us.

"What's going on?" I whispered to Hank on my left.

"No freakin' clue," he answered.

"Oddest thing I've ever witnessed," Dima said as she squinted up the hill. "Why aren't they charging us? We're outnumbered by a shitload."

"We want Essie McGee and Hank Wilson."

A Wolf I recognized from the zoo had shouted the demand.

"There will be no bloodshed if you hand them over without a fight."

"I don't know about the no bloodshed part," a gorgeous male Dragon with an evidently vicious streak purred. "I quite enjoy a little friendly bloodshed."

Dima hissed next to me and smoke wafted from every orifice on her head.

"Daddy?" I asked.

"Yep, but not for much longer," she replied evenly.

"Nice."

"Along with a little spilling of blood, I'd like my daughter to come home. Her loving father misses her so," the Dragon spat sarcastically.

"I'll see you dead first," Dima yelled across the field.

"Now that's not a very respectful way to speak to one's sire," he said silkily with narrowed eyes and fire coming out of his nose.

The feral Wolves growled and pawed at the ground in agitation. I suppose they figured we were a lesser evil than the Dragons. They didn't really like our little mixed species group, but they absolutely despised the Dragons.

"Respect is given where respect is due," Dima shot back to her very displeased father.

"I'm having a problem here," Dwayne called out. "You see, I just had the grounds seeded around my home and you douchecanoes are stepping on it. This makes me grumpy. You are not getting Essie or Hank."

Dwayne paced dramatically as he spoke to the Wolves.

"They have entirely too much to do with planning their wedding. There is not time for them to be incarcerated and tortured by idiots who don't know their heads from their asses. And you," he pointed to Dima's father with his middle finger and a huge smile on his face, "are not getting your daughter."

"Who do you think you are, Vampyre?" an old Wolf yelled.

"I'm Dwayne the Gay Vampyre Drag Queen Priest with a Keen Dress Sense and Fabu Abs. I am the wildly proud father of eight daughters and I moonlight at a wedding shop I also model for. Most importantly, I am your worst nightmare along with my somewhat violent friends slash acquaintances slash occasional mortal enemies… "

"Who want to marry your Cow daughters," Vlad chimed in.

"Yes, well, that's a conversation for another day... or century," Dwayne muttered with an eye roll. "My frenemies like to decapitate things. Say hello to Vlad, Edward, Barnabus, Bones, Dimitri and Spike!"

"Is this a joke?" the Council Wolf growled and began to pace the hillside. "We are your supreme rulers. You will hand over the prisoners or we will take them."

"It's Aramini," Hank said softly. "One of the members who want the reveal."

"Is Gades with him?" I asked as I scanned the crowd.

"He is," Hank ground out. "Only those who want the reveal are here. Interesting."

"I think we know now which Council members are in cahoots with the Dragons," I stated the obvious.

"Our mission should be over," Hank said as he ran his hands through his hair and grunted in disgust.

"Yep, it should, but I'd have to say it's definitely not."

"Affirmative."

"If we live through this can I ride you like a cowboy tonight?" I asked.

"I have no problem with that," he said with a lopsided grin.

"TMI," Dima muttered with a groan. "Some of us are single."

"Sorry," I said insincerely.

"Right," she said with a snort. "Get your head in the game."

"Will do."

The Dragons were up on the hill to the left and the Wolves to the right. They stood about six hundred feet away. Both groups were against us, but they were not together by anyone's stretch of the imagination. The sound of screaming and a body running at us made me pull my Glock and a dagger. The Vamps got ready to shred the attacker and the feral Wolves howled with fury.

"Stand down," Hank yelled. "We know her."

Angela was a bloody mess as she tore forward away from the Council Wolves and ran as if her life depended on it. They gave a halfhearted chase, but she was near death and they didn't seem to care. What was wrong with my people?

"Angela," I cried out as she fell in a heap at my feet.

I was so relieved to see her, but some of the others were not. It was fast and I was so concerned with Angela I was almost unaware it was happening. Almost.

I shifted to my Wolf on instinct as the female feral Wolf my Granny had refused to fight dove forward and went for Angela's neck. I used my body to block her and rolled with her into a now destroyed flowerbed. I wasn't sure if Dwayne's shriek was because I was in danger of biting it or because we'd just wiped out several thousand dollars worth of Knockout Roses.

She bared her teeth and snapped at me as she struggled to get back to Angela. She was strong and large and she wanted Angela—bad. Why in the hell did everyone want to kill my boss? She was a pain in the ass, but being one was not an offense that merited death. I felt the Vampyre blood in my system burst free and flow through my body. My need to fight the female wolf was intense. She was not going to kill what was mine. Only I could kill what was mine...

Wait. Where did that come from?

She hissed and growled. Hank shifted and had my back. The male feral Wolf, who I also recognized, had hers. The Vamps floated above ready to dive in at my first sign of distress. I needed no help whatsoever. I blocked her every move to get back to Angela and her frustration was evident. However, she refused to engage me. What was her problem? Did she fear me? Why in the hell would she fear me? I was smaller and clearly not as old or as skilled as she was.

She made the mistake of looking away and I pounced. I held her pinned under me and she whimpered only once before she offered her neck to me in submission. Why? Why was she doing this?

"Kill her," Angela hissed. "Kill the bitch. She wants me dead. Kill her. Now."

Angela was both frightened and furious. She had to be in shock from repeated beatings, but what she wanted from me was wrong.

It would be so easy to follow orders, but I had stopped taking orders from Angela several days ago. I wasn't going to start now and kill a Wolf that had offered its throat to me. To do so would be cold-blooded murder. I would kill—it was part of my job, but only when necessary or provoked. Period.

I backed off of the female Wolf and gave Angela a withering look as I shifted back to human.

"Bring her in the house," I told Pat and Harley, referring to my boss. "She's in no shape to fight."

"I told you to kill her," Angela rasped out as blood poured from a cut over her eye and from her nose.

Holy hell, they'd worked her over good.

"You'll be happy later that I followed protocol and didn't kill a defenseless being. You'll be safe inside."

"When I tell you to do something, you do it," she screamed as she let Pat and Harley lead her inside. "No one is listening anymore."

I noticed the Aramini and Gades chuckling at the scene. The Dragons appeared bored and the feral Wolves pinned me with stares.

"What?" I snapped at the ferals. "What do you want? And where are the rest of you? There are supposed to be thirty of you... well, I guess twenty-three because of the other day, but..."

"Thirty," Hank said in shock. "There were thirty."

"Ferals?" Dwayne asked confused.

I felt cold and hot at the same time. My head was light and I felt a little like I was floating above myself. It was all in front of us the entire time...

"Agents. Thirty missing agents presumed dead with no proof of death," I said as my body started to shake uncontrollably. "Oh my god," I shouted at the entire hillside. "Is this what you're hiding? Wouldn't the rest of the Werewolf nation be interested to learn that service to your government means you end up as an experiment with half of a fucking life? Is *this* why you want me? So I can be part of your game along with my parents?"

I wanted to peel my skin off and I wanted to throw up. I was fairly certain at this point I had almost just killed my mother. I had also dropped the f-bomb which was something Granny would wash my mouth out with soap for, but it felt right and Granny was inside.

Of course... now it all made sense. Granny had recognized her daughter and her son-in-law. She had been sure which was what had killed her. It's why those two Wolves stayed and protected her body... and it's why they were still here.

"This ends now," I ground out through clenched teeth. "All of the Wolves and Dragons on the hill die today. Are we all on the same page?"

"Yes, we are," Vlad said as he rubbed his hands together with glee.

"Cows, inside the house," Hank directed as the Wolves on the hill began to shift and howl.

"We will fight," Harley said as she and Pat came back out of the house.

"Absolutely not," I said. "Your blood will not be on my hands. Inside. NOW."

The howling of the Wolves and the unfortunate shifts of the dozen or so Dragons did not bode well for us winning. However, I was not going down without putting up a fight and I planned to take a few Council members with me.

I sincerely hoped I survived the day and I prayed I made it through with all of my limbs intact. I wanted to get married with all of my original parts. But I also hoped the two feral Wolves made it. I was pretty sure I knew who they were now, but I was too frightened to hope it was true.

The Cows ignored us and shifted, which was one of the most alarming things I'd ever seen. There were roughly the size of the cab of a Mac truck and their tusks were about five feet long. The gals were hairy and their eyes bulged to the point I thought they might fall out. No one would believe me if I described them. It was like your worst and strangest nightmare come to life... and they could speak.

Holy crap.

"Everybody stand back," Pat bellowed in a voice definitely more manly than girly. The Vamps flew around and squealed like girls. "It's gonna get stinky."

"Oh my hell," Dima sputtered as she pulled me back toward the house. "Are they going to kill my father with anal acoustics?"

"Very nice," I said as I pitched a throwing star at some incoming bad guys, removing a head and making the others duck for cover. "I'm impressed. I will accept that gross pun and raise you a booty belch, anal salute, cheek squeak and sphincter siren."

"I'm going to be ill, but I will counter your offer with a butt bazooka, a crack splitter, Horton hears a poo, and a nice bout of rectal turbulence," she shot back as she beheaded something flying low over her head. Thankfully it wasn't a Vamp.

"Can I play?" Hank asked.

"Of course," I told him.

"Panty burp, roar from the rear, air tulip, and ass ripper," he added proudly.

"I will marry you," I said with a grin. "Your disgusting mind matches my own. And *you* deserve my friendship," I told Dima. I gauged how fast the enemy was coming and how close the Cows would let them get before they let go with a blast of insane methane.

"Don't know if that's a compliment or a curse," Dima said as she backed farther away from the Cows. "Will we live through this?"

"Um... not sure," I admitted. "Stay upwind and hold your nose."

"How will I breathe?" she asked.

"Through your mouth," I said logically.

"Oh, hell no. Then I'll taste it," she gagged out.

"Point. Can't help you there," I said, as I pondered the situation and waited to see what happened next.

The Wolves and Dragons didn't want us alive, but they were hesitant in their attack. Possibly Hank's and my reputation for killing Dragons had surfaced. Or maybe they were simply too important to fight— something they usually left to the commoners—like me.

However, I didn't have to ponder it long. Nope. What I saw would stay with me always, even though I would pay good money to have it removed. The butt yodeling was only the tip of the iceberg. The rest was almost unexplainable.

The Cows turned, bent over and ran backwards toward the incoming aggressors. The Dragons and Council Wolves were confused and amused. Clearly they had no clue what was coming next. I believe their condescending shouts were their undoing. The Cows might have been satisfied with asphyxiating them, but the bovine slurs were what landed them in hell... which was where I assumed most of them were headed, one way or another anyway.

The booty bombs were in technicolor and they were loud. I now wondered if the explosions earlier were my Cow friends practicing. Dragons literally fell from the sky and Wolves curled into balls and convulsed as they gasped for air.

The Vampyres cheered loudly. Their fangs glistened as they blew raspberries and kisses to their bovine loves. The feral Wolves had backed up to the front porch and were clawing desperately to get in. I didn't blame them, but I didn't let them. I was unsure if it was to get to Angela or to get away from the smell.

The next part is what I wanted to close my eyes for, but morbid curiosity and healthy respect for five foot tusks made me watch. There was a reason Cows were feared. Dwayne's gals were no longer pacifists. They had found their inner killer with a vengeance and they were having a blast.

The Council Wolves and the Dragons... not so much.

Hank pulled me to the porch along with Dima and Dwayne. It was the first time in my life I relaxed in a battle. There was nothing for me to do. It was all being done for me... and Hank... and Dwayne... and Dima and the Vamps.

After the initial butt crack concert, the Cows went berserk. It was not exaggerated how poisonous their tusks were. A simple prick would have killed even the strongest paranormal. However, the girls weren't satisfied to poke and run. They were more into gore, shake, and hurl at least three hundred feet or so. They seemed particularly focused on the Dragons. This made sense, considering the Dragons had burnt their family alive.

It was like watching a warped child's version of what happened to bad guys. It was bloody, ugly and short. Giant clouds of purple Dragon smoke and small fires littered the lawn. Dwayne's grass would definitely have to be re-seeded. It was a freakin' mess.

"He got away," Dima cried out as she ran the grounds and searched for her father. "Damn it, he got away."

This was not good. At all.

"We'll find him and we'll kill him," I promised her as I stepped over the dead bodies of Aramini and Gades.

It would be interesting explaining this clusterhump to the rest of the Council. I had no idea if they would believe us or if they were all in on this sick game. Yet another big hurdle to not look forward to.

"Guys, back off." Hank growled at the feral Wolves as they continued to try and claw their way into the house. They were led by the two who were familiar to me. My instinct was to shift and help them—strange.

"I don't know if Dwayne will want you guys in the house if you're going to fight or cause trouble," I told them. "Tell me what's wrong."

I could feel their tension and I shared it. I had no clue why, but a feeling of unease skittered up my spine. It was strong and I wasn't able to push it to the side or ignore it. The Wolves had spoken to me once before and I was hoping now they would speak again.

"*She's in there with my mother,*" the female said. "*You must stop her.*"

What the hell was she talking about? Two things jumped around in my head. The fact I was correct—

the Wolf at my feet was indeed my mother because she referred to Granny as her mother. Then I lost track of my shock trying to figure out what the hell she was talking about.

"Oh shit," I yelled as I turned and burst through the front door when I figured it out. I looked wildly around for my granny. The feral Wolves were on my heels along with Hank, Dwayne and Dima.

And then I spotted her. She was seated on a dark brown leather couch which had been pushed up against a wall. There were no windows behind it and it had the best view of all the entrances and exits into the Great Room. Once an agent, always an agent. Granny had looked bad earlier—now she looked positively horrific. Angela had put her in restraints and she was bleeding from multiple wounds to her face and head. My stomach lurched as Angela held a large silver machete to my granny's neck. My boss was calm and she was smiling.

And she was about to die.

Chapter 21

"So this was your project?" I asked casually, pointing to the feral Wolves.

"All of you disarm or her head goes," Angela said tightly.

"Not a problem," I assured her as I took every weapon I had on my body off and put them on the floor, as did the others. "You want to explain?"

"You were supposed to die," she spat. "First with the Dragons in Hung and then with the Dragons in Illinois. Either would have killed your parents. It was part of the master plan to break them. How the hell are you still alive?"

She squinted at me as if I were a freak of nature...actually, I was.

"Just lucky, I suppose. How did you know we were in Illinois?" I asked, wanting to understand why a woman I liked and trusted had turned on me so viciously.

"You're tagged. I have GPS on you," she sneered. "When any recruit joins we chip them. We can protect you that way."

"Or conveniently find us and kill us," I added.

"Yes. That too," she added with a satisfied grunt.

It was fairly easy to get Angela to monologue. She liked to hear herself talk. Normally I tried to ignore her, but not today. I wanted to hear every word she had to say.

"Why? What did I do to you that I needed to die for?"

"*You exist*," Angela shouted. She grabbed Granny by the hair and ran the knife down the side of her face, creating a new scar and a new pool of blood.

What she couldn't see was the maniacal look on Granny's face and the long sharp Vampyre fangs that had dropped down for a visit. I'd say Angela had maybe five more minutes... and I wanted answers.

"Ooookay," I said as I sat down on the floor and got comfortable. "Tell me why my existence is such an issue for you."

"*You* should have been mine," she hissed as spittle gathered at the corners of her mouth.

How had I never noticed her crazy before? The feral Wolves, aka my mom and dad, growled low in their chests.

"I'm sorry. What?" Hers? How in hell should I have been hers?

"I wanted him. He should have been mine," she whined.

Granny rolled her eyes. I could see it was all she could do not to go ballistic on Angela, but I guess she wanted answers too. Angela didn't have any clue how difficult it would be to kill my Granny now—considering she was immortal.

"He never would have been yours," Granny snapped and clenched her fists. "He was engaged to his mate—my daughter. He never wanted you, you horrible stupid woman."

"*Shut up*," Angela shouted. "John never got the chance to know me because of her." She hissed as she stared daggers at my mother in her Wolf form.

"Whoa whoa whoa," I said, shaking my head as I tried to keep a lid on my need to tear Angela's head from her body. Hank's low growling beside me let me know he was on the same page. "You got spurned by my dad, so you had him and my mom put into an experiment that kept them permanently in Wolf form?"

"Yes. It was my idea," Angela crowed proudly. "I was revered for it by the Council members who were funding the project and by the scientists. We could take problem Werewolves and use them to create perfect fighting machines."

"That's sick, Angela. You're no different from Hitler," I ground out.

"Thank you," she said with a bow of her head.

"It was not a compliment, you piece of trash. I missed out on having a mother and a father all of my life because you're a jealous psycho. You have ruined the lives of countless people and families... thirty I know of, and all because you're mentally ill with delusions of grandeur."

"What kind of magic was used?" Hank demanded in a tone that made everyone in the room flinch, including Angela.

God, he was hot when he was scary.

"Like I'd ever tell you." Angela laughed and pulled on the few hairs left on her head. "It's my ticket to stay alive."

The sound of her hollow and pathetic laugh bounced around my brain and made me feel clammy and ill. No, she probably wouldn't tell the secret, but if anyone could figure out how to reverse a spell or find a chemical compound that could solve this problem, it was Junior. We probably didn't even need all the information.

"You were my partner," Granny growled angrily. "You took my daughter and my son from me."

"You didn't think I was good enough for him," Angela bellowed.

"What are you talking about?" Granny shot back, completely mystified. "I had no clue your sick mind was even going there. You only met John and Annie once!"

"Yes," Angela agreed moodily, "but then I followed him for a year and ran into him randomly on purpose. But no... he was too enchanted by your whore to notice me," Angela screamed as she went to cut Granny's face again.

"So finding me and hiring me was all just a game to you?" I questioned loudly. I was trying to distract her from slicing and dicing my granny while also trying to make sense of how someone could be so delusional. "You had this planned all along?"

"Yes, I did. And you're a whore just like your mother."

I was a lot of things, but whore was not one of them—not by a long shot. Don't know if it was the word whore, or her tone of voice, or the fact it had been a really long week for everyone, but her name-calling was the last straw. Much to Angela's shock Granny tore out of her restraints like they were made of tissue paper and turned on her with a fury like I'd never seen. I dove like an Olympic swimmer onto the couch just as my parents sprang from their spots across the room and went for her neck.

And then suddenly it was over.

I have no idea who ended Angela's life. I don't know if it was me, my mother, my father or my grandmother. It didn't matter. She was destroyed by the family she destroyed.

"Well, that was messy." Dwayne broke the silence with a ridiculous but accurate comment.

"All of this was because of unrequited love?" I asked in a daze as I backed away from the carnage that used to be Angela.

I stared at my parents and wondered what they looked like in their human form. I wondered if I would ever see them in their human form.

"Can you shift?" Hank asked as he got down low to examine the wounds on my parents.

Granny had already healed. Werewolf-Vampyre genes were clearly superior.

My father slowly shook his head no and pressed his body against my mother's.

"*Not all of the Wolves are like us,*" my father said to me. "*Most want nothing to do with normal Weres or humans. They're dangerous, but deserve a chance at rehabilitation if we find a cure.*"

"I agree," I said aloud. "He says some of the feral Wolves are dangerous and we need to proceed with caution, but they deserve a chance to live too."

"*You're beautiful, Essie, and I love you so very much,*" my mother said with a thick voice filled with sorrow. "*I am so sorry.*"

I grabbed Hank so I didn't fall to the floor as my knees buckled. After all the danger was over I was left with a massive amount of emotion I wasn't quite sure what to do with. I had wished my whole life that my mom and dad were alive… and now they were.

Maybe not in the way I had hoped for, but they were alive. I could have a relationship with them. We could be a *very* unconventional little family.

Slowly I crawled to the Wolves and wedged myself between them.

Granny looked on with a smile on her beautiful undead face.

I laid my head against their necks and breathed them in. They were mine. This by no means perfect, but it was something large—something large and wonderful.

My Granny was a partial Vampyre and my parents were Wolves twenty-four seven and I was...

I was a scattered girl who could shoot the teats off a cow in the next county over.

I was a girl without a job or a boss.

I was a girl who was wildly in love with her mate.

And I was pretty sure I was the girl who talked Dwayne into wearing the horrid poofy dress for her at her wedding.

Life was looking pretty damn good right now.

"Hank wants six kids," I told my mom as I traced the markings on her snout. "I say he's smoking crack."

"I want ten," Hank corrected with a chuckle. He sat down on the floor and offered his respect to my father by keeping his head lower than his.

"So not happening."

I giggled and punched his arm as my mother nudged him and licked his cheek.

"Jesus Hesus," Dwayne shouted, startling everyone. "Your daddy can give you away at the wedding!"

"Yes. He can," Granny said with glee and a fit of giggles. "Of course we can't invite any humans— they'd just flip if you walked down the aisle with a Wolf and then kissed it."

I glanced at my father who looked sad but hopeful.

"I would be so happy if you would walk me down the aisle," I told him as I ran my hand along the side of his enormous head.

His fur was soft and I had to fight a tremendous urge to curl up next to him and cuddle.

"*It would be my honor,*" he said gruffly and pushed his head against my hand.

"Done," I said with satisfaction and a huge hug for my dad. "Where's Dima?" I asked as I scanned the room.

"She went to check on someone," Dwayne said with a wink.

I was worried about her and her son, but we would stand by her one hundred percent.

"Um… sir," Hank said to my father. "It's a bit past the actual point of asking."

"Yes," Dwayne agreed. "They've been having sex for *years*."

"Oh my god, Dwayne," I shrieked and went to slap his bald head. "That is massively unnecessary information for my parents—and my granny."

"Correct, but it's so much fun to see the look on your face when I overshare."

"While it's all kinds of awesome for you, it's totally sucktastic for me. Do it again and you're wearing a plain old black tuxedo to the wedding," I informed him with raised brows.

His squeal of terror was music to my ears. It was difficult to make eye contact with my parents after the great reveal of my sex life, but what was done was done.

However, I was going to think of something to tell Dwayne's girls guaranteed to make him want to hide for a week or two. It was going to be a challenge, considering Dwayne had no filter and very little shame…

"Anyway, back to what I was saying before Dwayne started spouting all that fiction," Hank said while staring at the ceiling and trying to gather himself. "I love your daughter. I have loved her since the day I laid eyes on her. I just want you to know I will make her happy and love her for every moment I live."

My dad grunted his approval and my mom licked his cheek again. I simply stared at him.

"I love you so much it makes my teeth hurt," I said as I threw myself into his strong arms.

"My life is empty without you in it, crazy girl," he said with a grin.

"I hear there's a good Western on TV tonight," I said with my own silly grin.

"You don't say."

"Actually, I do say. And I can guarantee you're gonna love the show. It's a wild one."

"Essie," Granny said as she got up and loving ran her hands over her daughter and son-in-law.

"Yes, Granny?"

"We all know what you're talking about," she said with a wink and a smirk.

"*Shit,*" I muttered as I felt the heat crawl up my neck and land squarely on my face.

"It's okay, baby," Hank said as he pulled me toward the grand staircase that led to the second floor. "Trust me, they've all been there and wish they were again."

"He's right, sweetie," Granny confirmed. "Can I use my real cell phone now?"

"Sure, why?" I asked.

"Because I'm pretty sure I'm smarter now that I'm dead. I think I could kick that cheating computer's ass crack in Scrabble," she said seriously.

"Um… awesome," I said. "We're gonna go watch a western… maybe three."

"Or six," Hank said as he picked me up and took the stairs two at a time.

"Have fun," Granny called out as my parents howled their approval.

"I love you, Hank Wilson," I whispered when my family was finally out of view. "You make life so much more fun."

"And I love you Essie McGee soon-to-be Wilson. You make life worth living."

"You ready for a Western, cowboy?" I asked with a giggle.

"Never been more ready for anything in my life," he said.

Epilogue

The WTF Council accepted our version of the events with very few questions asked. I was shocked. Hank was not. It was a relief to know they were as surprised and appalled as we were at the creation of the feral Wolves and the bargaining with the Dragons.

There were several on the governing Council I thought were a little shady, but it wasn't the time or the place to call them on it. Thankfully the reveal to the humans was on permanent postponement due to the small fact the champions of the stupid idea were dead.

However, when they asked Hank and I to take over the seats of extremely indisposed and six feet under Aramini and Gades, we were both struck dumb.

Hank likes to tell the rest of the story, but I always stop him with the threat of withholding panty privileges. Granny would have a fit if she caught wind of my language.

The truth goes like this. They asked. We laughed hysterically.

They asked again. We laughed harder.

They asked a third time and it dawned on us they were serious.

We stopped laughing.

I then said, no f-bombing way would I be on the Council. Hank cracked up to the point he almost hyperventilated, which is very difficult for a Werewolf to do. The Council members, particularly Weterman and Dahn, were highly unamused by me and my colorful language. But I'd been through so much in the last few weeks I didn't really care.

I think I may have called Weterman an asshat at one point. Hank swears I did. I'm not as sure. I thought I called him an assjacket.

They asked us to hold off on giving them a real answer for a few months. I was clear though that if we decided to join their sorry old asses—*my words, not theirs*—there would be no more retreats in Wisconsin. All future retreats would have to be in Jamaica or Hawaii. My change of venue confused a few, but they didn't say no.

We hid my parents safely within the Georgia Pack. Junior welcomed them with open arms and expressed his fervent desire to find a spell or potion that would one day enable them to be human again. Most of the ferals joined the pack as well, but several went off on their own. This was probably not smart, but after having lived in captivity for so long we let them leave uncontested. Although if they caused problems or we discovered a cure, they knew they had to come back to the fold.

The new and improved Granny is a shock to all. No one ever saw a true hybrid. She is thrilled with the attention. She and Dwayne are now working on a musical tribute to *Twilight* in honor of Granny's new bloodsucker status. Apparently there's a pole involved and an array of nipple-less sequined bras. I hope to Jesus Hesus my parents never watch the show.

Speaking of JHC, aka Jesus Hesus Christ, we made the urban dictionary and the national news. Of course, the credit went to the churchgoers who claimed Jesus came to them through their TV sets during an episode of *The Voice* and told them the Lord's middle name was Hesus.

Going viral was all kinds of credibility ruining awesomeness. Dwayne has been canvasing everyone as to what the next new *thing* should be. We haven't decided yet, but *Moses Bilbo Waterparter* is edging to the forefront.

The Cows are now living with the Vamps, much to Daddy Dwayne's agony over the situation. My BFF threw a fit so large it caused a mini tornado. Thankfully nothing and no one was harmed except for Dwayne's collection of Dolly Parton wigs. He repeatedly threatens to dismember and chop to pieces any Vamp who makes his girls unhappy. He's quite specific about chopping them up and then putting the pieces all over several continents so it would take centuries to regenerate.

His detailed threat left most of us at a loss for words. However, Granny thought it was hilarious. Vamp humor... go figure.

Dima is the one I worried about most when the dust settled. With her father still alive she's gone into hiding with her son, Daniel. Dwayne is the proud owner of approximately three hundred homes around the world and gave Dima the keys to all of them. She has nine months and we have been working closely with her. If she finds a mate, we won't have to off her dad immediately. The main problem she has is most male Dragons are terrified to show interest in her due to her father's penchant for killing them. However,

272

she did keep mentioning a guy named Seth. Interesting.

Junior was on a mission to get Sandy, and his love campaign was going to hell in a hand basket fast. Against the advice of Dima and myself, he'd used the word boff in reference to Sandy four times. She'd of course caught wind of it since you couldn't sneeze in Hung, Georgia without everyone knowing. Sandy has been ignoring Junior for several weeks. He's been depressed and more determined than ever to get his girl. God help us all… especially Sandy.

"Do you think if I asked nicely Dwayne would pick out the invitations, the flowers and the cake for the wedding?" I asked Hank as I sat curled up on the couch in our perfect little bungalow in Hung, Georgia.

"I don't think you even have to be nice about it," Hank said, making a fine point.

All the Cows had insisted on eloping with their Vamps which almost sent Dwayne over the edge. He blamed the dead dudes for this and was prank calling them on a semi-daily basis.

"You're right. You know, we really will have to name our firstborn son after him," I said as I scrolled through the family pictures we'd had taken last week. They were a bit unconventional, considering some of us were in fabric and some in fur, but I thought they were beautiful.

Junior had been unsuccessful so far finding an antidote to the spell that had been put on my parents and the other feral Wolves. But I knew he would never give up. That was the kind of guy Junior was… just ask Sandy Moongie.

"Do we really have to?" Hank asked as he plopped down next to me and looked at the pictures.

"Yep, he convinced your mom he had to wear her dress. It might just mean we have to name all of our sons Dwayne."

"Like George Foreman?" Hank laughed. "Dwayne Jr, Dwayne the second, Dwayne the third and so on and so on and so on."

"Well, since I'm only blowing out two point five children, we could only have Dwayne Jr, Dwayne the second and Dwa," I explained to a laughing Hank.

"God, I love you, love you, love you," he said as he pulled me close.

"Should we go try and make Dwayne Jr?" I asked, running my hands over his broad chest.

"Wouldn't it be scandalous to be pregnant at the wedding?" he asked in mock horror as he slid his hands under my t-shirt and cupped my breasts. Shudders of pleasure shot through me and I arched to give him better access.

"I'm pretty sure my parents already know we do the nasty. How bad could a baby bump be?"

"Works for me," he said as he picked me up and carried me to our bedroom.

"You are so easy." I laughed as he tossed me on the bed.

"Only for you, Essie."

"Good thing you're mine then."

"Damn good thing," Hank agreed. Then he fell on top of me and let me know how much of a damn good thing it was.

And he was right.

It was a damn good thing.

A very, very, very, damn good thing.

THE END (for now)

Note From the Author

If you enjoyed this book, please consider leaving a positive review or rating on the site where you purchased it. Reader reviews help my books continue to be valued by distributors/resellers and help new readers make decisions about reading them. You are the reason I write these stories and I sincerely appreciate you!

Many thanks for your support,
~ Robyn Peterman

Visit my www.robynpeterman.com for more info.

Sign-up for my newsletter to be notified about future releases.

Excerpt from SWITCHING HOUR

Magic and Mayhem, Book 1

Chapter 1

"If you say or do anything that keeps my ass in the magic pokey, I will zap you bald and give you a cold sore that makes you look like you were born with three lips."

I tried to snatch the scissors from my cell mate's hand, but I might as well have been trying to catch a greased cat.

"Look at my hair," she hissed, holding up her bangs. "They're touching my nose—my fucking *nose,* Zelda. I can't be seen like this when I get out. I swear I'll just do it a little."

"Sandy... " I started.

"It's Sassy," she hissed.

I backed up in case she felt the need to punctuate her correction with a left hook. You can pick your friends, your nose and your bust size, but you can't pick your cell mate in the big house.

"Right. Sorry. Sassy, you have never done anything just a little. What happened the last time you cut your own bangs? Your rap sheet indicates bang cutting is somewhat unhealthy for you."

She winced and mumbled her shame into her collarbone. "That was years ago. Nobody died and that town was a dump to start with."

"Fine." I shrugged. "Cut your bangs. What do I care if you look like a dorkus? We're out of here in an hour. After today we'll never see each other again anyway."

"You know what, Miss High and Mighty?" she shouted, brandishing the shears entirely too close to my head for comfort. "You're in here for murder."

That stopped me dead in my pursuit of saving her from herself. What the hell did I care? Let her cut her bangs up to her hairline and suffer the humiliation of looking five. Maybe I wasn't completely innocent here, but I was no murderer. It was a fucking accident.

"You listen to me, Susie, I didn't murder anyone," I snapped.

"*Sassy.*"

"Whatever." She was giving me a migraine. Swoozie's selective memory was messing with my need to protect her ass. "Oh my Goddess," I yelled. "I didn't sleep with Baba Yaga's boyfriend—you did."

"First of all, we didn't sleep. And how in the hell was I supposed to know Mr. Sexy Pants was her boyfriend?"

"Um, well, let me see…did the fact that he was wearing a *Property of Baba Yaga* t-shirt not ring any fucking bells?"

I was so done. I'd been stuck in a cell with Sassy the Destructive Witch for nine months—sawing my own head off with a butter knife had become a plausible option. I was beyond ready to get the hell out.

"Well, it's not like the Council put you in here just to keep me company. You ran over your own familiar. *On purpose,*" she accused.

278

I watched in horror as she combed her bangs forward in preparation for blast off and willed myself not to give a rat's ass.

"I did not run over that mangy bastard cat on purpose. The little shit stepped under my wheel."

"Three times?" she inquired politely.

"Yes."

We glared at each other until we were both biting back grins so hard it hurt. As much as I didn't like her, I was grateful to have had a roomie. It would have sucked to serve time alone. And coming up with different female names that started with the letter S had helped pass the time.

"I really need a mirror to do this right," Sassy muttered. She mimed the cutting action by lining up her fingers up on her hair before she commenced.

I walked to the iron bars of our cell and refused to watch. Our tiny living quarters were barren of all modern conveniences, especially those we could perform magic with, like mirrors. We were locked up in Salem, Massachusetts in a hotel from the early 1900s that had been converted to a jail for witches. Our home away from home was cell block D, designated for witches who abused their magic as easily as they changed their underwear.

From the outside the decrepit building was glamoured to look like a charming bed and breakfast, complete with climbing ivy and flowers growing out of every conceivable nook and cranny. Inside it was cold and ugly with barren brick walls covered with Goddess knew what kind of slime. It was warded heavily with magic, keeping all mortals and responsible magic-makers away. At the moment the lovely Sassy and I were the only two inhabitants in the charming hell-hole. Well, us and the humor-free staff of older than dirt witches and warlocks.

I dropped onto my cot and ran my hands through my mass of uncontrollable auburn curls which looked horrid with the orange prison wear. I puckered my full—and sadly lipstick-free-lips as I tried to image myself in the latest Prada. The first damn thing I was going to do when I got out was burn the jumpsuit and buy out Neiman's.

"Fine. We're both here because we messed up, but I still think nine months was harsh for killing a revolting cat and screwing an idiot," I muttered as the ugly reality of my outfit mocked me.

I held my breath and then blew it out as Sassy put the scissors down and changed her mind.

"I can't do this right now. I really need a mirror."

It was the most sane thing she'd uttered in nine months.

"In an hour you'll have one unless you do something stupid," I told her and then froze.

Without warning the magic level ramped up drastically and the stench of centuries-old voodoo drifted to my nose. Sassy latched onto me for purchase and shuddered with terror.

"Do you smell it?" I whispered. I knew her grip would leave marks, but right now that was the least of my problems.

"I do," she murmured back.

"Old lady crouch."

"*What*?" Her eyes grew wide and she bit down on her lip. Hard. "If you make me laugh, I'll smite your sorry ass when we get out. What the hell is old lady crouch?"

My own grin threatened to split my face. My fear of incarceration was clearly outweighed by my need to make crazy Sassy laugh again. "You know—the smell when you go to the bathroom at the country club...powdery old lady crouch."

"Oh my hell, Zelda." She guffawed and lovingly punched me so hard I knew it would leave a bruise. "I won't be able to let that one go."

"Only a lobotomy can erase it." I was proud of myself.

"Well, well, well," a nasally voice cooed from beyond the bars of our cell. "If it isn't the pretty-pretty problem children."

Baba Yaga had to be at least three hundred if she was a day, but witches aged slowly—so she really only looked thirty-fiveish. The more powerful the witch, the slower said witch aged. Baba was powerful, beautiful and had appalling taste in clothes. Dressed right out of the movie *Flash Dance* complete with the ripped sweatshirt, leggings and headband. It was all I could do not to alert the fashion police.

She was surrounded by the rest of her spooky posse, an angry bunch of warlocks who were clearly annoyed to be in attendance.

"Baba Yaga," Sassy said as respectfully as she could without making eye contact.

"Your Crouchness," I muttered and received a quick elbow to the gut from my cellmate.

Baba Yaga leaned against the cell bars, and her torn at the shoulder sweatshirt dripped over her creamy shoulder. "Zelda and Sassy, you have served your term. Upon release you will have limited magic."

I gasped and Sassy paled. WTF? We'd done our time. *Limited magic?* What did that mean?

"Fuck," I stuttered.

"But...um...Ms. Yaga, that's not fair," Sassy added more eloquently than I had. "We paid our dues. I had to withstand Zelda's company for nine months. I believe that is cruel and unusual punishment."

"Oh my hell," I shouted. "You have got to be kidding me. I fantasized chewing glass, swallowing it and then super gluing my ears shut so I would have to listen to anymore play by plays of *Full House* episodes."

"*Full House* is brilliant and Bob Saget is hot," she grumbled as her face turned red.

"Enough," Baba Yaga hissed as she waved a freshly painted nail at us in admonishment. "You two are on probation, and during that probation you will be strictly forbidden to see each other until you have completed your tasks."

"Not a problem. I don't want to lay eyes on Sujata ever again," I said.

"It's Sassy," she ground out. "And what in the Goddess' name do you mean by *tasks*?"

Baba Yaga smiled—it was not a nice smile.

"Tasks. *Selfless* tasks. And before you two get all uppity with that *'I can't believe you're being so harsh'* drivel, keep in mind that this is a light sentence. Most of the Council wanted you imbeciles stripped of your magic permanently."

That was news. What on earth had I done that would merit that? I conjured up fun things. Sure, they were things I used to my advantage, like shoes and sunny vacations with fruity drinks sporting festive umbrellas in them, served to me on a tropical beach by guys with fine asses...but it wasn't like I took anything from anyone in the process.

"I'm not real clear here," I said warily.

"Oh, I can help with that," Baba Yaga offered kindly. "You, Zelda—how many pairs of Jimmy Choo shoes do you own?"

I mentally counted in my head—kind of. "Um...three?"

Baba Yaga frowned and bright green sparks flew around her head. "Seventy-five and you paid for none of them. Not to mention your wardrobe and cars and the embarrassingly expensive vacations you have taken for free."

When her eyes narrowed dangerously, I swallowed my retort. Plus, I had eighty pairs...

"And you, Sassy, you've used your magic to seduce men and have incurred millions in damages from your temper tantrums. Six buildings and a town. Not to mention your *indiscretion* with my former lover. If I hadn't already been done with him you'd be in solitary confinement for eternity. Can you not see how I had to fight for you?" she demanded, her beautiful eyes fiery.

"Well, when you put it that way..." I mumbled.

"There is no other way to put it," she snapped as her mystical lynch mob nodded like the bobble-headed freaks that they were. "Zelda, you have used your magic for self-serving purposes and Sassy, you have a temper that when combined with your magic could be deadly. We are White Witches. We use magic to heal and to make Mother Earth a better place, not to walk the runway and take down cities."

"So what do we have to do?" Sassy asked with a tremor in her voice. She was freaked.

Baba Yaga winked and my stomach dropped to my toes. "There are two envelopes with your tasks in them. You will not share the contents with each other. If you do, you will render yourselves powerless. *Forever.* You have till midnight on All Hallows Eve to complete your assignments and then you will come under review with the Council."

"And if we are unable to fulfill our duty?" I asked, wanting to get all the facts up front.

"You will become mortal."

Shit. My stomach dropped to my toes and I debated between hurling and getting on my knees and begging for mercy. Neither would have done a bit of good...There was no way in hell I could make it in this world as a mortal—I didn't even know how to use a microwave.

And on that alarming and potentially life ending note, Baba Yaga and her entourage disappeared in a cloud of old lady crouch smoke.

"Well, that's fucking craptastic," I said as I warily sniffed my envelope—the one that had appeared out of thin air and landed right between my fingertips.

"You took the words right out of my mouth," Sassy replied as she examined hers.

She tossed her envelope on her cot as though she were afraid to touch it and turned her back on it. I simply shoved mine in the pocket of my heinous orange jumpsuit.

"So that's it? We just do whatever the contents of the envelope tell us to do?" Sassy whined. "Okay, so we're a little self-absorbed, but I do use my magic to heal. Remember when I kind of accidentally punched the guard in the face? I totally healed his nose."

I laughed and rolled my eyes. "He was bleeding all over your one and only pokey jumpsuit."

"Immaterial. I healed him, didn't I?" she insisted.

"And then I zapped your skanky jumpsuit clean," I added, not to be outdone by her list of somewhat dubious selfless acts. "However, I get the feeling that's not the kind of healing magic Baba Yasshole means." I sat down on my own cot, still stunned by our sentence from the Council.

"You know what? Screw Baba Ganoush!" Sassy grunted as she grabbed her envelope and waved it in the air. I sighed and put my hand on her arm to prevent her from doing any damage to her task.

"Yomamma. It's Baba Yomamma, Sassy. And seriously—what choice do we have at this point except to do what she says? You don't want to stay in here, do you? I say we yank up our big girl panties and get this shit done. Deal?"

I stunned myself and Sassy with my responsible reasoning ability.

She made a face but nodded. "Baba Wha-Wha said we couldn't share the contents of our envelopes. There's no way in hell we can open these together and not share."

"Correct. Baba Yosuckmybutt is hateful."

"You want to get turned into a mortal?"

I shuddered. "Fuck no. So now what?" I asked as I played with the offending envelope in my pocket.

"See you on the flip side?" Sassy held up her fist for a bump.

I bumped. "Probably not. While it's been nice in the way a root canal or a canker sore is nice I think it's time for us to part ways."

Sassy grinned and shrugged and I answered with my own.

"So we walk out of here on three?" she asked.

"Yes, we do."

We both took a deep breath. "One, two, three…"

The door of our cell popped open the moment we approached it, clanging and creaking. We exchanged one last smile before Sassy hung a left and headed down the winding cement path that led to freedom. She made her way down the dimly lit hallway until she was nothing but a small, curvy dot on the horizon.

I clutched the envelope in my pocket with determination and sucked in a huge breath.

And then I hung a right.

Chapter Two

Dearest Zelda,

Apparently your Aunt Hildy died. Violently. You have inherited her home. Go there and make me proud that I didn't strip you of your magic. You will know what to do when you get there.

If you ever use the term "old lady crouch" again while referring to me I will remove your tongue.

xoxo Baba Yaga

P.S. The address is on the back of the note and there is a car for you parked in the garage under the hotel. It's the green one. The purple one is mine. If you even look at it I will put all of your shoes up for sale on eBay. And yes, I am well aware you have eighty pairs.

"Motherhumper, what a bee-otch—put my shoes up for sale, my ass. And who in the hell is Aunt Hildy? I don't have a freakin' aunt named Hildy. Died violently? What exactly does 'died violently' mean?" I muttered to no one as I reread the ridiculous note.

Goddess, I wondered what Sassy's note said, but we had gone our separate ways about an hour ago.

My mother was an only child and I hadn't seen her in years—so no Aunt Hildy on that side. My mom, *and I use the term loosely*, was an insanely powerful witch who had met some uber-hot, super weird Vampire ten years ago and they'd gone off to live in a remote castle in Transylvania. The end.

And my father...his identity was anyone's guess. In her day my mother had been a very popular and *active* witch. I suppose Baba *I Know Freakin' Everything* Yaga knew who my elusive daddy was and Hildy must be his sister.

Awesome.

I hustled my ass to the garage and gasped in dismay. In the far corner of the dank, dark, musty-smelling garage sat a car...a green car. A lime green car. Even better, it was a lime green Kia. Was Baba YoMamma fucking joking? Why did I have to drive anywhere? I was a witch. I could use magic to get wherever I wanted to go.

Crap.

Did I even have enough magic to transport? Could I end up wedged in a time warp and stuck for eternity?

And what, pray tell, was this? A Porsche? Baba Yoyeastinfection drove a Porsche...of course she did.

I eyed the purple Porsche with envy and for a brief moment considered keying it. The look on Boobie Yoogie's face would be worth it. Another couple of years in the magic pokey plus having to watch my fancy footwear be auctioned off on eBay was enough to curb my impulse. However, I did lick my finger and smear it on the driver's side mirror. I was told not to look at it. The cryptic note mentioned nothing about touching it.

Glancing down at my orange jumpsuit I cringed. Did they really expect me to wear this? What the hell had become of me? I was a thirty-year-old paroled witch in orange prison wear and tennis shoes. My fingers ached to clothe myself in something cute and sexy. Did I dare? How would they even know?

Wait…she knew I called her old lady crouch. She would certainly know if I magicked up some designer duds. Shitballs. Orange outfit and red hair it was.

Thankfully the car had a GPS, not that I knew how to work anything electronic. I was a witch, for god's sake. I normally flicked my fingers, chanted a spell or wiggled my nose. The address of my inheritance was in West Virginia. How freakin' far was West Virginia from Salem, Massachusetts?

Apparently eleven hours and twenty-one minutes.

It took me exactly forty-five minutes of swearing and punching the dashboard to figure that little nugget out. Bitchy Yicky was officially my least favorite person in the world. However, I was a little proud to have made the damn GPS work without using magic or blowing the car up.

***

Five hours into the trip I was itchy, bloated and had a massive stomachache. Beef jerky and Milk Duds were not my friend. Top that off with a corn dog and two sixty-four ounce caffeinated sodas and I was a clusterfuck waiting to happen.

Thank the Goddess New England was gorgeous in the fall. The colors were breathtaking, but they did little to calm my indigestion. The Kia had no radio reception, but luckily it did come with a country compilation CD that was stuck in the CD player. I was going deaf from the heartfelt warblings about pickup trucks, back roads and barefoot rednecks.

Pretending to be mortal sucked. Six more hours and twenty-one minutes to go—shit. Sadly I found myself longing for even the hideous company of Sassy. Being alone was getting old.

"I can do this. I have to do this. I will do this," I shouted at the alarmed driver of a minivan while stopped at a traffic light in Bumfuck, Idon'tknowwhere.

"I'm baaaaaaack," something hissed from behind me.

"What the fu…?" I shrieked and jerked the wheel to the right, avoiding a bus stop and landing the piece of crap car in a shallow ditch. "Who said that?"

"I diiiiiiiid," the ominous voice whispered. "Have yoooooooou missssssssed me?"

"Um, sure," I mumbled as I quietly removed my seatbelt and prepared to dive out of the car. Maybe I could catch a lift with the woman I'd terrified in the minivan. "I've missed you a ton."

"You look like shiiiiiiit in ooooorrrrangeeeee," it informed me.

That stopped me. Whatever monster or demon was in the backseat had just gone one step too far.

Scare me? Fine.

Insult me? Fry.

"Excuse me?" I snapped and whipped around to smite the fucker. Where was he? Was he invisible? "Show yourself."

"Down heeeeere on the floooooor," the thing said.

Peering over the seat, I gagged and threw up in my mouth just a little. This could not be happening. I pinched myself hard and yelped from the pain. It *was* happening and it was probably going to get ugly in about twelve seconds.

"Um, hi Fabio, long time no see," I choked out, wondering if I made a run for it if he would follow and kill me. Or at the very least, would he get behind the wheel of the Kia and run me over...three times. "You're looking kind of alive."

"Thank youuuuuuuu," he said as he hopped over the seat and landed with a squishy thud entirely too close to me.

I plastered myself against the door and debated my next move. Fabio looked bad. He still resembled a cat, but he was kind of flat in the middle, his head was an odd shape and his tail cranked to the left. Most of his black fur still covered him except for a large patch on his face, which made him resemble a pinkish troll. He didn't seem too angry, but I did kill him. To be fair, I didn't mean to. I didn't know he was under the wheel and I kind of freaked and hit reverse and drive several times before I got out and screamed bloody murder.

"So what are you doing here?" I inquired casually, careful not to make eye contact.

"Not exxxxxxactly sure." He shook his little black semi-furred head and an ear fell off.

"Oh shit," I muttered and flicked it to the floor before he noticed. "I'm really sorry about killing you."

"No worrrrrrries. I quite enjoyed being buried in a Prrrrraaada shoeeee box."

"I thought that was a nice touch," I agreed. "Did you notice I left the shoe bags in there as a blanket and pillow?"

"Yesssssssssssss. Very comfortable." He nodded and gave me a grin that made my stomach lurch.

"Alrighty then, the question of the hour is are you still dead...or um..."

"I thiiiink I'm aliiiiive. As soon as I realliiiized I was breathing I loooooked for you."

"Wow." I was usually more eloquent, but nothing else came to mind.

"I have miiiiiiiisssed you, Zeeeeldaaaa."

Great, now I felt horrible. I killed him and he rose from the dead to find me because he missed me. I should take him in my arms and cuddle him, but I feared all the jerky and Duds would fly from my mouth if I tried. He deserved far better than me.

"Look, Fabio...I was a shitty witch for you. You should find a witch that will treat you right."

"But I looooooovvve you," he said quietly. His little one-eared head drooped and he began to sniffle pathetically.

"You shouldn't love me," I reasoned. "I'm selfish and I killed you—albeit accidentally—and I'm wearing orange."

"I can fix that," he offered meekly. "Would that make you looooooove meeeee?"

I felt nauseous and it wasn't from all the crap I'd shoved in my mouth while driving to meet my destiny. The little disgusting piece of fur had feelings for me. Feelings I didn't even come close to deserving or returning. And now to make matters worse, he was offering to magic me some clothes. If I said yes, it was a win-win. I'd get new clothes and he'd think I loved him. Asshats on fire, what in the hell was love anyway?

"Um...I would seem kind of shallow if I traded my love for clothes," I mumbled as I bit down on the inside of my cheek to keep from declaring my worthless love in exchange for non-orange attire.

"Well, youuuuuu are somewhat superficial, but that's not alllllllll your fault," Fabio said as he squished a little closer and placed the furry side of his head in my lap.

"Thank you, I think."

A compliment was a compliment, no matter how insulting.

"You're most welcome," he purred. "How would you know what loooooove is? Your mother was a hooooooker and your poor father was in the darrrrrk about your existence most of your liiiiiiiife."

"My mother was loose," I admitted, "but she did the best she could. However, my father, whoever the motherfuck he is, just took off after he knocked up my mom. And P.S.—I'm the only one allowed to call my mom a hooker. As nice as the fable was you told me about my dad…it's bullshit."

"Noooooooo, actually it's not," Fabio said as he lifted his piercing green eyes to mine.

"Do you know the bastard?" I demanded, noticing for the first time how our eyes matched. That wasn't uncommon. Most familiars took on the traits of their witches, but I wished he hadn't taken on mine. It would make it much harder to pawn the thing off on someone else if he looked too much like me.

"I knoooooow of him."

"So where the hell is he if he knows about me now?" My eyes narrowed dangerously and blue sparks began to cover my arms.

Fabio quickly backed away in fear of getting crispy. "Asssssssssss the story goes, a spell was cast on him by your mooooooother when he learned of your existence. From what I've heard he's been trying to break the spellllllllll by doing penance."

I rolled my eyes and laughed. "How's that working out for the assmonkey?"

"Apparently not veeeeeeery well if he hasn't shown himself yet."

I considered Fabio's fairytale and wished for a brief moment it was true. Maybe my father didn't know about me. I always thought he didn't want me. That's what my mom had said. Of course she was certifiable and I'd left her house the moment I'd turned eighteen. I did love her but only in the same way a dog still loves the owner who kicks it.

Fabio's story was utter crap, but it was sweet that he cared. Other than Baba Yopaininmyass, not many did.

"Where did you learn all that fiction?" I asked as I eased the lime green piece of dog poo back onto the road before the police showed up and mistook me for an escaped convict.

"Yourrrrrrrr file," he answered as he dug his claws into the strap of the seat belt and pulled it across his mangled body. "Evvvvvvery familiar gets a file on their witch."

"Here, let me," I said as I pulled the strap and clicked it into the lock. "Was there anything else interesting in my file?"

The damn cat knew more about me than I did.

"Nothing I caaaaaan share."

I pursed my lips so I wouldn't swear at him—hard but doable. I wanted info and I knew how to get it. "What if I reattached your ear? Would you tell me one thing you're not supposed to?" I bargained.

"I'mmmmm misssssssssing an ear?" he shrieked, aghast.

"Yep, I flicked it under the seat so you wouldn't flip out."

His breathing became erratic. I worried he would heave a hairball or something worse. "Yesssssss, reattach it, please."

I opened my senses, and let whatever magic Baba Yasshole had let me keep flow through me. Light purple healing flames covered my arms, neck and face. Fabio's ear floated up from under the passenger seat and drifted to his head. As it connected back, I had a thought. It was selfish and not...

"Hey Fab, do you mind if I fill in the fur on your face?" It would be so much easier to look at the little bastard if I didn't see raw cat skin.

293

"Ohhhhhhhhhh my, I'm missing fur?" He was positively despondent. Clearly he hadn't looked in a mirror since his resurrection.

"Um, it's just a little," I lied. "I can fix it up in a jiff."

"Thhhhhhank you, that would be looovely."

The magic swirled through me. It felt so good. The pokey had blocked me from using magic and I'd missed it terribly. The silky warm purple mist skimmed over Fabio's body and the hair reappeared. Without his permission I unflattened his midsection, reshaped his head and uncranked his tail. It was the least I could do since I'd caused it in the first place.

"There. All better," I told him and glanced over to admire my handiwork. He looked a lot less mangled. He was still a bit mangy, but that was how he'd always been. At least he no longer looked like living road kill. "Your turn."

"Your Aunt Hildy was your father's sisssssster and she wasssss freakin' crazy," he hissed with disgust.

"You knew her?"

"Ahh no, but sheeeeeee was legendary," he explained.

"Why the hell did she leave me her house?" I asked, hoping for some more info. I'd already assumed she was my deadbeat dad's sister. I wanted something new.

"I suppose you will take ooooover for her," Fabio informed me as he lifted and extended his leg so he could lick his balls.

"Get your mouth off your crotch while we're having a conversation," I snapped.

"Youuuuu would do it if youuuuuu could," he said.

"Probably," I muttered as I zoomed past six cars driving too slow for my mood. "But since I can't, you're not allowed to either."

294

"Can I dooooooo it in private?" he asked.

"Um, sure. Now tell me what crazy old Aunt Hildy did for a living so I know what I'm getting into here."

"No clue," Fabio said far too quickly.

"You know, I could run your feline ass over again," I threatened.

"Yeeeeeep, but I have six lives left."

I put my attention back on the road. "Great. That's just great."

Coming Soon #

Visit *robynpeterman.com* for more information.

Sign-up for my newsletter to be notified about the release date.

Excerpt from *Ariel: Nano Wolves 1*

By
Donna McDonald

Copyright 2015 by Donna McDonald
Reprinted here with permission of the author.

Book Description

Being a living experiment wasn't part of the scientific career she'd planned for herself.

Despite her sharp scientific mind and her degree in bio-molecular genetics, Dr. Ariel Jones hasn't figured out how her life changed so much in a single day. Before she can blink and ask about what is going on, she is injected with a billion nanos and some very potent wolf blood.

Now she can suddenly turn into a giant white wolf with the bloodlust of a starving animal. And she's an alpha...or so she is told by the even larger, very male, black wolf who was used to create her. Hallucination? She wishes.

Whether human or wolf, Reed talks in her head and tells her how to handle things...or rather how to kill them...starting with the men who hold them all captive. Too bad he can't tell her how to put her life back like it was.

There are perks to being a werewolf, such as meeting sexy werewolf guys like Matthew Gray Wolf. Science labs aren't exactly overrun with sexy men in white coats.

Ariel also doesn't mind learning about a side of herself she never knew existed. It's great changing into a real wolf whenever she wants, but being a living experiment wasn't part of the scientific career she'd planned for herself. Neither was falling for the local werewolf alpha, but what else is a newbie werewolf caught in her burning time going to do?

Chapter 1

Dr. Ariel Jones blinked at the bright lights overhead as she woke. Finding herself naked and strapped to some sort of gurney, she turned her head and saw two women similarly strapped to gurneys beside her. One was weeping steadily. The other was glaring at a fixed spot on the ceiling.

Her scientist brain got busy immediately, trying to figure out what had happened since she'd come to work that morning. Her typical day at Feldspar Research always started at five in the morning to accommodate the light limitations of living and working just outside Anchorage, Alaska.

She had processed the new set of blood samples waiting for her in the lab and instantly reported the unusually rapid cell mutation she had seen happening under the lens of her microscope. Then at about ten o'clock, she'd gone for a direct meeting with Dr. Crane, who had asked to speak with her in person about what she'd found.

One minute she had been drinking coffee and talking with a colleague. The next she was waking up naked in...where was she anyway? Looking around more, she finally recognized the place. It was where they had brought the giant wolf.

Sniffing the air, she could indeed smell the pungency of the trapped animal. It was what had bothered her most. From what she knew, he'd been here longer than she had worked for Crane. The one and only time she'd seen the wolf in person had been more than enough. He was the biggest animal she'd ever seen and bigger than any she could have ever imagined.

Now she was here—in the same room where they had kept him. The discovery brought her back to her own pressing problem of waking up naked and restrained without knowing why. A thousand thoughts raced through her mind, none of them pleasant.

"So good of you to join us at last, Dr. Jones. I've been delaying things and waiting for you to wake up. I didn't want to start the injections while you were still under the effects of the mild sedative we gave you earlier."

"You put drugs in my coffee this morning," Ariel stated, somehow sure of it even before her bastard employer nodded and smiled.

"The sedative was the fastest way to obtain your physical cooperation. Time is critical. We don't know how long the window of opportunity from your findings will remain open. You told me several weeks ago you had come to Alaska because you craved more out of life than sitting in a lab doing research. Well, I'm about to make your dreams come true in a way you have never imagined."

Ignoring her accelerating heartbeat, Ariel decided she wasn't going to get emotionally alarmed until there was a greater reason to do so than simply being naked and unable to free herself. She was used to thinking her way out of bad situations. She just needed to remain calm, ask questions, and figure out what was really going on.

"I would like to know the purpose of your actions. Are you planning to take physical advantage of my helpless condition? Who are the two women next to me? What role do they play?"

Dr. Crane smiled. "So many questions. Of course, I expected someone like you would have them. You're going on a scientific adventure or at least your body is. The three of you are about to become the next step in the evolution of our species. But I guess it's rather bold of me to theorize such a result without any proof yet. Part of the excitement is considering all the possibilities. Now I know your circumstances are a bit alarming at the moment, but if this experiment works, you'll become an extremely valuable asset to our military. Even the most highly trained K-9 units won't be able to compete with your animal skills. Alaskan wolves are quite superior to canines in nearly all areas. Everyone studies their predatory actions for just this reason."

"I still don't understand, Dr. Crane. I thought Feldspar was testing wolf fortitude to glean survival information for living in extremely harsh environments," Ariel said, discreetly testing the restraints around her wrists again.

"Oh come now, Dr. Jones. That sort of work is barely fit for a second year university student. You are here because you personally possess several strands of DNA in common with our latest Feldspar wolf acquisition. He's been rather solemn since we informed him of your findings. He's glaring at us steadily which I take as the highest compliment about your discovery. It's as if he senses what we are about to do to the three of you."

"Dr. Crane, are you saying you're communicating with a wolf? Don't you think that assumption is a bit odd?" Ariel asked.

"Not at all. I sincerely wish we could be communicating with his human side, but we've purposely kept him from shifting back to his human form by the silver collar around his neck. I think it helped greatly to leave the six silver bullets someone put into him too. He was initially impossible to capture in his wolf form. If his pack had been nearby, I doubt we would have. In fact, I don't know who exactly did capture him. I found him both shot and tranquilized with a note pinned to his collar when someone activated the alarm on the back door of the lab."

"I'm sorry Dr. Crane, but you sound like some crazy mad scientist out of a movie. What are you going to do to us? Seriously? You don't have to make up such wild stories. I assure you I won't be reduced to hysterics by hearing the truth," Ariel demanded.

"Still the skeptical scientist, I see. In just a moment, I'll happily explain the rest to you. Since what's going to happen to you is beyond your control, I don't see any benefit from not telling you the whole story." Dr. Crane waved at the man assisting him. "Proceed with injecting the weeping one on the end. I cannot tolerate a weeping female. She is highly distracting. I can't talk to Dr. Jones over her constant whining."

Ariel's head whipped over, straining to see the gurney at the end. She saw the woman's body arch when a plunger was placed at her neck directly on the carotid artery. Whatever was in the injection, they wanted it to hit all parts of her body quickly. To her surprise, the man rolled the woman's head, and shot a second plunger directly into the woman's brain stem. The woman seized, strained at her straps, and

301

then fell silent. If the second injection didn't paralyze her spine, its content would be in every brain cell in less than ten minutes.

"Now administer the sedative and move Heidi to the last cage. Come straight back and process Brandi next. I'll take care of Dr. Jones personally."

Ariel looked back at the man speaking so calmly. He looked at her and offered a shrug.

"The sedative is to help keep you calm during the worst of your genetic transmutation. We're not completely without conscience. I see no need for any of you to suffer more than necessary. Since you're the first of your kind, we don't exactly know how much the transpecies mutation process hurts. Our captive wolf shifter has been quite unwilling to share any information, assuming he can still speak in his wolf form. We haven't been able to ascertain it one way or the other."

The woman directly beside her was still as quiet as ever. So far, she had not made a sound. Ariel listened to the gurney with the now unconscious Heidi being pushed to the far end of the room. She listened to a cage door being opened and straps being undone.

"Please continue your explanation, Dr. Crane. Did I find something important this morning?"

"Yes, you did. I applaud you for being as smart as your resume indicated. People usually lie on those you know. Somehow I knew right away when we met that you were being honest. It was quite the stroke of luck your blood also showed excellent—most excellent—counts of nearly everything required for the experiment. When I personally saw the metamorphosis strand in your DNA, I was literally as giddy as a schoolboy. The strand is missing from your fellow subjects."

"I did my doctoral thesis on the metamorphosis strand. Most in the scientific community don't even

302

think its real. But I've seen it. People who have it tend to die fairly young. It's one of the reasons I left New England and came here. I wanted to explore the world a little before I came down with some disease I couldn't survive."

"Yes. Human subjects with the strand do tend to die young. But extending your doctoral hypothesis, I also believe the strand has a higher purpose in those who possess it. So when I saw from the extensive health exams Feldspar required that you personally had the strand, I just couldn't pass up the opportunity. Roger, I said to myself, what would happen if someone extremely intelligent suddenly became a wild animal? Would the person be able to control their carnal nature enough to use their intelligence in their animal form? The chance to discover the truth was just too much to pass up. Now you get to benefit from the very discovery you made this morning, Dr. Jones. It's too bad the global medical community will never know anything more about you except for the unfortunate accident which burnt your body to ashes today when you went into Anchorage for lunch. Alaskan winters can be terribly challenging on vehicles, as I'm sure your gurney mates can also attest to since they suffered the same fate."

Ariel flinched when she heard the woman beside her hiss and swear at the depression of the plunger at her neck. When her brain stem was shot, the woman shrieked loudly and nearly broke the straps with her arching. The sedative calmed the woman instantly, but it had the opposite effect on Ariel. Starting to panic at last, because she knew the same fate would be hers, Ariel renewed her efforts to escape and twisted against her restraints. Unfortunately, she lacked the strength to break them.

She listened to the second gurney being wheeled down the hall. Again a cage door opened. Moments later, she heard it close and a key turning in a lock.

"Who gave you the right to do this to us, Dr. Crane? I came to Feldspar to do research for you, not to *be* your research. What you are doing is illegal and immoral."

"I know. I do feel a little bad about hiring you under false pretenses, but your discovery this morning stacked the odds in favor of your participation. My benefactor is most anxious to see some evidence that the transpecies mutation process can work. If even one of you survives the change, he will fund me for at least another two years."

"You're the sickest, sorriest excuse for a scientist I've ever met," Ariel declared.

Dr. Crane nodded as he lifted the first injection into the air above her. "Not anymore. Now I'm the scientist who has figured out how to make werewolves. As far as I know, I'm the only one like me on Earth. My services will be highly sought after when I show them a brilliant scientist in her wolf form."

Ariel called out and felt fire crawl under her skin as sizzling hot liquid entered her bloodstream. "*Nanos?* You injected me with nanos? It feels like a billion ants crawling on the inside of my skin." She saw Crane lift an eyebrow at her knowledge, but then so did she. She wasn't even sure how she knew what they were giving her.

"You're very sharp, Dr. Jones, much too sharp to spend your life doing research. I picked women as initial test subjects because they could be physically restrained the easiest. I did not plan on using a woman who would be able to figure out what was going on. But that's what makes life interesting. Now the next injection has to go directly into the brain steam for best results. I'm sorry for the extreme pain it causes. Judging from your fellow test subjects, the pain won't last more than a few moments."

Ariel fought as the assistant turned her head and held it still while Dr. Crane positioned the plunger. The depression happened quickly. Pain more intense than anything she'd ever known shot through her head and had her calling out. Before her consciousness faded, her last thought was that Dr. Crane had lied to her. She had been spared nothing. Her head exploding from the inside was what dropped the eventual black veil over her thoughts.

She never felt the sedative working at all.

Chapter 2

Ariel shook with cold as she came up out of a deep, drugged sleep. Naked and shivering, she determined that she was lying on a small cot.

As she struggled to open her eyes, she could just barely make out the forms of Dr. Crane and his white-coated asswipe of an assistant. They were staring into the cages where they'd stashed the other two women who had been captured alongside her. There was a bunch of growling and hissing which kept getting louder as the men talked.

Dr. Crane looked extremely pleased with whatever was happening. The knowledge pissed her off, but her dark thoughts of doing vicious and hideously cruel things to both men surprised her.

Ariel lifted a pale hand in front of her face, which blurred out of focus, but finally came back in. So far, nothing overly unusual had happened to her body, unless you counted the sick headache she had at the moment. She felt strange though—very strange. Her stomach growled with fierce hunger and there was a steady fire burning between her legs. Those two white-coated bastards had better not have touched her. If they did, she was cutting off their man parts and throwing them in the recycler. Later, when she was more alert, she promised herself she would check her body closer.

A loud clanging against the bars of her cage had her covering her ears. Sound—all sound—hurt terribly and increased her headache. A percussion band played in her head as she fought the pain.

"I'm afraid your doctoral thesis is now a complete failure, Dr. Jones. Apparently, the metamorphosis strand is a deterrent to transpecies mutation as well as being something to shorten a person's life. Now I have to decide what to do about you. We can't just turn you loose in society and have you telling everyone what we're up to here. You were certainly a waste of a couple billion very expensive nanos we can't get back. Sadly, you've become the only failure case, rather than the pinnacle of our success."

It took her a lot of effort, but Ariel finally managed to manipulate her hand enough to get her middle finger to stand up alone. Crane's laugh at her silent rebellion grated on every nerve she had, not to mention how much his voice hurt her ears.

"When I get out of here, I may kill you just to watch you hurt," Ariel croaked, her mouth dry as dust.

Crane laughed harder and walked away. At his departure, the growling and hissing in the cages next to her ceased. When the room was totally silent once more, she drifted back into a peaceful oblivion where she could pretend nothing had happened.

***

Dr. Jones—Ariel. Wake now, but do not shift. Wake in human form. Think of yourself as human and you will be one.

Ariel rolled to her side on the canvas cot and tried to pull the scratchy cover she'd found over her naked body. Even with her knees scrunched up, it was far too short. She covered her eyes with a hand as she fought off the nightmares which were now continuously talking to her. There must have been hallucinogens in what they gave her.

I am not a hallucination. I am Reed—a three hundred year old alpha. You are a two day old version. It is very wise of your wolf to hide itself from those who seek to harm you.

Ariel groaned and rolled to the other side. "Head hurts. Stop talking to me."

I know you are in pain, but you must fight off the drugs now. Crane returns soon. He is planning to move you to another facility and dissect your body to find out why conversion failed with you. They have identified another experiment victim and she arrives tomorrow. You must rescue the others and kill Crane before he can turn more.

"Kill Crane? Sure. I'd love to do that," she repeated, covering her eyes with her hands.

Yes. I regret the extremeness of the step, but Roger Crane must not be allowed to continue his work. You will have to destroy the lab as well. Accidents happen all the time in Alaska. I doubt Feldspar Research will fund any other scientist if we completely destroy the proof of Crane's success.

"O—K." she said groggily, working her body into an upright position. Sitting up hurt as much as anything else did. "And I thought my divorce was traumatic. Either my nightmares are getting bossy or I'm hearing real voices in my head."

Putting a hand up to her head, she rubbed the base of her skull where they had shot something into her brain stem.

"Hey nightmare, since we're on a speaking basis, do you know what the hell Crazy Crane shot me with in the back of my head?"

My blood—I believe. He took it at the pinnacle of my wolf's lunar cycle. Since I was already in my wolf form when he caught me, hitting the lunar pinnacle was evidently strong enough to cause a species turning. I had heard the legends, but human turnings have not been done since the middle ages. Packs prefer to propagate organically. Unfortunately, Crane found a way to take the choice from me.

Ariel laughed. Her intuition spoke to her all the time, but it usually didn't announce she was a wolf in human form. "Hey Nightmare, are we going to keep talking in my head?"

Yes. I am your alpha. You are an alpha in training. So yes—we will talk in your head—until we can do so differently. I cannot shift from my wolf until the bullets and collar are removed from me. Silver has a restraining effect.

"Being shot with your blood doesn't make you my dad or anything, does it?" Ariel could have swore her nightmare wolf tried to laugh. He huffed like a dog doing it.

No. But it does make you my responsibility until you take a mate who can look out for you. Being part of a pack is like having a large family. I think you might like it once you understand it.

Ariel snorted. "So I'm an alpha. Does being alpha mean you're top dog or something?"

We are canis lupis, not dogs. Alaska is home to more than eleven thousand wolves. More than half are what humans call werewolves. This is what you have become, Ariel Jones. You are now both human and wolf, as are the other two females. They are your charges and the first of your pack. They are your responsibility and will look to you for guidance on how to adjust to their new lives.

His comments—which she was starting to believe weren't just voices in her head—had Ariel standing on wobbly legs and walking to the bars of her prison.

In the cages next to hers, two multi-colored wolves paced restlessly. They were less than half the size of the black wolf, but still real enough to convince her she wasn't just having a nightmare. Oh no—she was living one.

"Brandi. Heidi. Relax. We're going to escape. I promise." When both multi-colored wolves sat and turned to her expectantly, Ariel shook her head. She knew their names and could command their obedience. Though she'd never been a person given to swearing, there were no normal words to express the enormity of her shock. Was she truly going to one day be a wolf as well?

"Un—fucking—believable," she whispered. She turned her head until she saw the edge of the giant black wolf as he leaned against one side of his cage. "Reed? Is the giant black wolf you?"

Yes, Ariel. The giant black wolf is me. You should see the alpha of the Wasilla Pack. Matt's wolf is even bigger.

She felt like peeing herself when the black wolf turned his head and met her gaze like a human would during a conversation. He had the greenest eyes she'd ever seen on a man or animal. They were filled with a kind of determination she'd never felt before, but had a feeling she was about to get an education in it.

Crane returns. I know it is him. His stench will haunt me for the next hundred years of my life.

"Okay. I'm wide awake now and mostly willing to believe you," she said, hoping all three wolves understood she was working her way to acceptance as fast as she could. She went back to her cot and huddled under the short cover. "Hey Reed, did I get bigger or something?"

Yes. And you are strong enough to kill the men who will be trying to kill you. You have to try, Ariel. It is important to me that you and the other women survive. When they open the cage to take you out of it, call your wolf to help. She will be more than happy to answer. I've been helping you hold her back until the time was right.

"My mind is having a hell of a time trying to believe all of this is real, but I'm sure as hell not ready to die. Let's say I believe you. What does my wolf look like?"

Until she comes, none of us will know. I just hope she's big and strong. Rest now and pretend to be weak. You do not want them to know what you really are until it is too late.

Ariel leaned back on the cot and tried to look as pathetic as possible so her captors would believe she was just as harmless as they assumed she was.

Inside, she was praying that Reed—or whatever inner voice was helping her survive—was right about her being able to free them all.

##Available now # #

Visit *donnamcdonaldauthor.com* for more information.

ROBYN PETERMAN BOOK LISTS
(in correct reading order)

HOT DAMNED SERIES
Fashionably Dead
Fashionably Dead Down Under
Hell on Heels
Fashionably Dead in Diapers
Fashionably Hotter Than Hell

SHIFT HAPPENS SERIES
Ready to Were
Some Were in Time

MAGIC AND MAYHEM SERIES
Switching Hour

**HANDCUFFS AND HAPPILY EVER AFTERS
SERIES**
How Hard Can it Be?
Size Matters
Cop a Feel

If after reading all the above you are still wanting more adventure and zany fun, read *Pirate Dave and His Randy Adventures*, the romance novel budding novelist Rena was helping wicked Evangeline write in *How Hard Can It Be?*

Warning: Pirate Dave Contains Romance Satire, Spoofing, and Pirates with Two Pork Swords.

About Robyn Peterman

 Robyn Peterman writes because the people inside her head won't leave her alone until she gives them life on paper.

Her addictions include laughing really hard with friends, shoes (the expensive kind), Target, Coke Zero Cherry with extra ice in a Styrofoam cup, bejeweled reading glasses, her kids, her super-hot hubby and collecting stray animals.

A former professional actress with Broadway, film and T.V. credits, she now lives in the South with her family and too many animals to count.

Writing gives her peace and makes her whole, plus having a job where you can work in your underpants works really well for her. You can leave Robyn a message via the Contact Page and she'll get back to you as soon as her bizarre life permits! She loves to hear from her fans!

Visit **www.robynpeterman.com** for more information.

20321030R10174

Printed in Great Britain
by Amazon